Where We Left Off

SAPPHIRE HALE

CONTENTS

Sapphire Hale

PLAYLIST

I Hate Everything About You – Three Days Grace

Dirty Thoughts – Chloe Adams

You Don't Get Me High Anymore - Phantogram

Meddle About – Chase Atlantic

Breath – Breaking Benjamin

Fire Up The Night – New Medicine

Bodies – Drowning Pool

Wasted – Juice Wrld x Lil Uzi Vert (Huken x Murkish)

Villain I'm Not – Three Days Grace

Jealousy – Pale Waves

Casualty Of Your Dreams – Maggie Lindemann

Small Town Boy – Dustin Lynch

Hurricane – Luke Combs

American Nights – Morgan Wallen

Uncover – Zara Larsson

Grace – Lewis Capaldi

Snap – Rosa Linn

Until The End – Breaking Benjamin

Life Starts Now – Three Days Grace

CHAPTER 1

Present

I pull my arm back and smash my fist into the side of the truck bed.

Wow. That went so much worse than I had anticipated.

I yank my hand back before it can become impaled, clutching it to my chest, and I stare horror-stricken at the truck.

Instead of getting onto my bike and riding home, I'm standing in the centre of Phoenix Falls' town square in a piss-pouring thunderstorm, the college-prep books that I just borrowed from the library tucked safely into my tote (and, therein, tucked safely inside of a water-proof carrier bag), because some asshole has parked their truck directly in front of my bike, blocking me in so that I can't escape the ever-growing crowd beginning to infiltrate into the town's diner.

It's dark, my glasses are smudged, and I failed to realise that this truck is a thousand years old. The panels are peeling metal in small exploding sections. I don't even want to look at my hand. I glance at it anyway and gag a little.

That looks like a *lot* of blood. Even though I pulled back quickly I can feel sharp stings all over my fingers and knuckles. I'm going to need to run my hand under a cold tap for the next ten years.

"Are you okay?"

I startle and whip around upon hearing the voice, but the sharp subsequent waft of air awakens my injury anew. I hiss and frown down at my hand, my black hood shielding my face from the rain.

"Shit, is that blood? You want me to drive you to the hospital?"

Something about his tone stirs like honey in the bottom of my stomach and I feel a slow trickle of lava begin to course through my bloodstream.

Deep and husky.

Concerned.

Familiar.

I look up, allowing the rain to finally lash against my skin as my hood falls backwards, and I suck in a quick sharp breath.

Not only am I about to lose my hand, I'm going to have an aneurism.

Streaks of water are gushing down his tan cheekbones and his hair is plastered, dark and tousled, to his forehead. Rain is running over his lips in a way that feels explicit.

And his eyes are on mine.

"Riv… River?"

Eyes. Lips. Eyes. Lips. His gaze flicks between them like he can't choose which deserves his attention more.

I stumble one step backwards, puddle water spitting up my calves, and it snaps him out of his reverie.

Good. He doesn't get to daydream about me anymore.

Tate. Coleson.

The best friend that I ever had.

Who then became the *worst* friend that I ever had.

2

He squares his shoulders and his voice becomes stiff and strained. "River. If you would like I can take you to the hospital, and we can go and get your hand checked."

If I would like. What a concept. It's a bit too late for that now, isn't it Tate?

"It's fine," I snap, even though by this point an at-home amputation is likely. His shoulders flex when he hears my voice and he moves like a shudder just ran down his spine.

"River, please." His voice is so much deeper than it used to be, and his body has doubled in size. He was always tall, but now I'm snapping my neck just to get a look at him. I wonder if I could wrap my hands fully around the thick base of his throat. "What happened here?" he asks, eyes lingering momentarily on my mouth, before they drop back down to my hand. "What were you doing?"

What am *I* doing? What is *he* doing? And, more importantly, what is *he* doing *here*? Tate's family left town just after he turned sixteen, but now that he's almost nineteen and a high school graduate I guess he could have moved out. He could have moved back.

He could have been back for a while.

"I'm leaving," I say and I turn back around, ready to scrape the shit out of the truck bed whilst I extract my bike. I hope the spokes are extra spiky today.

"Wait," he says, and his tone is suddenly lighter, entertained almost.

I narrow my eyes in suspicion.

"Did you punch this truck?"

I turn around and see him looking at the sight of the crime. Evil metal nubs sticking out of the panel. I don't think that I even dented it.

A pity.

"It almost crushed my bike," I say.

Why am I even talking to him? *Rot in Hell, Tate.*

I can hear him laugh softly as I try to squeeze between the truck bed and the bush behind it to access my bike for

3

retrieving.

Asshole.

But then an engine revs and I'm no longer being juiced as the truck drives three feet forward. Tate puts the truck into park and then steps out of the driver's side, leaning his bicep against the door with a playful glint in his eyes.

"I'm glad that I got over here before you slashed the tires."

What an excellent idea.

He rounds the other side of the bed and pulls up the tarp, squinting up at me against the beating rain. "Put the bike in the bed. I'll take you to the hospital."

"Uh, no way," I say and I give him an *as if* eyebrow raise as I mount my bike.

Suddenly he's in front of me, gripping the handlebars in his big drenched fists.

"You can't be serious," he says, his voice hard.

I look up and I wish that I hadn't. He's so close to me that I can almost taste the rain radiating off his warm skin. His jaw is so tense and his eyes are so hard that he's practically vibrating.

"Riding a bike. No helmet. In a rainstorm." He glances down at my bloodied fist. "One handed."

He looks furious, which fills me with evil glee.

I ring my little bell.

"Move, please."

His hands grip tighter, jaw flexing. His white knuckles are making me sick with pleasure.

Why do you care so much, Tate?

"Don't do this, River."

I push off the ground to get my foot on the pedal, which is, admittedly, concerningly slick. The front wheel shoves into the leg of his denim jeans and reluctantly he takes a step back. He thrusts his hands in his pockets and pierces me with a deep, molten glare.

I'm almost shimmering with satisfaction.

"Stay away from me," I warn him with narrowed eyes, and then I kick back off the blacktop and speed away as fast as I can.

*

As soon as I rounded a few corners I was off my bike, washing my wounds with the remnants of my water bottle and fixing my knuckles with four plasters. Yes, I am a plaster-carrier – as it happens, a danger-prone girl like me can never be too anal.

I throw my bag in my room and I look out of the window. It's pitch black except for the street lamp, completely obscuring the view of the house in front of me.

Good.

I meet my mom in the kitchen as she's putting potatoes in the oven. When I go to wash my hands so that I can start making the salad she notices my hand and sucks in a breath.

"Jesus, what happened?" She asks. Then, "Did you spray perfume on it?"

Perfume on a wound is our home's answer to disinfecting injuries. I don't think my mom has taken me to a hospital since I bust my lip at the age of seven. She's made me very DIY.

I completely omit telling her about the incident with Tate's truck. I never want to think about it again, purely because I never want to think about *him* again. I skirt around the subject and tell her that I'll give it a spritz later.

Once our dinner is ready we sit down at the table, café jazz playing softly from my laptop on the counter.

"So this Friday," she starts, and my stomach sloshes with unease because we don't usually have plans. I do school. She does work. That's the routine. My mom is a professor at the college campus that's a twenty minute drive from here and, as her miniature, it's the same vision that she's been grooming into me since before I was born. Work hard, stay in a regimented system, and you'll always be protected. Bonus points if you secure a fortune from an Ivy League billionaire – if not, revel in your chastity, daughter, 'cause that's what mama wants.

All the more reason why I don't mention Tate. My mom has literally no idea what went down between us – hell, I don't think she even knew that he *existed* – and he definitely doesn't prescribe to the future she's mapped out for me.

If only he didn't prescribe to the secret future I had mapped out for *myself.*

"I want you to meet him," she finishes.

Okay, I may be a killjoy in my own life but I'm not about to screw up my mom's new secret boyfriend situation. He's been taking her out for dinner, and walks, and more dinner every weekend for three months straight, and I've never even met the guy. I don't stalk-watch them from my bedroom window as they disappear from the driveway. I don't look out of my window full-stop.

"I want to meet him," I agree with a nod, although my tone sounds a little offended because I hate the fact that she's thinking that I would put an obstacle in the way of her happiness. "What time is he coming over?"

"Hmm," she says, her mouth suspiciously full of my sliced-to-perfection lettuce. I narrow my eyes on her and stop her wrist when she goes for another forkful.

"*Hmm?*" I inquire.

"We're going to his place," she says quickly, and then she rams in the forkful that I was preventing, smug with speed.

I can handle this, I can handle this. I don't want to embarrass her by being her untrusting hermit daughter so I say, "That sounds lovely," even though I think that she just triggered my IBS.

"I hope so," she says, her eyes trained on a potato. "Wear something nice, please," she adds.

My stomach sinks a little.

"Yes mom," I murmur, and I shut up for the night, my chest constricting tightly.

*

"That's the house," my mom says, pointing.

It's the same as all of the others. Cute porch. Clean lawn. Only this one also has a hot tan lumberjack smiling at us from the garage entryway.

My mouth falls open but I quickly snap it shut in case he can see us as visibly as we can see him. No way am I going to inflate his ego.

He's over six foot, and I mean he is *well* over six foot. His skin is so tan that it leaves no doubt in my mind that he must work outdoors. From the stretch of his shirt I can tell that he's ripped. The only negative thing about right now is the fact that he's wearing a shirt *at all*.

I spin a full ninety degrees in my seat to face my mom. "*That's him?*"

Her mouth tilts up into a little self-satisfied smile as she manoeuvres into the driveway. I can't help but notice the fact that the drive is empty, meaning that this man purposefully moved *his* ride so that his girlfriend's would have an easy fit. My heart squeezes.

I mean, I'm practically jealous. From one look at this guy-slash-god I can tell that he is everything my mom has ever told me to stay away from. I'm being presumptuous but the initial vibe that I'm getting is: outdoorsy; wears a suit no more than once every three years; and owns a cowboy hat un-ironically. Why can't I have one?

When I glance back at him again, this time I peep the contents of his garage. My brow creases. "Why does he have so many saws and shovels?" I ask.

My mom laughs as her eyes flick over to the garage. "He owns a joinery company. He's as normal as they come."

Now I'm really jealous. He closes the garage as my mom

puts the car in Park and he comes over to open her door for her. I'm frozen in wonder as he helps her out and gives her a peck on the cheek, saying something to her in a voice like maple syrup.

I take a few deep breaths but somehow they make me feel even more anxious, so I decide to fuck the breathing and just get out of the car.

Once I close my door I'm met with sparkling oceanic eyes and deep bedded dimples. High-five mom.

"River," he drawls, a handsome smile playing on his lips, "I'm so happy that you're here."

Wow. Me too.

He points at himself and says, "Mitchell, but call me Mitch. Or Mitchell. Whatever's your preference."

One of his arms is wrapped around my mom's shoulders and he ushers me with his free hand, saying, "Please, come inside."

Mitch and my mom are inside the doorway by the time that I make it to the top of the steps. It's still light out, but there's a welcoming glow emitting from the entryway, not to mention the *smell*. No way can a guy this hot also cook. I glance at my mom again and wonder if she did witchcraft to summon this man.

"I hope you're hungry," he says as he takes my mom's coat. His accent is so thick that I could pour it over pancakes. "My son insisted on making the food tonight and he's kind of awesome when it comes to cooking."

He glances over to the kitchen and calls, "Tate, get out here!"

Instantly I pause.

Tate?

What?

My eyes flash to the direction of the kitchen and I watch as Mitch's son steps out. He holds a kitchen towel in one hand and he's sweeping tousled hair out of his eyes with the other when his gaze meets mine. His body instantly stills and his expression turns to pure shock. He clutches the towel in his fist with renewed vigour.

Mitch smacks him on the back and grins at me. "I hope you don't mind having a step-brother!"

My stomach drops and I swallow hard.

Oh.

My.

God.

CHAPTER 2

Three Years Ago

I quickly shut my locker as I hear the doors to the hallway swing open.

This year's class of sophomore boys is truly terrifying. I think it's because they're taller than the juniors, and the seniors are too depressed to care about keeping up a reputation anymore. I'm only a freshman but everyone can see the hierarchy. I know exactly whose radar to avoid this Fall.

I don't know the one at the front but he has black hair, big shoulders, and he's dripping with rain. Suddenly, he pulls his arm back and then slams it forward, launching the basketball in his hand like a missile. It whacks down on the floor so hard that it is re-propelled against the ceiling, before it bounces along the rest of the corridor away from its handler.

I don't blame you little guy. Keep bouncing.

"Get that for me?" Shoulders is talking. It's pre-period so the hallway is rammed and, almost comically, the entire corridor turns to see who he has graced with his attention.

My mouth goes dry.

He's leaning back with the two other alphas and he's staring dead into my eyes. The one to the right snorts like that's the best joke he's heard in the past four weeks. Dirty blond tousled hair and eyes that look like they could cut you. He thinks that he's a stud, but he has the ugliest smirk that I've ever seen.

And to the left?

Tate. Coleson.

The tallest boy in the school, whose chocolate brown hair is in perpetual disarray. Rich tan skin, long black eyelashes, and a silver chain with a little cross dangling over the buttons of his shirt. I stalk-watch him every morning from my bedroom window.

The boy across the street.

Tate folds his arms across his chest until the patter of the basketball completely ceases, and then he turns his gaze to me.

A luscious grip tightens painfully in my chest.

Before I can turn myself off and on again in a bid to find some coherent words, I watch Tate shoot Shoulders with a withering look, lips parted like he's about to say something, but then we're figuratively saved by the bell.

A junior grabs the ball and runs it back to its owner, a puppy dog look in his eyes that begs *Please let me join the team!*

And then the actual bell sounds.

I immediately turn right and speed-walk down the hallway, the ominous thud of the basketball pounding again and again behind me as the sophomores dawdle their way to their next poor unsuspecting teacher. For some reason I hope that they're on their way to a male teacher. I don't like the thought of Dirty Blond anywhere near the female staff.

*

I walk my bike to the back of the house and then come around to the porch, unlocking the front door. I wash the school germs off my hands, make a drink, and then head to my room.

I have my favourite Breaking Benjamin CD already in my stereo so I hit play as I shrug out of my uniform and look at the house in front of me. Are my curtains open? Yes, but I'm not putting on a show. Tate's mom, Pamela, and her new uniformed boyfriend work late every day, and Tate has extracurriculars until it's almost dark out, so no one's going to see me.

I don't know what sports he plays on which days, but I know that he does almost everything. Football. Basketball. Swimming, but that's off campus. His arms were built to lift heavy things, and he has the biggest hands that I've ever seen. I watch them like a vulture as he handles his food in the cafeteria.

I sit on my bed once I'm out of my school clothes and I pick up the book that we're reading in Literature. I finish off the remaining sections in less than an hour and then reward my torture with a non-school book for fun. I shimmy down against my pillow until my neck is at a dangerous ninety degrees and I read until my mom is home and the outside is dark enough for me to need to put on a lamp.

Then I hear it. The door across the street slamming shut. I smile as I feel a little fire ignite in my belly.

I always hear him when he's leaving.

I crawl to the edge of my bed and rise from my crouching position so that I can see his porch through my window.

He has something tucked under his arm and he looks really pissed off. He looks pissed off every night.

I see him walk to the top step of the porch and then he pauses. Mmm. He's wearing the long-sleeved top which goes under his football jersey, giving me an explicit eyeful of his insane quarterback shoulders. He's slipped into a pair of blue denim jeans – the proper workingman's type, not the showy designer ones – and his tan hands are flexing like he's cracking his knuckles one by one.

Then he looks right at me.

Shit, shit, shit!

I jolt like I've just been electrocuted, my heart bouncing like that goddamn basketball, and I throw myself back against my pillow, shuddering hard.

That is the hottest boy that I have ever seen my life. I spend a lot of my time wishing that I wasn't straight because the guys at school totally suck, but for Tate Coleson I make the exception. How did he get so big? I bet he's going to have loads of fun doing who-knows-what with all of the other popular people tonight. Some girl is going to get the full-force of his up-close attention and have the best night ever. He'll definitely kiss her. Maybe he'll do even more.

I grab my baby-pink teddy bear and clutch it tightly to my chest.

I don't look out of the window again for the rest of the night.

CHAPTER 3

Present

No, no, no.

Tate's eyes are trained on mine and a small wave of rage shudders through my body. I hide my bashed up hand behind my back and narrow my eyes at him in displeasure.

I'm planted in the doorway and I'm emitting serial killer vibes. Undeterred Tate steps in front of me, albeit cautiously, and he inhales deeply before swallowing hard. I watch as his thick Adam's apple rolls up and down in his throat.

"River," he says. His eyes sparkle as he outstretches his hand to me. His *right* hand. Ha. As if I'm going to let him see the terrorised state of *my* right hand after the other night's incident. I offer him my left one instead.

The corners of his lips twitch and I drop my hand completely.

"How's the other one?" he asks.

"Amazing," I lie. My hand is so swollen that I might actually lose it.

"Did you get it checked?"

"No," I admit in a rare moment of honesty. This seems to irritate him, which makes me perk up a little. I spot the silver crucifix hanging over his shirt and say, "I have been praying though."

My mom has gone into the kitchen so I turn my attention to Mitch, but my expression glitches when I realise that he has been watching our entire exchange. Scrambling, I gesture to the dining area with my thumb and ask, "D'you want me to set it up for you?"

Mitch cocks an eyebrow at me, and I see the exact same squint in his eyes that was in Tate's a moment ago. He too is holding back on some dark little joke.

"You're our guest," he scolds, taking the coat that I had half-shrugged off my shoulders before I had my step-brother-sized seizure. "Take a seat. I'll pour you a drink."

My head is spinning because I can't believe that this is happening. We manoeuvre to the table and Mitch hands me one of the glasses before working on opening a bottle of soda. I stay standing as I take in the room. He has in fact already set up the table, a detail which I had not observed whilst my insides began unravelling like linguini. The furnishings are dark wood and the accents are wine red. No clutter and innately primitive. Sexy. I brush one finger across the polished tabletop and the oil from my print mars the surface.

When I look back up at Mitch he's watching me *very* cautiously. I have a horrible feeling that he is somehow in my head, and not just in the conscious surface. He's submerged in the dark and nasty stuff that I want to keep repressed. He's looking at the thoughts that I'm not even allowing *myself* to look at.

"I'm glad that I'm finally meeting you," he says, pulling the bottle away from the lip of my glass. "Obviously your mom has told me a lot about you, but I'm sure that you'll be even better in person."

He gives me a guarded smile but from the look in his eyes I think he means it. Only I don't understand why he is the one putting his guard up. He's acting like he's hiding something and it's putting me on edge.

I hear Tate leave the vicinity as he walks back inside the kitchen.

I put the drink down and stare at Mitch as I purposefully shove my glasses back up my nose. It's a gesture that says, *Look at how innocent I am. So small and inoffensive.* Then I fold my arms across my chest because I mean business. "Thanks. I just want whatever is best for my mom. If that's you, then good."

Mitch rocks on the back of his heels and observes me with a slow nod. Suddenly I decide that I'm being too nice. I've hard-wired myself to never be nice to a guy again, so I elect to throw him off a bit.

"And if not," I continue conspiratorially, thinking back to his garage, "I've already seen where you keep the murder tools."

Mitch's eyes widen and then he throws his head back in a dazzling laugh, one hand clutching his wide muscled stomach. I literally can't believe that my mom has pulled this guy. When he drops his head forward again he sighs with a lazy smile, basking in my threat.

I know that smile.

"I knew you'd be even better in person," he says and he gives me another winning grin as he leaves the dining area. I let out a shaky breath as he disappears. It's amazing that now that he thinks I'm unhinged – even in jest – the air is suddenly clear. He's real smiles and belly laughs.

Men.

In a desperate bid to recoup my brain cells I keep to myself at the back of the house, looking through the window into the back garden. It looks like the guys have almost finished building themselves a pool. I don't let myself think about that for too long.

It takes three minutes for Mitch and – Jesus Christ – *Tate* to put the dishes on the table, and then Mitch is summoning me like the demon that I am back to the dining area.

I sit down and force a smile at Mitch. "Thank you," I say to him, well aware that I should be saying this to Tate. My least favourite person in the world. My future *step brother*.

There's a dangerous slosh in my stomach.

Mitch points to my right hand with the serving spoon. "So what happened to your hand?"

I shovel a forkful of mashed potatoes into my mouth. They're really tasty, which is annoying.

I glance over the table and a shiver ripples up through my neck, prickling my cheeks. I don't feel too guilty staring though, because Tate's eyes aren't on my face – they're on my hand, too.

I turn to Mitch and give him a light-hearted, would-you-believe-it shrug. "I knocked it on something."

I see Tate shift in his seat out of my peripheral vision. "I'll take off the bandage and check it out after dinner for you, if you don't mind," Mitch says, pouring himself a drink.

I do mind, but I think that it's getting worse by the hour, so I silently concede and get back to my annoyingly good potatoes. Over the next hour I focus on psychoanalysing Mitch's interior décor. He's very woodsy, which makes sense considering his job. I wonder if he made this table. I wonder if *Tate* made this table. My cheek's heat up as I picture him rubbing down the dark oak top.

Get me out of this house.

When everyone finishes eating Mitch insists on inspecting my hand, so I sit on the couch as he undoes the bandages and he lets out a little hiss once my hand is bare.

"How long ago did you do this?" he asks, already rummaging in his first aid kit for something. Hopefully an axe.

Tate is standing over us looking incensed with his arms folded across his chest. I bask delightedly in his discomfort. "A few days ago," I reply, with a nonchalant shrug. When Tate's gaze moves from my hand to my eyes I do a sort of self-satisfied smile. His eyes narrow.

"Dad, she needs to go to the doctor's."

What's it to you, Tate?

Mitch doesn't look up at his son but he nods in agreement. "The cuts aren't deep but there are multiple, and it's swelling because one of them must've become infected. Hopefully only one of them. We'll get you antibiotics tomorrow."

I shake my head at Mitch. "I can go on my own - I don't need you to come with me."

Mitch looks up at me once he finishes applying some sort of gel. "Your mom said you don't drive," he responds.

That's kind of embarrassing, especially since I kind of like cars, but I brush it off. "I don't, but she can take me some time. I'm not putting you out."

Mitch frowns. "Your mom's going to be pretty busy at the storage unit tomorrow."

Now it's *my* turn to frown. "My mom doesn't even have a storage unit. What are you talking about?"

Mitch folds his lips in on themselves. My mom sits down on the free armchair like an Angel of Doom. I glance up at her and she gives me an unnervingly innocent smile.

"River, I'm sure that you're wondering why you're meeting Mitch today," she begins calmly. I sit back a little so that I have enough vantage to look at her fully. "As I mentioned, Mitch is an amazing joiner." Her pause makes me prickle with nerves. "So I wanted you to meet him before I let you know that he will be doing the refurb on our house."

My brow creases in confusion. What? I don't know why she would want our house refurbished, but that doesn't seem like an issue, regardless. Why are they acting like this is an issue? Am I *that* hostile?

I shrug my shoulders and say, "Okay."

No-one says anything else. Mitch is staring at my mom. My mom is staring at me. I want to stare at Tate and find out if he knew about our parents, but my gut tells me that this is a freshly unveiled nightmare for him too.

I look back at my mom, my suspicions rising by the second. "Aaaaand...?" I prompt.

"Well, obviously he's going to be in the kitchen to do the cabinets, because the whole thing is going to be coming out. And he might also do a shelving-unit in the living room, for the TV and some displays – you know the sort," she says casually.

I don't know where she's going with this.

"So because he's going to be doing all of that, we thought, why not spruce up the upstairs too? Maybe matching cabinets in the master bedroom and then, um-" she pauses momentarily. Then she starts speaking a mile a minute. "We thought it might be beneficial to knock through the office wall so that we have three large upper rooms, instead of just two large, two small."

I blink at her like an extraterrestrial. Why would I care about any of this? I mull over her words for a moment.

Then I look back up at her.

"But if you knock through the office wall, you'll-"

You'll be in my bedroom.

I'm not going to be able to stay in my bedroom.

Which means-

"So whilst Mitch and Tate and the boys on the team help out at *our* house, he thought it might be handy if we just... stay with them. Here." She smiles.

The last particles of air leave my lungs.

"Well," Mitch interjects, "Tate doesn't technically live here – he has his own place – but obviously he can crash here anytime." Mitch is looking pointedly at Tate, who has turned slightly in our direction now, as he makes that last point.

WHAT?

Then Mitch faces me. "It's just temporary, and it won't be too long. But during the time that the team and I are working on your room," he lifts his hands in a sorry defeat. "You won't be able to stay there whilst we're doing that."

There are a lot of thoughts going through my head right now. Firstly, why the hell is my mom renovating our house in the first place? It's been the same way since forever and I didn't think she cared about splashing out on fancy interiors.

Secondly, if I can no longer use my room, and we're going to be bunking here-

"So where am I going to be sleeping?" I ask.

My mom and Mitch look at each other. Then their eyes flicker to Tate.

Right.

I shouldn't have even asked.

I know exactly which room I'm going to be sleeping in.

CHAPTER 4

Three Years Ago

Music is basically a free period. We've had a subbie teacher since the start of term, so giving us a textbook and telling us "have at it" is the extent of his pedagogical capacities.

I'm a good student but I'm not a drip, so after fifteen minutes of shuffling and reshuffling the papers in my bag I ask if I can go to the bathroom. Like a godsend he says yes without even thinking about giving me a toilet pass. I grab my bags with ninja agility and whip out of the doors, ready to get some actual studying done in the library.

I take the stairs on the left up to the second floor and round the corner of the Computer wing because the library is up past English and the detainment rooms, right at the other end of the school. Outside is a miserable grey colour and my heart swells with joy. I love this weather. The rain trickles down the panes in a never ending cascade and, if we're lucky, in a minute or two we'll get a rumble of thunder crackling in the distance.

I'm walking quickly past the next stairwell junction

between the Lit classes when I see them. One of the science teachers is walking with purpose to the Detention Office, and filing behind him is a trail of three smug-looking jocks. They're slowly swaggering like they're just going for a mid-afternoon stroll and, from the state of the white shirts that are clinging wetly to their sophomore swim-team muscles, it looks as though that's what they were just caught doing. Outside. During fourth period.

It's the guy with the black hair who notices me first. Shoulders, I do recall. He's wearing his tie around his head for the full *I hate school* effect and his canines flash blindingly white with every arrogant guffaw. If I had to pigeonhole him in the yearbook I would rank him as "Most Likely To Secretly Be A Vampire".

In order to avoid them I would stop and pretend that I was about to open up a locker but, after last week, there's the potential that they'll remember that my locker isn't actually on this hallway, so instead I fiddle with my bag, buckling and unbuckling the fastening, whilst trying to not pass out at the sight of Tate Coleson.

Tate gets a nudge on the arm and he looks up at me mid-laugh.

I'm so dazzled that I can't breathe. I consider unbuckling my bag again so that I can take a gasp on my inhaler.

The amazing thing is, he doesn't stop smiling. He's still laughing from somewhere deep in that unbelievably broad chest of his, and he's grinning in that sexy-cocky way. He has a badly behaved twinkle in his eye and I feel it pulse brighter the closer I get.

Dirty Blond snaps me out of it.

"Jeeeeee-*sussssss*," he groans loudly, rolling his eyes like this is the most annoying moment of his entire life. "Give me a fucking *break*, already."

Tate glances over at him, still laughing, and puts him into a rough headlock. The other boy snorts and they disappear into the naughty boys' pen, shaking the rainwater out of their hair like a pack of wolves.

The teacher who was accompanying them waits outside of the room and barely spares me a glance. A small female student, wearing glasses and a skirt from Goodwill? No way would she be ditching class.

I slow my pace before I turn for the library and I risk a glance in the direction of detainment room. Through the porthole window I see the three of them, hands behind their backs as they listen to their slap on the wrist scolding. Two of them are facing forward, struggling to keep their smirks at bay. The other one has his head ducked towards the door, eyes alight and molten, with a grin tugging at his lips.

My heart shivers with pleasure as I rush towards the library.

Tate Coleson just smiled at me.

*

I feel like I'm on a sugar high. Tate Coleson is a chocolate caramel sundae injected straight into my bloodstream. I have so much energy during my hour in the library that not only do I finish tomorrow's Math practice paper, I also finish my French assignment for next *month*.

I'm a junkie. Gimme, gimme, gimme.

When the bell for last period sounds I consider skipping another class. I could easily be ill and in the bathroom – my disappearance from Music would match the alibi. I want to mill around the Detention Office and see if he's still in there. I want him to grin at me again. I want to be so close to him that I can see all of the colours in his eyes.

I also want to push that dirty blond friend of his out of the window.

Why is Tate friends with him? He seems like a jerk.

I go to my Design and Technology class and end up

making a mock-up poster for the Homecoming dance. It's mainly dark navy except for the text, and in the centre I overlaid an in-motion shot of a girl twirling so fast that all you can make out is her waistline and the lifted hem of her baby pink dress. Cliché but cute. It probably won't get picked anyway.

My good mood exceeds the final bell and I'm still a little shimmery when I'm cleaning up the dishes after dinner with my mom.

I hear the door slam outside from across the street, but I'm so zoned into my History notes that I don't go to the window and check. Okay, the main reason why I don't check is because I'm scared that one of these days I'm going to see him with a girl. It's a fully-fleshed out nightmare that I sometimes traumatise myself with for about an hour and a half before I go to sleep.

I am truly insane.

Once I finish highlighting and annotating my History notes I stuff the work into its binder and kick back my chair. I'm just stretching my neck, hair cascading down my shoulders and my arms lifted over my head, when I notice him.

It's literally eight p.m. and I swear that Tate left his house at around half six. I leave my lamp on, because I don't want him to notice the change, but I sink down further in my chair so that he's less likely to catch me as I stare.

He's sat on the top of his porch steps in his hoodie and track shorts, and with what looks like a homework binder and paper pad laid out behind him, under the shield of the porch roof. His elbows are bent up on top of his large tan knees and he has his hands splayed over his ears on the outside of his hood. His eyes are shut tight and his fringe is falling over his face, dripping a little from where the rain has caught him.

What. The. Hell.

I thought that after his sports practices he came home to eat and then left again to hang out with his friends.

Has he been sitting out there alone *every night?*

Cautiously I stand up and reaching out slowly I turn off my lamp. Tate senses the change like an animal and his eyes shoot up to my bedroom window. I wonder if he can see me. As I contemplate this I remember that I didn't change out of my uniform tonight and, suddenly impish, I decide that maybe now is as good a time as any.

I slip my fingers into the knot of my school tie, gently ease the length through the loop, and then I throw it onto the floor next to my school bag.

Tate sits upright.

So you *can* see me, Tate.

I'm feeling bold and I like it. I tug my sweater vest up at the sides, slide my fingers beneath the hem, and then I pull it over my head, before dropping it to the floor with the tie.

He's really on the edge of his seat now. Shirt? Skirt? What could possibly be next?

I move over to the ledge so that I can see him clearly through the rain that's streaking my window. We're watching each other like two primates in the wild. Neither of us has blinked in the past thirty seconds.

I'm going to be sneaky this week. Every day that I hear the slam of the door I'm going to wait for ten minutes and then see if he's still outside. Then I'll wait an hour and check again. By Friday, if I realise that he's been sitting outside of his house every single night, I'm going to do something about it.

But for now?

I flick the top button of my shirt through the hole and then I whip my curtains shut.

CHAPTER 5

Present

Tate's former bedroom is in the attic.

Although I did start silently haemorrhaging when Mitch told me where I would be sleeping, I am quietly buzzed about residing in the attic, as it will really facilitate my hermit agenda.

But I couldn't stay to check it out after dinner. I was weirdly wired and there was this energy in the house that was getting too charged, so I decided that, after Mitch took me for my hand appointment this morning, I would permit myself an unaccompanied house tour. In solitary. Completely alone. Every stalker's dream.

Mitch took me back to my mom's, I ingested my antibiotics, and then they left together to start putting boxes in her secret storage unit. I was given a large navy suitcase to decant my essentials into so I piled in winter clothes, my skincare bits, and about thirty books too many, before attempting to start working on the zipper. Impossible, obviously. I took out the skincare and whipped it shut.

Naturally it starts pouring down when I realise that my raincoat is at the bottom of the case so, needing an alternative, I pull on a hoodie instead and then I head out of my mom's house.

Mitch and my mom were supposed to be back by now so I decide to wait for them in the little shielded bit over our front door - that is, until I see another truck pulling up onto the street.

It turns out that the scraggy metal death-trap I pitch-forked my fist on was Mitch's, and the sexy black Ford truck I spotted on his curb yesterday belongs to Tate. Before he has a chance to park in front of the driveway I yank up the suitcase handle and begin speed-wheeling it to the sidewalk.

He opens his door and drops his legs down over the step. He's so tall that his feet are planted on the curb, knees bent.

"Backpacking?" he asks, with one large hand still gripped around the steering wheel. I can see the tendons of his forearm flexing through the sleeve of his shirt.

I walk right up to him and then make a sharp *fuck-you* left turn, heading down the street.

"Get in the truck and I'll put your case in the backseat."

I ignore him and I continue ignoring him, even as I hear him jog up to me, puddles of rain splashing loudly against his boots.

"You'll drown in this weather," he says, a teasing lilt in his bass tone.

I scowl up at him and my glasses streak with raindrops immediately. I keep walking though, stubborn bitch that I am.

He steps in front of me and blocks my attempts to skirt around him. He's wearing a long-sleeve shirt and it's plastered to his chest. I can see every curve and ridge of his torso.

Every. Single. One.

"You don't have to shotgun with me, you can ride in the back with your case if you want." His voice is quieter now and he looks a bit dejected. And also flushed.

Interesting.

Without a word I U-turn back to the house, dragging the case behind me as the rain lashes at my face. I feel him pluck the case from my hand and I watch as he jogs ahead of me to his truck, opening one of the back doors and sliding it inside.

I roll my eyes at him as he shuts the door. Then he re-opens it, remembering the unlikelihood of me wanting to shotgun with him.

"I'll drive," I say, and I hold my hand out for the keys.

He folds his arms over his chest. I wish that my glasses were clearer so that I could get a better view. "You don't have a licence," he replies flatly.

I make an impatient grippy motion with my outstretched palm. "I'll risk it."

"Get in the car please. You're getting really wet."

I am actually. My hoodie weighs about fifteen stone.

I turn away from him and hop into the back. He closes the door behind me, surprisingly gently. When he gets into the driver's seat I realise that I've got a horribly perfect view of him thanks to the rear-view mirror. I slink down in my seat to avoid him catching any glances.

"Your case weighs a lot," he says as he pushes off the curb and starts making his way to Mitch's house.

I look down at my hand. "I had to stock up on knuckle-dusters."

His eyes meet mine briefly and then he looks back at the road. "Would you like some music?"

I stare at him in the rear-view mirror, my mouth agape. *Surely* he wouldn't-

His fingers move, hovering over the radio button. They pull back slightly. Then he presses it. There's a CD in the player and I recognise it immediately. This is *my* CD. The car is quivering with tension and I don't think that either of us is breathing anymore.

When he pulls up to Mitch's house I scramble out of the truck before he's even stopped the car. I drag my case out with me and it thuds painfully against the pavement. I wouldn't be surprised if that registered on the Richter scale.

Tate steps out of the driver's side and closes the door, looking down at me hesitantly. The rain runs like sweat over his skin.

"I'll take you to… your room," he says cautiously.

My room.

His room.

I swallow but maintain my glower, albeit blinking a bit weirdly because of the torrential downpour. "Okay."

His eyes stray to my outfit – a severe hoodie, oversized-men's-jeans, ball cap situation – and a pained look creases his brow before he turns to the house and unlocks the door.

Wow, I look so bad that it caused him physical pain.

When he unlocks the door he pushes it open and then steps aside so that I can enter first. A little flicker licks at the dry campfire in my stomach. I stomp it out immediately.

We both leave our shoes under the porch roof outside before heading in. Once we're inside he says, "If you leave your hoodie in the kitchen I'll put it in the dryer for you."

I refuse to remove any items of clothing in front of him. "I'll chance the pneumonia," I respond dryly.

He stares down at me, a tense flex in his jaw. He turns to disappear into the kitchen for a moment and when he comes back out I hear the hum of the heating system. He doesn't look at me again as he ascends to the bedroom.

My bedroom.

I know why he's being so amenable and he damn well ought to be. I hope that he is ridden with guilt over what he put me through.

When Tate opens the bedroom door, he looks at me

over his shoulder, like he's thinking of letting me through first again. The stairwell to the attic is so narrow that pressing past him would undoubtedly result in me getting totally rolling-pinned, so he thinks better of it, chest heaving, and heads into the room.

There's a tiny flutter in my chest when I drink in the room. It would be cramped for most people but, at my height, it's cosy. Dark curtains, pillow cases, and quilt covers. A lamp on each side, framing the bed. The downpour outside creates a calming, repetitive thumping sound against the roof above us, and there's beautiful bespoke wood panelling everywhere.

It's rustic, and my little loner heart loves it.

I press my hand into the black comforter and the bed gives a little squeal.

"I'll leave you to unpack," Tate says in a deep, strained voice. I look over to him and he's standing rigidly in the doorway, his hulking body stiff with discomfort. "Should I close the door?"

I turn fully around so that I'm facing him head on and I give myself three seconds to appreciate why I feel so uncomfortable around him. Tan skin flushed with the sting of the rainstorm. Chocolate brown hair now a tousled, dripping mess. His hard-earned manual-labour muscles twitching with the need to break some logs with his bare hands. Did I mention that he's more than a foot taller than me? Because he is.

He's standing in my damn bedroom. I'm going to be sleeping in his damn bed. He's my mom's boyfriend's son.

And he was the worst thing to ever happen to me.

I flip back towards the bed so that I'm no longer facing him and I pull my sodden hoodie up over my head.

"You should definitely close the door."

CHAPTER 6

Three Years Ago

We were never pre-assigned seats for Biology so it's one of the only classes wherein I get to sit next to my best friend Kit. Her name is actually Kitty but she insists on the shortened version because it sounds more curt. *Take-no-shit Kit.* Very appropriate.

She's sweeping her long black hair into a ponytail whilst Mr Miller draws a DNA ladder on the whiteboard when she gives me a nudge with her elbow.

I look over at her and her fierce cat eyes are locked onto mine like a target. How is she not the most popular girl in school? She's definitely the hottest. For some reason people always avoid the nerds.

She hisses over to me, "Did you submit your poster to the Homecoming committee?" just as her overly-stretched hair bobble snaps and flies across the room, Pablo Picasso at the whiteboard evidently none the wiser.

I nod at her. Kit is on every committee available. It's her attempt at forced social interaction, which she says is for the maintenance of her natural animal requirements, otherwise she would undoubtedly avoid our classmates like the plague.

"You better have," she continues, pinning her hair back with a red clippy-grip instead. "No way am I letting Madden's get picked."

I write "*I don't think mine is very good*" on a scrap piece of paper and push it over to her.

She pushes it back to me and whispers, "This note is better than Madden's poster."

I don't know who Madden is but I laugh and get back to copying Mr Miller's diagram into my Bio book. I glance over at Kit and she's drawing a severed penis with a sad face on her hand.

Once Biology class ends and we try to get out of the room we have to shove our way through the bulging swarm because there's a blockage in the upper corridors. Everyone is pressed up against the window panes, trying to get a glimpse at the outside sports courts.

"That sophomore team is annoyingly good," Kit remarks as I put my biology book into my locker. "It's going to be so gross when some of them go pro, and whenever we see them on TV we'll remember what assholes they were in high school."

We push past the wall of bodies and make our way downstairs.

"Wanna objectify them a bit?" she asks, craning her neck over the students by the windows as we walk down the corridor.

"We'll only encourage them," I say.

In reality, the reason why I don't want to look is because I have purposefully been avoiding Tate Coleson all week and I know that he will be out there scoring hoop after hoop with the other sophomores. I watched him like a sleuth all of last week and in a stomach-sinking twist it turns out that he *does* sit outside alone every single night.

There's something that none of the girls at the windows know.

Kit slips into a small gap and peeps out at the court. She sighs dramatically. "I hate this. Why couldn't I be more gay? This feels so anti-feminist."

We have one more minute until the next bell for class so I wait with her as she watches the court melancholically. I stand with my back to the window, my heart thumping hard as I think about what I'm going to do when I see Tate outside again tonight. I'm so nervous that my hands are sweating. I rub them down the front of my skirt and I shakily re-tie my ponytail.

"Oh my God, incoming," Kit hisses, and she shoves herself against me as the crowd moves away from the doors to make room for the players heading inside to the water fountain. I keep my eyes on my shoes but I can hear the bass tones of their voices as the joke around and get their drinks.

"Cocky pricks," she whispers. Then she adds, "Whose penis do you think is the tiniest?"

The bell will ring any second now so I push myself off the wall and turn to walk to class. I feel Kit behind me but I can sense her potent glower on the boys up ahead.

"The blond one," I whisper to her, and she nods earnestly in agreement.

As we approach them I feel a wild animalistic pull and I can't seem to stop myself from shooting a glance towards the big sweaty bodies lounging around the fountain. The boy with spiky black hair is drinking directly from the spout, his eyes on us as he lets the water gush between his lips, over-spilling only slightly. I look away, mortified but also mesmerised, and my eyes naturally find the most beautiful thing in the area. Tate's smooth tan skin is glistening with sweat and rain, and his hands are fisted low in the pockets of his basketball shorts. His eyes are scorching, like liquid fire, as they pierce into mine. They burn a message deep in my brain that says *I know what you know about me.*

I send back *I know that you do. And I'll see you tonight Tate.*

*

Now that the moment is here I am a lot less confident in my plan. I know that I shouldn't be going out there – we haven't exchanged one word to each other in our *entire lives* – but he seems so depressed and alone. If I was in his... *giant* shoes, I would want someone to look out for me.

I go to my window and look down at Tate's porch. His head is ducked just outside of the porch roof, allowing the rain to run down the tousles of his hair, and his hands are gripping his head, pressing firmly against his ears.

Enough.

I run quietly downstairs, not wanting to disturb my mom from her work in her office, and I quietly unbolt the door. Once I'm outside I look up at Tate's porch, and to my surprise he is now on his feet. It's as if he knew that I was about to come out here. It's as if he was awaiting me.

I'm instantly fifty times more nervous than I was a minute ago, so I watch my feet as I step in puddle after puddle instead of looking up at his face. It takes all of ten seconds to get across the street and then I'm standing right in front of him.

I risk a glance at his face and he's frowning down at me, large tan hands clenched at his sides.

"You shouldn't be over here," he says in a commanding tone. He almost sounds like he's disappointed in me. I'm actually a little confused as to why I'm over here myself, so I shuffle on my feet for a moment, my wellies squelching.

I glance at the door behind him because I can hear sounds coming from inside, his mom and her boyfriend both home from work for the day.

"I... I brought you something," I croak out. I'm

embarrassed and breathless because I have never spoken to this boy in my life, and now I am deciding to technically give him a present. I hold my hand out and cringe for being such a weirdo.

His brow creases even further. "What's this?" he asks. He's looking at me like I'm insane, which is probably accurate.

My stomach has folded into itself so many times that I don't think I'll ever be able to eat again.

"I know – sorry – this is so weird, I didn't mean it like that. It's just – well – because you live across from me… and sometimes I see you out here… and I thought that this might help – it's stupid, sorry, I'll just-"

I begin to retract my arm but he swipes his hand out and holds my wrist to stop me. I'm so surprised that I gasp, and then drop the object in my hand. He darts his other hand out and catches it before it hits the ground.

Basketball players.

"It's a CD player," he says, no longer frowning as his eyes search mine. Tate Coleson is one of those rare people who have incredibly beautiful eyelashes, and his irises sparkle like sugar crystals. When I look into them I feel like I'm falling inside of a kaleidoscope.

"Yes," I admit.

"Retro," he replies, smiling.

Smiling.

I shake my head. "It's… archaic. Very primitive. I'm sorry. I just thought…" I trail off.

I don't have any new gadgets even though I'm at the top of my Computer Tech class. I know the other kids have smaller, sleeker, non-battery-powered devices, but I don't mind. It makes me feel like I'm from a different generation, and in turn it makes the rebuffal of people my own age hurt a little less.

Then I realise. "Obviously you don't want to listen to music anyway – otherwise you would be using your phone.

Sorry – *again*." I reach up to take back the player but he shoots his hand up and holds it over his head with his stupid basketball player arms.

"My mom gives me technology curfews, and I'm not allowed to go out on weeknights," he says. "I'm supposed to be studying and I don't like doing it when her boyfriend comes over is all."

He brings down the device and holds it between us. He swallows hard.

"So… you're letting me use this tonight?" he asks. We look into each other's eyes again and I think about how his warm fingers are still firmly wrapped around my wrist.

I nod. "You can use it tomorrow night too if you'd like. And the next night. And the night after that."

Shut up, shut up, shut up.

He ducks his head, shaking it slightly, and when he straightens his posture I can see that his eyes are glittering in the glow of the golden porch sconce.

"Thank you," he says. His voice is deep and thick. I think that it's the nicest voice that I have ever heard.

I look up at him with a small smile. "You're welcome. I guess." I laugh nervously, which makes him laugh too.

"Can I look inside?" he asks.

He's talking about the player, but it feels as though he's about to look inside my brain.

I nod again.

He pops open the top and he cocks his head to look at the inscription on the disc. It's my Breaking Benjamin *Phobia* album. The writing is miniscule and it doesn't even have the album title on it – the sticker mainly occupies a smouldering brown and black Celtic knot, flecked in a way that makes it look like an iris, and the band name and record label border the circle in silver print so tiny that I'm not sure if you can even read it in this light. He squints at it for a long time to try and decipher the text, but after a while his lips twitch with a small smile and then he spins the CD with his middle finger playfully.

There's a gentle flutter in my tummy when he does that.

"You're a little emo," he says with a laugh, but he says it in an endearing way.

I feel my cheeks heat but I don't feel as embarrassed anymore so I'm smiling now too.

"I'll give it back to you tomorrow morning before school," he says.

Instantly, my stomach drops like a tonne of bricks.

He must notice because then he bends his knees a little so that we're at more of a similar height and he locks my gaze in with his.

"And then tomorrow evening you can come back over here again," he adds. Then he pauses, eyes wide like he just said something incriminating. "I mean, you can bring it back over here again." He gives me a nervous smile, eyebrows raised as he awaits my answer.

I can feel my heart in my stomach. It's thumping like I'm going to be sick and pee my pants at the same time, but kind of in a good way.

I scrunch up my nose, blush, and smile simultaneously, and his eyes are glowing when I meet them with mine.

"Okay... yes, sure, okay. See you tomorrow," I say, and a warm feeling spreads through my chest.

Dimples appear in his cheeks. "See you tomorrow, River."

CHAPTER 7

Present

"I can't believe that we're going to be submitting our college applications soon. We're, like, literally adults now," Kit says as she affixes her sweat-guard wristbands.

I pull up my Gym socks, frowning. "I don't want to go to college," I say. "I want to live on a farm."

She nods in agreement and we head out onto the track field. Mud squelches onto our trainers as soon as we step onto the grass. We hop across it like it's quicksand until we reach the paved track, scraping our heels against the side of the path to get the dirt off.

"Have you picked your colleges yet?" she asks.

I shake my head as we set off round the trail. "Anywhere with good scholarships," I say. "But I wasn't kidding about the farm."

"I know. I just want to be a housewife."

The ultimate feminist win: thriving off the patriarchy for our own evil gain.

"You'll be a senator or something," I say, my breathing

a little heavier now. My brain is picturing my inhaler with little pink love hearts around it. "You're the kind of person our nation deserves."

She snorts lightly. "I hate public attention almost as much as you do. I want to live in the shadows like a vampire."

I glance over at her and see that she's biting the side of her lip, an anxious expression on her face as our soles slap the track.

Changing the subject, Kit asks, "Are you helping with the Halloween dance this year?"

I chew it over. "I'm not sure," I say slowly. "My living situation just got a little weird."

She points her laser eyes on me. "Do tell."

Now I'm gnawing on my lip too. "My mom and I just moved in with her boyfriend. It's only temporary, and he's fine, but..." I trail off. I don't know if I should mention Tate. For the entire duration of our friendship Kit and I have barely ever spoken about boys, for the solid reason that if our lives were a movie we would die if it didn't pass the Bechtel test. Plus I hate thinking about Tate, simply because it hurts that I have to hate him.

I stretch my back as we jog. "Actually, maybe I should help out – and not just with the design stuff. Maybe this is a great excuse to get out of the house."

"And it'll look good on your college applications," she adds.

College applications that I don't even want to apply for, I don't add. There's a palpable pain that comes with not living your life for yourself but I know better than to go against my mom. She's done well in her life – stable job, nice home, semi-normal daughter – and, let's not forget, she's the reason why I'm running around this track right this very second. I owe her my life. The least I can do is try to give it to her.

I change the subject back to the Halloween dance, and

we talk about it until my thoughts about college applications and Tate Coleson are almost forgotten.

Almost forgotten.

＊

I thought that temporarily moving into Mitch's house with my mom would result in awkward encounters and forced politeness, but it hasn't required any adjusting at all. My mom and Mitch are out at work all day, and I eat dinner in my room, so we rarely even cross paths. I'm basically a lodger in my new little attic-cave but I love the space so much that I don't really mind.

By Friday this feels normal.

The sky is ominously overcast this evening. My mom and Mitch are staying at his brother's place tonight and they offered me to join but the thought of being introduced to another step-something made my stomach curdle, so I shook my head and told them that I needed to work on some homework.

In my warm, yielding bed.

I'm fully unpacked now, which was easy considering the fact that I didn't bring much to begin with. I don't *have* much to begin with. My clothes are in the drawers under the bed and my books are piled in miniature stacks around the border of the room. My mom retrieved my bath stuff from the house, so they've been stored in the cabinets by the headboard. I kept the black bed sheets because I'm emo – or maybe I kept them because I'm a weirdo. Either way, I kept the sheets, and I found no incriminating items belonging to the room's previous resident as I worked my way around it.

Trust me, I checked.

And I was very thorough.

I put my drink on the nightstand and shimmy my pyjama pants down my legs so that I'm just wearing my top and underwear, before sliding beneath the sheets with my book. The cotton quilt feels cool on my bare skin and I shudder as I slink further into the mattress, the rain thudding repetitively on the window pane outside.

I'm almost unconscious when I hear it. Loud voices outside. Getting nearer. And then the sound of the front door being unlocked.

The sound of the front door being unlocked.

I shoot up in bed, shoving my glasses back up my nose as I try to ease the crick in my neck from jolting so suddenly.

There are voices in the house.

I didn't even think to shut my bedroom door because I'm home alone tonight. I can hear multiple male voices, fanning out downstairs. Loud and clear.

Obviously it's not going to be my mom and Mitch, but whoever is here has a key…

I tighten my grip on my book, pause for a moment, and then gently extrapolate myself from the duvet. I pull my pyjama pants back on, and then check outside the window for any familiar trucks. I catch sight of a large black Ford and my tummy clenches.

Fascinating.

Time to investigate.

I pad out of my room with stealth and grace. No one has ever moved so silently. When I reach the top of the stairs to the ground floor I see shadows moving across the living room. They're playing music through someone's phone and I hear the hiss of bottles opening. I look down at my healing fist contemplatively.

"River?"

I snap my head up and my breath gets caught in my throat.

Tate is standing at the bottom of the stairs in nothing but a pair of denim jeans and his silver crucifix. His torso is the best colour I have ever seen, like piping hot caramel. He has one hand shoved in his front pocket, and the other is running through his hair.

And, unless my brain is glitching, there is a large dark tattoo – something like a cross and storm clouds and maybe some scripture – enveloping his swollen bicep.

I haven't seen him since he deposited me in his former bedroom, so this feels like a lucid dream.

I put on my annoyed face and cross my arms. "Breaking and entering?"

His eyes trail down my body, a somewhat reluctant look in his gaze as he takes in my outfit, and then he lets out a breath, eyebrows pinched. He glances to the living room and then back to me, warily. He advances one step forward so I take one step back.

"I thought you were at Jason's tonight," he replies.

Who the hell is Jason?

"I do not know anyone by that name," I say in a dignified voice.

He bows his head and breathes out a laugh. His abs ripple. This feels like a test from Satan. I want him to lift his face so I can see his smile, but he hides it from me until the laugh has passed.

He grips the bottom of the banister with one hand, the tendons in his arm flexing. "Jason is my uncle," he clarifies. He glances down my outfit once more and then suddenly looks up at me with heated, taunting eyes. The corners of his lips twitch. "*Our* uncle."

Did he-

Before I can think of a retort, one of Tate's friends rounds the corner and pulls up to lean on the other side of the staircase. He's just as tanned as Tate and most likely the same age but his hair, peeking out from a backwards baseball cap, is light gold, surfer style.

He folds his arms across his chest.

"Sup," he says, jerking his chin at me before surveying my outfit. I think that it gets worse every time someone sees it. Then he looks over at Tate. "Who's that? If that's your dad's girlfriend I'm gonna lose my shit."

Tate is still looking at me. "She's not his girlfriend."

His friend nods, sated. "Who is she then?"

One second.

Two seconds.

Three.

I cock my eyebrow at Tate and he narrows his eyes.

"She's living here whilst we do her refurb."

I smile like the smug little bitch that I am. I feel like I just won an argument.

His friend looks back at me. "I'm Caulder. You legal?"

Tate spins around. "What did you just say?"

Caulder laughs and takes a sip from his bottle, eyes glinting playfully. "We should see if she wants to come down for a drink is all."

In the space of one second Tate starts ascending the stairs looking like a serial killer. I instantly start walking backwards, double-speed, and we reach the back of the landing at almost the exact same moment.

"What are you doing?" I ask, breathless with confusion.

He's ushering me without touching me, the demand radiating from his exposed skin. I acquiesce partially because I don't want to get trampled, but also because I'm the same height as his solid pectorals and this arrangement gives me time to perv.

"You're going upstairs."

I reply "I am upstairs" because I'm a wise-ass.

"You're going *up*-upstairs."

"What if I want a drink?"

I stop abruptly at the bottom of the attic stairwell and he has to catch himself on the frame of the entryway to prevent us from toppling body-into-body.

Tate is blazing with frustration when he looks down at me. "You're not having one. I'm going to make everyone leave. I didn't know that you were home tonight."

Back to the ushering.

"Stop herding me," I grit out, irritated. When I get no response, I choose violence. "Are you inviting girls over or something? Having an orgy on the sofa? Some saint you are. I expect a fucking deep clean by tomorrow morning."

His voice is rougher than gravel. "You want a deep clean?"

This time when I whip around to face him he actually does crash into me. His chest knocks against my left shoulder, but before I can stumble backwards he hooks his right arm around my waist to prevent the fall.

There is a heart-stopping split-second wherein we look at each other, wide eyed, in disbelief over the past five seconds. That he just said that. That our bodies are touching again. It isn't even skin on skin but I feel his rigidity and heat seeping through the fabric of my top. My glasses are slipping down my nose so I shove them back up with a shaking hand.

Then I'm furious.

I bend my arms up and thrust my elbows into his chest, hard. He doesn't budge but I manage to claw my way out of his arms anyway. I'm sprinting up the stairs and my heart is thundering in my chest because I can hear him racing on my tail. I push into my room and purposefully spin around so that I can look at him whilst I slam the door in his face but he drives his arm out, stopping it.

"You can't come in here," I say quickly, and I raise a *so-there* eyebrow at him.

He glances over my shoulder. "I like what you've done with the place."

He knows that I haven't changed a damn thing since he was last here. I narrow my eyes on him.

"Thanks. Your visitation's over now. Tell Caulder I said hi."

He glances down at my pyjama pants. "Are you cold in here? You're dressed for Antarctica."

I pause for one stomach-sinking moment because with that comment he's hit a nerve, but I quickly shake it off. "I'm toasty. Did you know that you're naked?"

He's eyeing up my little stacks of books. Thank God he's far enough away from them to make the titles illegible. Then he glances over at the bed, a crumpled mess with my current read enthroned on the pillow like a little smut shrine.

Tate looks down at me and folds his arms across his chest in an attempt at male modesty. His biceps bulge against his nipples in my peripheral vision.

"Are you staying in tonight? It's Friday." He sounds genuinely concerned.

"I am very busy," I reply.

"What are the little tabs for?" His eyes are back on the book stacks, much to my horror.

"I tab the useful bits of information. Vivid and grotesque murder scenes, for example."

He runs his hand through his hair. "You just keep them out on the floor like that?"

I scowl at him as he continues surveying the room. *What is he still doing here?*

His breathing becomes a bit weird and I notice that he's looking at my laundry pile. It's topped off with the little baby pink bra that I need to hand wash because of the black lace trim. I can smell thunderstorms and pheromones radiating off his hot damp skin and he drops his eyes and swallows, a subjugated blush spreading across his cheekbones.

He takes a step back, avoiding my eyes. "I'm... sorry about tonight. I'll get everyone out of here, five minutes tops."

Then he turns around and begins trudging down the stairs, hands in his pockets.

When I put my hand on the door to finally close it, a thought crosses my mind as he reaches the last step.

"I want a lock on my door," I call down the stairs.

He pauses with his back to me for one moment before he looks back over his broad shoulder and meets my gaze, under a veil of wet tousled hair and stunning black lashes. His eyes twinkle with something that I can't put my finger on.

Then he rolls his shoulders and exhales deeply.

"Trust me, I'll fit one."

CHAPTER 8

Three Years Ago

By the following Monday Tate knows the order of the track list and every lyric to my Breaking Benjamin *Phobia* album.

On the second evening that I went to give him the player again he looked a lot happier than he had the previous night. He had his hands shoved in the pockets of his hoodie and a gorgeous smile tugging at his lips.

When I went to hand it to him I noticed that he had put out some folded up blankets to sit on, which was unusual because I'm pretty sure that he had never done that before. He was blushing a bit when he saw me looking but then he stood up extra straight and said, "I was wondering if you wanted to listen to it with me tonight?"

How did his eyes get so sparkly? I said yes, of course, and we sat down, taking one ear bud each. I was holding the top step of the porch in a death grip because his pinkie finger was so close to mine and he flexed it a few times as if he could sense the attention.

At the end of the week I had become more comfortable,

so I asked him if I could unfold the blankets and lie down whilst we were out here. Being a full-time swat was kind of tiring, and I could use the resting time.

Tate was eager in agreement. He was so on board with the idea that he even went back inside to get the pillows from his bed for us to lie on.

We were near the end of the album when I heard it. I was only wearing one ear-bud so I could still hear the noises from around us, and, being a nerd and all, the rustle of pages caught my attention. I opened my eyes and looked over at Tate, thinking that maybe he was asleep, so I took the headphone out using the hand that wasn't next to his and I sat up.

Twisting my head I looked at the binder laid out behind us and I gently opened up the first page. It was stacked with old test essays, only it looked as though none of the questions had been answered yet. Maybe these were his revision papers that he was yet to go through. I softly moved over a few more leaves until I got to one that was dated this week, again empty, but this one had a circled letter *F* at the top, and a *see me after class* scribbled underneath it.

Was Tate failing his classes? The thought made my brow pinch. From what I could tell, Tate was smart. He was articulate and considerate, two skills that take a developed intelligent brain. I pondered it some more and then realised that maybe it was because of all of the sports that he has been doing, taking his time away from his studies – and that isn't necessarily a bad thing, especially if that's the kind of physical profession he would rather do after he finishes school – but it did explain why he would want to hide this stuff from his mom and her boyfriend.

I couldn't help the ten-tonne drop in my stomach, though. My mom would never approve of him.

Suddenly I looked down and Tate's eyes were on mine. He didn't blink because he knew what I was seeing, and a soft pink flush spread across his cheeks.

Without a word I put the headphone back in my ear and lowered myself down so that I was facing him. Neither of us closed our eyes this time. It was like we were speaking to each other without saying any words.

Then I felt it. The warm brush of his long fingers against mine, the gentle rub of his knuckles on my skin.

He looked down at our hands and then back up at me through beautiful black lashes.

And then our fingers entwined.

*

I slink into the swivel chair next to Kit as our Computer Tech teacher momentarily leaves the room, and I hand her back her memory stick that I saved the updated Homecoming poster to.

"You emboldened the theme?" she asks.

"Yes." We're having a 1950s theme because apparently it's compulsory for all high schools to do that at least once.

"Thank you. What are you going to wear? I'm going to wear a suit - maybe a leather one," she says.

There will be no competing with that.

I scrunch up my nose. "I might not actually go to Homecoming as an attendee." My stomach feels weird just thinking about it. Watching people have fun in their big social circles as I cling to my one friend in her all-leather suit.

The teacher comes back into the room, oblivious to the alteration in the seating plan, so I stay planted in the chair in the hopes of not getting caught.

"Of course you're attending Homecoming," she whisper-scolds. "I expect an outfit update by next week."

After class we head to our lockers to pick up our gym clothes. I twist the key, pulling open the little door, and as I go to grab my sports bag I see a piece of folded paper that I don't remember putting there. I blink at it for a few moments like it's an extraterrestrial. I assume that, whatever it is, it was slipped under the bottom of the door frame so I grab a pen from my bag and slip it between the fold, lifting it with neurosurgeon-level caution.

It's a type-written note, printed from one of the computer labs by the looks of the borderline translucent paper, and my chest flutters as I read it.

Please meet me after last bell, or you'll be BREAKING Tate's heart :)
Location: parking lot, big tree

I smile at the paper and then slide it gently into my satchel. There's a little skip in my step as we make our way to the gym.

*

I thought that I would beat him to the meet-up because the gym is right next to the lot, but once I'm out of the doors I see that Tate is already by the tree.

But he's not alone.

The guy with the black hair is standing next to him and they're both wearing their track gear. There's a cold pattering of rain and it's kind of windy but my blood has gone cold for a whole other reason.

Why is someone else here?

By the time that Tate sees me my smile has vanished and I'm nervously pushing my glasses back up my nose. He's leaning against the tree and his friend is toying with something small in his hands. When I'm about six feet away Tate pushes himself off the trunk and he smiles down at me.

I don't smile back. Instead, I look pointedly at his friend, who gives me a smug knowing grin in return.

"This is Madden," Tate tells me, and he tugs at my shirt sleeve to pull me closer to him.

Madden? I give him a frosty once-over. So *this* is the guy that Kit was talking about.

"Right," I say, ice pooling in my stomach.

"He knows who you are," Tate says, the smile still on his lips as he tries to slip my fingers into his.

I shrug him off.

Madden rolls his eyes and fixes me with a cocky, meaningful look. "I was just waiting with him whilst Your Highness was taking her sweet time in the changing rooms," he says, folding his arms over his chest. "Trust me, I don't want any part in this." He jerks his chin at Tate. "See you in five."

Madden strolls away and Tate laces our hands together, his smile still in place. "Madden's cool, I promise. He's not like Huddy."

I look up at him. *Huddy*. So that's the name of the dirty blond.

"Are you unhappy to see me?" he asks, ducking his head down so that our eyes are level. His *eyes*. I'll never get over them.

I shake my head, feeling self-conscious and out of my depth. "Sorry, no, that was weird of me. I just didn't expect... I'm sure he's awesome." I muster up a small smile.

Tate pulls the hair tie off my wrist and pushes my curls back from my face, holding them gently in his fist before securing them with the band. When the ponytail is in place he moves his mouth to my ear and whispers mischievously, "Not as awesome as *me*."

I laugh and he pulls back, a satisfied swell in his chest.

"Look, I had to meet you today because I'm not going home after practice. I'm heading to Mad's with the guys so I won't be home tonight for our thing. I wish I didn't have to, but I'll be back tomorrow, so I'm not flaking, I mean it."

There's a sad drop in my tummy knowing that I don't

have my favourite part of the evening to look forward to tonight, but there's also a little flash of lightening in my chest knowing that this is now *our thing*.

I smile so brightly that I think it offends him. Then I laugh, which makes things even worse.

"That's fine, Tate," I say, my voice tinkling with joy. I'm on another sugar high. "That is so fine, I promise."

It's my turn to give the *please forgive me* eyes.

He nods warily and then drops his head, blowing out a little laugh. "God, you're so cool."

I choose not to correct him.

He pulls me closer than before, closer than I have ever been to him, until our chests are almost touching. I can smell the cool rain radiating off his warm caramel skin. His hands are so big and sturdy that I want to be covered in them.

Our faces are only a few inches apart. He's looking down at my mouth so I look up at his. A water droplet runs over the curve of his bottom lip and I think about how it would feel if I were to catch it on my tongue.

His eyes flick back up to mine, now piercing and aflame. He ducks down and presses the raindrop on his mouth against the flushed skin of my cheek. My skin is icy cold and his lips are molten. My blood pumps fast. I think that he might have just added ten years to my life.

He pulls away and squeezes my hands tightly in his. I feel that same compression around my heart. I let go before he has the chance to, moving my hands to grip the strap of my bag.

He puts his hands in the pockets of his shorts and gives me a perfect departing smile.

"I'll see you tomorrow, River."

CHAPTER 9

Present

"What the hell is that?" My mom is looking sceptically out of the front door into the bed of Mitch's truck.

He throws her a cocky smile. "Wanna have a go?"

She looks thoroughly mortified. "If that's yours, I'm out of here right now."

I look out of the door with her. In the back of Mitch's truck there is a monstrous black motorbike. I have never seen one this up close before and, from its raised position in the bed, it's way bigger than I was expecting.

"Not mine," Mitch replies, and he shoots me a piercing look.

"So what exactly are you doing with it?" my mom asks, arms folded across her chest.

Mitch swaggers to the mouth of the bed and leans against it with his palms behind his body. "*I* am not doing anything with it."

I sense the presence of a large warm body standing close behind me so I refuse to turn around. It feels like I have a lighter licking up my spine, and my stomach swirls with heat.

Tate's arm grips the doorframe above my head and he rubs it with his thumb. I pretend that I don't see it.

My mom steps out of the doorway but Tate stays positioned at my back anyway. I remind myself why I hate him as my body masochistically soaks in his heated pheromones.

My mom looks between Mitch and Tate.

"Your son rides a motorcycle?" she asks. She has an intrigued look in her eyes now that she knows it isn't her boyfriend who is going to risk life and limb on the road, but her voice is laced with displeasure.

"He does motorbike races when there are comps on the weekends. There's an enclosed track just outside of town, but it's out of use when we get all the rainfall, so this will probably be the last event until next spring. Which means I get him on-site full-time for the next few months." Mitch winks at Tate, but my stomach jolts as if it was aimed at me.

Tate slides his thumb down the doorframe and then back up. It feels as though he's pressing it against my spine.

His bass timbre hits me from behind, impossibly deep and chocolate-cake rich. "Are you coming, River?"

I decide to risk my life. "To watch you get beaten by thirty other men on motorcycles? Of course I am."

I feel his body tense and I get all warm and fuzzy as I watch his forearm flex with rage. I disguise my smile by fiddling with my glasses.

My body sighs with relief as I walk out of the doorway and onto the porch, extrapolating it from the heady mixture of his heroin cologne and my violent hormones. I give Mitch a cheerful look which makes him eye me suspiciously.

"What time are we going?" I ask innocently.

Mitch flicks a glance at Tate and then back to me. "Comp starts at six, so you have all day to do whatever else.

Schoolwork or..." He waves his hand around, trying to think of some other things that seventeen year old girls might do on their Sundays.

My mom prods one of the wheels like it's a lab specimen. "Count me out," she says, her mouth twisted with concern.

I shoot her a glance. "Can I still go, mom?"

She doesn't look at me, still absently observing the bike. "You want to watch a bike show?" she asks, her voice dubious. She exhales a light laugh through her nose. "Sure honey." She wipes her fingers on her pants and then walks back up the drive, heading to the yard.

I'll take it.

I smile luxuriantly at Mitch and he has an amused glint in his eyes as he folds his arms across his chest.

"You got any clothes to wear tonight?" Mitch asks.

I'm affronted. "Of course I have clothes."

"Yeah, but clothes *for this*." He taps the bike with the back of his hand.

I wriggle a bit.

"I want you to blend in, River. I don't want it to look like I brought a sacrifice."

I frown up at him. Why is this always the sticking point? Okay, yes I wear prescription glasses, and clothes are unusually large on my body, but why do other people care so much about what *I* am wearing? What would they *prefer* for me to wear?

Tate's voice sounds from the doorway. "I have some things that she can wear. She just needs her own shorts."

I shake my head at Mitch. "Absolutely not."

Mitch holds his hands up and backs away from me.

I spin around to face Tate but my stomach instantly sinks. He's wearing saw-dust covered jeans and a taut black t-shirt. My chest is constricting more tightly than the cotton wrapped around his pecs. I can't believe that he was almost mine.

"I am not taking a single thing from you," I say in as steady a voice as I can manage.

He folds his arms and the tattoo on his bicep bulges. "Tell me whose bed you're sleeping in again?"

I mirror him and cross my arms too. "I'm sure that you have slept in all kinds of beds, Tate."

He raises his eyebrows and I swear that his fingers almost go up to touch the cross on his chain. He looks displeased.

"It doesn't have to be like this," he says. It sounds like he's pleading.

There's a horrible shooting pain deep in my oesophagus but the words tumble out of mouth anyway before I can stop them.

"I hope that you lose tonight, Tate."

And then I storm off, stomach churning.

*

After our conversation Tate locked himself in the garage and I heard all sorts of hacking and drilling sounds, so I imagine that he's making some sort of voodoo doll. I quickly got changed and fled to Kit's house.

I am naturally artsy and Kit is naturally morbid so the Halloween dance banners are coming along exceptionally well. Everything is orange, purple, and black, and I'm actually looking forward to being at some kind of social gathering.

Which reminds me.

I roll over so that I'm directly in front of Kit and I stare at her until she looks up. She yelps when she sees the intensity of my gaze.

"Oh my God, *what?*" she exclaims, a shiver rumbling through her.

"I have a fashion related question," I say.

She is thoroughly astounded. She adds a final leg to one

of her dangly black spiders and sets down her brush. "Go on," she encourages.

"It is purely for malicious purposes," I confess.

She nods. "As it should be."

"I was wondering..." I swallow, my stomach fluttering with butterflies. "Do you have a top that is super cute... but also violently inappropriate that I could possibly wear this evening?"

She blinks at me. Her eyes roam over my slouchy jumper and wide leg jeans. She nods like she's dreaming.

"Are you sure?" she asks as she pulls out a secret, hidden garment from one of her under-the-bed drawers.

"Yes. Just for tonight," I add.

Kit bids me to close my eyes and then she places the item in my hands. She actually puts it on a cushion first, for extra drama.

I look down at it and then give her a shy smile.

"Thank you, Kit," I say. "It's perfect."

*

Mitch and Tate pull up to collect me from Kit's house at five, and then we reach the race location with time to spare. I have my secret top on underneath my jumper and it's making me emit a devilish glow.

Tate can sense it. He keeps looking at me in the rear-view mirror because he knows that I am up to something.

But I can also sense something secretive shimmering beneath *his* unyieldingly composed façade, piquing my interest and annoying me senseless.

He hasn't said anything to me since my volcanic eruption on the driveway and, if I'm being honest, I don't blame him.

As we pull up I look down at the lit-up track. Now I understand my mom's hesitance: this looks dangerous. It doesn't seem as though it would fit many racers, so maybe only a few bikers race at a time. There's a crowd all the way around the track, and behind that I see stalls set up by sponsors and merchandise vendors.

When we get out, Tate dismounts his bike and disappears without a second glance.

Now I feel like I'm Mitch's daughter. He takes me to a food stand where he gets a hotdog for himself and fries for me, and then we make our way over to join the rest of the audience.

It is *really* hot near the stadium lights. I keep pulling at the neck of my jumper but the air is so still that it isn't helping. Now that I'm going to *have* to expose my stupid little revenge ploy it doesn't seem like such a good idea.

"You wanna take that off?" Mitch is watching my tussle with the jumper with a dubious expression. "I'll hold your fries."

I surrender. I hand him the fries and shed the jumper, sighing at the relief of having it off my skin.

"Jesus Christ!"

It seems that Mitch cannot be trusted to hold my fries. The fries are everywhere. They're on the ground. They're on my jumper. Mitch is looking at me with such a dismayed expression that it confirms that this top was an excellent choice. He picks my jumper off the floor, not even bothering to wipe it off.

"Put this back on. Right now."

I pluck the jumper from his hand and then drop it back to the dirt.

"River, what the fuck are you thinking?"

Wow, he really is like a dad.

"Tate cannot see you like this," Mitch says. "In fact, Tate cannot see *other people* seeing you like this. He's going to go insane."

I narrow my eyes at Mitch and everything becomes clear.

Mitch *knows*.

I never told my mom *anything*, but from Mitch's expression I know that he knows.

And that makes his concern even more absurd.

"I can wear what I want Mitch," I say as I collect my droopy little fries from the dirt and put them back into the carton.

He has his hand over his mouth like he's trying to decide which neuro-pathway to take in his man-brain. A or B.

"After Tate's race I want you to put that back on," he says, his voice stern and authoritative. Then he turns away from me without another word, waiting for the race to begin.

I can't tell which one is Tate because everyone on the track is riding a big black bike, but when I hear Mitch yelling I realise that he's right behind the lead. Mitch is shouting something about "cat and mouse" as the bikers skirt precariously over the twisting bends, and then when the first racer speeds over the finish line Mitch is vehemently fist-pumping the air.

I watch as Tate takes off his helmet. His hair has stuck against his forehead in a sweaty tousled mess and his perfect smile is visible all the way from here.

I turn around and head back to Mitch's truck.

I've only been walking a minute when I hear it.

"Hey, I know you – *whoaaaa*, how's it going?"

I look up and I'm met with the sight of Tate's friend from the house the other night. Caulder. So he must be one of Tate's motorbike buddies.

His shirt is off – it really is hot under these lights – and he's wearing heavily branded biking pants. There's a rigid V slicing up either side of his abdominals, and, most obviously of all, Caulder's eyes are magnetised to my chest.

"Hey," I say, putting my hand on my hip. It feels different talking to a guy who isn't at school with me. He doesn't have any preconceptions and therefore I can be whoever I want to be.

"Hey," he says again, before blinking hard and looking up. "Caulder," he blurts out, hand outstretched. Obviously he doesn't remember telling me his name.

"River," I say, and I brush past him, leaving him hanging.

"Hey, wait!"

I smile as I hear him chase after me. Tate is going to *looooove* this.

"What are you doing here? If you tell me that you ride I'm going to have to marry you on the spot."

I roll my eyes, ascending the hill to get to where the truck is parked.

"Let me get you a drink. You're not here with Tate are you? Doesn't matter, we can hide from him."

Some friend he is. I wonder if all of Tate's friends are this shitty.

He sees me stop next to Mitch's truck and he nods his head.

"So you *are* here with the Colesons. Damn. Come hang out with me for a bit anyway."

I lean my stomach against the side panel of the bed, looking out at the post-ride track, and Caulder leans next to me.

"Cute glasses," he says, and I can feel the heat radiating from his skin closer to me than before.

I turn to look at him, eyebrow cocked, but he really is cute. His eyes are sapphire blue and his hair is Californian gold. He senses my appraisal and he tilts a little closer, a knowing twinkle in his smiling eyes.

It only takes five seconds and then he's on the floor.

Tate hauls him by his shoulders and Caulder's back hits the dirt with a painfully loud thud. Tate's thighs straddle Caulder's hips, one hand pinning down his collarbones, and he smacks his palm across the side of his temple. I watch them over my shoulder with science-experiment curiosity.

"What the hell did I say to you the other night, Caul?" This is a voice that I have never heard before. It's so calm that it's scary. My stomach dips knowing that this display is for me.

"Nothing happened, bro!" Caulder is confused which is understandable. There is no logical reason as to why Tate would be acting out like this over me, especially given what *he did* three years ago. But, for some reason, I can sense it. I can still feel it deep in my bones on the most innate primitive level that this is for *me*.

Tate shoves Caulder's shoulders into the ground as a departing warning and then he stands, brushing the dirt off his knees with big tense hands.

I twist back towards the truck and I look straight ahead so that my back is to him. The truck bed dips with a groan as Tate's hands grip the panel on either side of my waist.

"River," he says, in a low and deadly voice. "Look me in the eyes, right now."

I ignore him because I know that that's what will annoy him the most.

I feel the hot firm grip of his palm on my shoulder and then he turns my body with ease to face him.

His brain explodes.

The thing about never showing your skin? When you do show it, it's a *really* big deal. Tate's chest swells on impact and he bends slightly at the middle, as if I just punched him in the gut. His hands have curled into fists on either side of me, forearms stiffening as he swallows hard. His eyes flash to mine and they are frenzied, desperate, wild.

Then Caulder shuffles to his feet behind him and the light goes out like a switch.

Tate spins around a launches a fist into the side of Caulder's jaw, his head snapping to the left and sending him stumbling into the side of someone else's car. Tate stalks him like an animal, grabbing his shoulder and swinging his arm back as if he's going to punch him again, but suddenly the little crowd around us gets involved, and guys are pulling them apart, restraining their arms and wrists.

Mitch appears and he grapples with Tate until he's on the passenger side of the truck. He shoves him through the door, slams it shut, and then hauls Tate's bike into the back. Mitch comes to stand in front of me, eyes livid and steam practically oozing from his tan skin.

"What the hell are you doing to him, River? He could get disqualified for that," he bites out, arms shaking at his sides.

I stand my ground. *Nothing compared to what he did to me, Mitch.*

"Just get in the truck, and don't say a word." He storms to the driver's door and heaves himself inside.

It's officially the tensest ride of my life. When we arrive back at Mitch's, Tate whips out of his dad's truck and quickly gets into his own, kicking the vehicle into reverse and racing off the driveway with dangerous speed.

Mitch turns to me, his face candy-apple red with a syrupy sheen.

"For that, you're grounded. Forever," he commands, and then he thunders into the house, shoulders rolling like a Viking.

I feel smug with satisfaction as I enter the house after him, all until I reach the bottom of the stairs to my room in the attic.

There's a pain in my gut as I see something sat carefully just outside my door. Mitch and my mom are in his room now and the landing is totally silent. I slowly ascend the steps, my eyes locked on the object, and my stomach sinks deeper and deeper until I feel nothing but emptiness inside.

Please don't be what I think you are, please don't be what I think you are.

My hand flies up to my mouth and I feel a horrible prickling behind my eyes.

Now I know what he did when he locked himself in the

workshop all day.

At the top of the stairs, wrapped up with a little ribbon, there is a tiny perfect wooden bookcase.

CHAPTER 10

Three Years Ago

"Are you alright?"

Kit is looking at me weird as I put some of my finished homework into my locker. For some reason each leaf of paper feels like it weighs eighty tonnes today and I cannot for the life of me carry the excess for one second longer.

"I'm fine," I say in an embarrassingly weak voice. My stomach actually convulses when the words leave my mouth. I rest my head against the locker above mine, not even caring about all of the germs that will now be embedded into my forehead.

What is *wrong* with me today?

"You look all pale and sweaty." She manages to say it in a friendly way.

"I feel a bit-" I take off my blazer and flap my arms about, trying to get the cool air to heal me osmosis-style. "I feel like I might be about to pass out."

"Hmm," she muses as we start walking to class. "Maybe it's your blood sugar. Do you want a Starburst?"

She rummages in her bag.

"Actually, I've only got the green ones left, and that might send you over."

I sigh. She is not wrong.

When we get to class I take my seat like a zombie. I don't even know which class we are in, so I just start pulling everything out of my bag in a heavy-lidded daze. Kit gives me her water bottle before she goes to her seat at the other side of the room and I absorb the liquid like a sponge. Then my stomach starts to hurt even more.

By the end of class I have coloured in all four corners of my notepad, gradating them from dark inky black, to dove grey, and then to the white of the page. I have also managed to not pass out, which feels like a very significant achievement right now.

Kit helps me stuff my things in my bag and then we are out of the room, standing next to a set of doors that lead to the courtyard. The air, fresh with recent rainfall, feels so good that I want to go outside and curl up like an animal on the concrete. Right after I've ripped out my intestines.

"We have one more hour – are you sure you don't want to go home? You can keep the water bottle by the way."

My heart is thumping in my ears, making her sound like she's underwater. "I'll get you a new one," I say, guilt-ridden because of my grossness.

"Please don't. All I ask is that you don't die because you're the only friend that I have."

That pierces the veil. I look over at her and she's shuffling on her feet, half wanting to make sure that I'm okay and half scared about not making it to class on time.

I have to be there for her.

"One more hour," I gurgle out, and we turn back down the corridor.

*

I face-plant my bed as soon as I get home. My glasses are now entrenched in my skull. I shuck off my skirt, tights and sweater vest, and I try to become one with the quilt. Am I dying? If I am at least I won't have to do that French listening test next week.

When my mom gets home she immediately stomps up to my room.

"Amazon delivery," she sing-songs dryly. "Thanks for keeping the front door unlocked. I'm here to murder a small teenage girl."

I groan and roll over, looking up at her stern face.

I expect her to start a lecture but her eyes drop down to the bed and she makes a small knowing sniff.

"*Oh*," she says.

I look down too.

Oh.

"River, why didn't you tell me?" she asks, her tone disappointed.

There is a small circle of blood on my bed. I sit up and look down at my underwear, and there is a small circle of blood there too.

My mom stopped getting periods when she hit an early menopause a few years ago so I don't really have any second-hand experiences to go on. I've never had a period before.

I'm so amazed by the sight that I stop feeling the pains for a minute.

"It must have just happened," I say, my tone awe-struck. RIP my underwear.

"Right, I'm going to go out and get you some pads and Ibuprofen. Stay right here."

Honestly, where does she think that I will go? My own body is stabbing me from the inside and I have sweat running down my forehead. I hear her close the front door and I roll back on my stomach, into my little blood patch.

Then there's another knock at the door.

Ugh. Why is she trying to torture me? Is this her way of forcing me out of bed so that I *have* to lock the door from the inside? Why can't she lock the door from the *outside*?

By the time that I reach the bottom step I feel like hell again. Too much jiggling. I catch sight of myself in the mirror and Kit was right. I am all pale and sweaty.

I open the door and my stomach drops.

Tate Coleson is an imposing presence when he's standing in your doorway. He's not even sixteen yet and he's already six foot tall. His face is in the shadow of the porch roof, making his skin an even deeper tan, and when he meets my eyes he looks hard and angry.

Then his face changes completely.

"River, what's wrong?"

All of a sudden I can't stand anymore. I want to put my head between my knees but that would look weird in front of Tate, so I opt for lying down on the tiles instead.

"I'm fine," I lie. From down here on the tiles the lie sounds believable. I think that I might be passing out. When I peek up at Tate he doesn't look convinced.

"River, please can I come in?" His whole body is straining in the doorway. He looks so desperate that I want to say *no* and then continue watching him put up this agonising fight with the invisible barrier, but instead I sigh and acquiesce.

"You can take the player, Tate. It's in my room." *Just leave me here to die.*

He's at my side in an instant, one hand cupping my head so that it isn't touching the tiles and the other entwining our fingers.

"What is it? What happened? I saw your mom leave. Tell me, River."

Suddenly I have this horrible recollection of what I am wearing. Luckily due to my short height the white shirt that I have on technically looks oversized, but still, if he looks any further-

"Tate, please don't look down," I say urgently.

Obviously Tate's eyes immediately flicker downwards and he sees exactly why I am melting like a puddle on my mom's tiles.

His eyes are back on mine in a second, his expression bashful and guilty.

"I'm sorry," he says, "I didn't mean to."

He moves the hand that was in mine up to my cheek and I groan in an agonising way. He flashes a wary glance to the front door and then back down to me. He does this a few times. Then he scoops me into his arms bridal style, knocks the front door closed with his shoulder, and starts carrying me up the stairs.

"I might bleed on your arm," I whisper.

He breathes out a small laugh but mainly he looks like he's hurting.

He's hurting because I am hurting.

At the top of the stairs he asks, "Which room is yours?" as if we haven't been staring into each other's windows for our entire teenage lives.

Both of our bodies are a bit tense now. I vaguely lollop my arm in the direction of my room and he carries me into it, fingers gripping into my thighs tighter than before. He cautiously settles me on my bed like a priceless one-of-a-kind artefact.

I roll onto my side as he crouches down next to me, and I wince as my stomach cramps.

"What can I do?" He's stroking my cheek with impossible gentleness. "Is there any way to relieve it?"

Is this what men are like? Surely not. Maybe I am dead.

Then he asks, "Can I touch your stomach, River?"

My eyes flash to his and my head spins a little. It is highly unlikely that having a man spread his palm over my stomach is going to relieve the pain inside of me.

And yet.

"Yes," I say quickly.

"Thank you," he replies, and he gets to his feet, towering over me.

I roll onto my back and look up at him.

Slowly he pulls up his sleeve and he splays his hand a few inches above my stomach. The air between my tummy and his palm is pulsing aggressively with anticipation. His fingers are so long and his knuckles are so big that I have to grip my sheet to prevent myself from wriggling. I must be emitting all sorts of violently explicit pheromones because his jaw is clenched and throbbing.

He eases his fingers out across the white cotton of my shirt and then he gradually begins to press the large expanse of his warm palm against my lower stomach. The heat from his skin sinks in through the fabric and I can instantly feel it submerging into my body. I arch my back up higher so that he can touch as much as possible and his hand presses even firmer into me. I push my head back into my pillow and the soft surface plumps up indulgently around my cheeks.

When I hear the hard sounds of ragged breathing I flutter my eyes open. Tate instantly looks away from me, a deep blush spreading across his cheekbones. I look down at my stomach and I can see the tension rippling through the thick tendons of his forearm. The possibility that I am responsible for his flushed demeanour makes me feel sparkly all over.

"It feels okay now, Tate."

My voice is all husky. It's foreign to both of us and it startles him. He pulls his hand back like my body just burnt him and he holds it behind his head, giving me a satisfying display of taut abdomen.

"My mom will be home in a few minutes. Do you want to take the player?" I nod over to the corner of my room where my CD player is longingly looking out of the window over at Tate's porch.

Tate lets out a long breath and shakes his head. He sits down next to my feet and the bed squeaks in delight. "I only want to listen if I'm with you," he says quietly, hands gripping his knees. Then he looks up my body until his eyes finally meet mine. "Only with you."

A warm feeling spreads inside of me.

"I'm sorry I didn't come over today, I was dying," I say apologetically. I tuck my knees up so that I can hide my underwear.

He shakes his head, and a finger brushes up my calf. "I was being greedy, I shouldn't have done that," he says. "You don't have to come to see me every day anymore - it's not fair to you. I'm going to start planning things. I want to spoil you." Then he looks up at me with a playful smile. "Are you going to let me spoil you, River?"

I laugh delightedly under his attention but then a car drives past the window and it snaps us out of the moment.

It wasn't my mom but it could have been.

He pulls the discarded cover from the side of my bed and tucks it snug around my body.

"I can't believe that I'm in your bedroom," he whispers tenderly.

"Don't look at anything," I whisper back. My eyes flick nervously to the stack of romance books by the door.

He smiles. "I haven't. But I want an in-depth tour the next time that I'm here."

Next time.

He crouches beside me again and murmurs, "I want to look inside every single one of these drawers", as he runs his fingers down their ridges. I shiver like he's running his fingers over me.

He grins.

Tate pushes himself up and carefully eases my glasses from my face. He sets them on the dresser the right way up, which makes my OCD shudder with delight, and then he leans over, covering me in the warm smell of his golden skin. He presses a firm kiss to the top of my cheekbone as he whispers me goodbye.

My cheek tingles even after he slips out of the house. I fall asleep with the feeling of his warm palm pressing heat and pleasure deep into my womb.

CHAPTER 11

Present

Mitch is keeping me under intense surveillance now. As my punishment for "deliberate incitement" I have to stay back at school each afternoon until Mitch finishes work for the day at my mom's, and then he picks me up, takes me to his place, and sends me to my room.

What he fails to realise is that this is pretty much what I did every day anyway, so essentially the only change is that he is now giving me a lift home.

The one thing that I *am* disappointed about is the fact that I am not allowed to attend the Halloween dance anymore. I'm okay to help set it up on the night, but then I'm getting picked up and – surprise, surprise – sent back to my room. I hadn't really wanted to go in the first place, but now that the option has been taken away – especially after all of my artistic investments – it has given me a good reason to mope about whenever I see Mitch.

My other punishment is that Mitch wants me to help out with his business and "earn my keep", which is obviously just code for "provide free labour". It's not *my* fault that Tate can't control his rabid hormones.

Mitch is sat with me at his kitchen table, showing me his very basic website. I tell him that it matches him perfectly and now I'm sentenced to washing his dishes for the rest of the week on top of all of my other punishments too.

I placate him, mainly to try and undo the dishes situation. "Yes, I can fix it," I say. "It would be handy if you could provide some before and after refurb pics, and maybe some photos of the team so that buyers know what they're getting." I don't tell him that I'm picturing his entire crew standing shirtless around a truck, holding planks of wood over their swollen sweaty shoulders. "If you give me the email login details I can set up a few social pages too, to spread a bit of awareness across the channels."

Mitch is distractedly thumbing the Halloween dance poster that I designed.

"Is this what you're gonna do at college?" he asks.

I pull a face and shake my head. "No," I mumble. I don't actually see the point of going to college to "study" about a skill that I already have, not to mention all of the limbs that I'll have to sell to fund it, but I know that in the real world you have to prove yourself with a college name and a grade sheet if you want to get a job. None of this matters anyway because I've been prepped to do exactly what my mom wanted of me since before I even started high school.

He nods but doesn't say anything. Then he puts down the poster and says, "Okay, you're hired." The "for free" is unspoken here.

After Mitch and I work out the basics, I trudge up to my bedroom and scrunch myself onto the quilt, pulling off my glasses and smushing my face into the cotton.

"*Uggghhhhhh,*" I groan and I pull my slippers off with my toes. It's grizzly outside, not raining but heavily overcast, and my window is open a crack, filling up the room with pinching cold air. I roll over just so that I can pull my school sweater over my head when there's a knock on my door.

I sit bolt upright. I fumble with my glasses until they're back on my face and I flatten my sweater back down.

"Yes?" I ask. Why is my heart in my throat?

The door opens a couple of inches and Tate is standing before me. Faded denim jeans and a t-shirt clearly selected to antagonise. The veins in his tan forearms are bulging, meaning that he must have been going pretty hard at the refurb today. We also now have matching wounded hands wrapped up in gauze, due to my incident with Mitch's truck and Tate's scene at the motorbike race. Even though I shouldn't care, I feel a hot flicker in my stomach knowing that I still illicit some primal hold over him. He's holding a toolbox in one hand, and he's gripping the top of the doorframe with the other.

He holds up the box. "You want me to fit that lock in your door?"

I'm clutching onto the quilt for dear life. His voice is so deep I can feel it in my bones. Mainly my pelvic bones.

I narrow my eyes on him anyway. "Fine," I say, and I roll onto my stomach so that I don't have to look at him.

I hear him suck in a breath behind me and then the floorboards sound as he steps back out of the room. I glance over my shoulder and I see that he has partially closed the door so that he can start unscrewing the pieces on the outside handle. Only the large curve of his right shoulder is currently visible so I do a quick sweep of my room to check for anything incriminating. The little wooden bookcase next to my bed is probably one of those things. I nimbly lean forward and fling my pyjama top over it.

I shuffle back against the pillows and pick up the college brochures that I've been collecting from the school library. I wasn't lying when I told Kit that I would apply for the places with the best scholarships, even if it is unlikely that I get one of them. It'll be good to leave this town, even if my soul is begging me to stay.

After a few minutes the door is pushed open again and Tate is standing there, hesitant and rigid. "Can I come in?" he asks, his voice stiff.

He hasn't been in this room since it became *my* room. I feel like if I invite him in he'll suddenly reveal that he's a vampire and suck out all of my blood. I look at the perfect white teeth biting into his bottom lip and I picture them sinking lusciously into my neck.

I throw the brochure down and he looks at it with narrowed eyes. I fold my arms across my chest. "If you must," I acquiesce, feigning boredom.

He steps inside and the room instantly becomes smaller. Darker. He's filled it with his size, scent, and pheromones, and now when I take a breath I'm breathing him in. He places down the box and pulls a tube from his pocket. It must be some sort of joiner's grease because he squeezes the gel onto his fingers and then he starts rubbing it in circles around the screws.

The brochure slips off my lap and onto the floor, causing Tate to glance at me over his shoulder. He takes in my dazed expression and heavy breathing, and a glint flashes in his eyes. He turns back to the door and drops down, picking up his tool as he begins unscrewing the bolts. The muscles in his shoulders are hard under my gaze.

"So," he begins, voice husky. "Did you enjoy the race?"

I think about the fact that I have the fastest motorbike racer in this town wearing out the knees in his jeans as he screws a lock into my bedroom door, and my stomach slowly pools with heat.

I lean down under the pretence of picking up the college booklet, but really I'm watching his hands force the metal out of my door. "I didn't not enjoy the race," I admit.

He's silent for a moment as he tries to work that one

out.

When the handle is released he holds a new one in place and he pushes in the tip of the first screw. Then he asks in a low tone, "What was your favourite part?"

I'm looking at his tousled brown hair, scruffy from where he's ran his fingers through it, and the smooth skin of his thick tan neck. I picture him towering over Caulder... overpowering him... *in my honour.*

"There was this really thought-provoking bit near the end," I say.

Tate fits the last screw on the setting for the inside handle and then he stands up and walks to the end of the bed that I'm resting on. He throws down his manual drill and I can see the outline of his crucifix pendant protruding through the thin cotton of his t-shirt. His eyes are on me, submerged in his sheets, as he takes the rag from his back pocket and wipes the oil from his fingers.

"Oh yeah?" he asks.

I nod slowly.

"And what kind of thoughts did it provoke exactly?" He's looking down at me with dark unyielding eyes, and his bass tenor reverberates through me.

His eyes flicker down to my hand resting against the quilt and he surreptitiously leans forward and takes my wrist.

My skin is suddenly on fire. His body is ten times warmer than mine and he's thawing me out, inch by inch. His fingers press firmly between the delicate ligaments and I suck in a breath as I realise what he's doing. My pulse point throbs under his touch and his eyes burst into flames.

He releases my wrist and picks up the drill, looking down at me on the bed. "Those kinds of thoughts, huh?" he taunts. His denim-clad thighs are pressed against the mattress.

"Are you finished?" I ask bluntly.

His fingers clutch at his belt buckle and he tugs it to the

side, as if in discomfort. "Is there anything else I can do for you?" he asks. I ignore the feel of his eyes roaming up and down my body.

"Leave please so I can lock you out."

He breathes out a laugh and paces back to the doorway. "Whatever you want," he mutters, eyes flashing dangerously close to the little camouflaged bookcase.

"Such a gentleman," I grumble dryly and I sink back against the comforter. I look at my college brochures and I want to hurl them out of the window.

He shakes his head and walks out of the room. "Only with you."

CHAPTER 12

Three Years Ago

Kit isn't at school today, so when I enter the cafeteria I check the bench along the left wall for any solo seats. There's one on the edge, away from the bustle of the kitchen and the till, so I slink into it and set all of my stuff down.

It was kind of humid this morning so a lot of people are in especially sunshiney moods. Most students buy their food at the cafeteria and today's selection does look pretty good. Slushies and fruit salads and some ridiculously cute cupcakes. I always felt odd being one of the only lunchbox kids, but Kit doesn't mind and that makes me feel less weird.

I drop my satchel next to my feet and pop my food container onto the table.

"Hey beautiful," a warm voice murmurs gently from behind me.

I startle and my heart starts pounding excitedly but I keep my body still. *He's doing this at school?* I look over to

Tate's usual table on the other side of the room and his friends are laughing and shaking their heads at him.

"Hey," I say. "You shouldn't be over here." I speak quietly, so that no-one else on the bench can hear.

"I had to come and check on my favourite girl," he replies easily. I can feel his smile radiating beside my cheek and it makes me squirm with butterflies.

But then reality sets in.

"Tate, they're going to make fun of me," I say, still holding my unopened lunch box, head down. They already *are* making fun of me.

I feel him step back and then suddenly my stool is swivelled around to face him. His tie hangs loosely, the way that the popular boys wear it, and from this angle he looks ridiculously tall and intimidating. His expression is self-assured and a little smug.

"They're not allowed to make fun of you. No one's going to say anything to you about this because, if they do, they'll have to deal with me." He flashes me a cocky boyish smile. "You're mine."

I try to ignore the flutters in my tummy because I know that this dynamic isn't really in my favour.

"They think that I'm your prey."

He grins even wider. "You *are* my prey. But you're also-" He fishes out the chain from under his shirt and holds the cross pendant up to me. "-the answer to all of my *prayers*."

I duck my head to hide my smile at that one.

"I want you to come over to mine after school today," he says. "When I was out this weekend I bought some things for you. Well, for us. But really they're for you."

He wants me to go into *his house*? I think I'm sweating. I clutch at my tie and try to loosen it so that I don't faint in front of him in the cafeteria. Understanding what I'm doing, Tate hooks two fingers under the knot of my tie and he gently pulls it forward, easing the fabric from around my neck. Then he runs his thumb down the length of the tongue until he reaches the tip in the cavern of my lap.

I'm breathing like I just ran a marathon. Thank God I don't have Gym later.

"I can't come," I say.

He gives me a sad frown.

"Why not?" he asks. He places the hand that was behind his back on the table to my rear, leaning closer.

"I have homework," I answer.

"You can do the homework at mine. Then, as your treat, I'll show you your gifts."

I look up at him from under my lashes and he's bearing down on me, eyes sparkling expectantly and tan skin aglow with excitement.

I shuffle on my stool and touch my tie in the places where his fingers have just been. "If my mom comes home and notices, she'll think that you're my boyfriend or something," I mutter, ashamed to even insinuate such a thing.

He straightens his spine and his chest doubles in size. I cringe. *I know. What a repulsive thought that will be for you, Tate.*

But then he says, "Good," in a hard, sure voice. "It's about time that you had a real man in your house."

I squeeze my eyes shut because I have no control of my emotions. I think I'm about to pee my pants.

I can feel as Tate bends forward again so that his face is right in front of mine and I peep one eye open. He's smiling. "Is that a yes?" he asks.

I scrunch up my nose.

"Don't give me that look like you don't want to," he scolds. He's joking, but I can tell from his voice that he's a bit nervous too. My heart swells.

"Fine," I sigh. I roll my eyes like I'm bored of him, but really I want his fingers running down my tie again.

He inhales deeply, a satisfied grin on his face. Then he whispers, "See you after school, River."

He pushes off the table and walks casually back to his

friends. I can hear them rebuking him for his stint, but I don't have any intentions to look over at them and let them ruin my mood.

When I turn back to my lunch box I squeeze back a smile.

On top of the small grey lid is a red velvet cupcake, topped off with a little heart.

*

After the final bell I head to my locker to grab my jacket and I shrug it on in a pink love-heart daze. The thought of going into Tate's house is giving me butterflies. Before final period had even ended I saw him and Madden leaving the school grounds which made me feel like maybe he was excited too. Maybe he's making sure that he gets home before me so that everything is just right. I watched them out of the classroom window until they disappeared from view completely.

I close my locker door but I gasp once it's shut. I take in the sly face next to me and try to calm my breathing.

"Hey *River*," he says patronisingly, eyes narrowed into slits. His mouth is curved into a smile, but it looks more like a snarl to me.

I swallow and fumble the key out of the locker door.

"Um, hi," I say quickly. I don't want to talk to him. It's Huddy, Tate's friend with the dirty blond hair. He jabs his hand into my arm, trying to get me to shake it.

"We haven't been properly introduced," he continues. "Seems a bit selfish of Tate if you ask me. You wouldn't happen to know what he's doing after school today, would you?"

My eyes widen in shock and he sneers knowingly. When I don't take his hand he grabs mine and squeezes it hard. I feel like my blood is going to be crushed out of my skin.

"Has Tate told you who I am?" he asks, our hands still

compacted together.

I tilt my chin up. "Yes," I say. "You're Huddy."

His face splits into a wide grin. "Of course he'd say that," he laughs. He swipes his tongue out over his bottom lip and he gives me a once over. Then he leans forward and says with relish, "I think you'll find that my name is *Hudson*."

I force my hand out of his and I frown nervously into his smug face.

I get it. His name is Hudson. My name is River. Whatever.

He folds his arms over his chest. "I'm not surprised that he didn't tell you. I wonder what other things he hasn't told you." He cocks his head in a way that makes my heartbeat thump dangerously. Whatever it is that he's insinuating I don't like it. He coughs loudly, dismissing his digression for the moment, and he continues, "But what is so special about *you* anyway?"

I'm wondering the same thing about him. *Why would Hudson be one of Tate's best friends?*

"You're just a goody-two-shoes nerd bitch who doesn't even own a pair of straightening irons," he says bitterly and then he yanks his fingers through a knot in my hair. I gasp at the sting in my scalp and then I clamp my mouth shut. "What the hell does he even do with you?"

He takes one pace forward and I step back on instinct. His eyes flare with the rejection and I swear his neck flushes red. He fishes something out of his pocket and flicks it at my chest. It hits off my jacket and lands on the floor, but I don't take my eyes off him to look at it.

"Don't worry, I'll get to know you soon enough," he says, his voice low and menacing. Then he turns on his heel and swaggers down the corridor.

I look down at the floor and instantly jolt backwards in distress.

The item that he threw at me was a condom.

CHAPTER 13

Present

"I think that we out-emoed ourselves with this one."

Kit swirls the ladle through the vat of red fruit punch, scooping up some of the skull-shaped ice cubes and then plopping them back in. A slew of punch droplets splash across the front of her white school shirt, making it look like she just went nuts with a machete, and she nods in approval.

We both stayed back after the final bell to set up the hall for the Halloween dance tonight. Yellow CAUTION tape is pinned around the room and spider's webs laced with fairy lights are flashing from the walls. We made a DIY pampas grass corn maze in the entry, lined with flickering electronic candles and an army of bed-sheet ghosts, and we tried to carve a couple jack-o-lanterns but that shit is hard. We also listened to Drowning Pool on loop before the dance began, so there is not a single brain cell left in either one of our heads.

I watch our schoolmates under the neon lights as they

acclimatise to a party on school grounds. The girls are mainly comparing costumes and dancing together, whilst the guys watch them stalkerishly from afar. When the boys start chasing their crushes around the room, I know that the dance has really begun.

"Sucks that you have to leave me here stranded," Kit shouts over to me, emphasis on *sucks* because she's wearing prosthetic fangs. "We did such a good job tonight."

I agree. I feel like I'm in an episode of *The Vampire Diaries*. I kind of want to stay and watch the dance but Mitch is keeping good on his word about incarcerating me for the rest of my life, so I'm due for a pickup in around five minutes.

I sigh sadly and let her feed me an extra-large marshmallow.

We jump down from the appetisers table so that I can grab my coat and satchel from the janitor's closet and then we circle back to the snack station. There's a group of juniors milling around in front of us, masks lifted on top of their heads whilst they cluster around the drinks. God knows why they're taking so long. Once they finally vacate the area Kit scoops me a red cup of punch, heavy on the ice skulls, and screams in my ear, "One for the road!"

I fake-sob as I hug her goodbye and then I make my way to the exit, taking a mouthful of the punch as I go.

It's a combination of every remotely Halloween-sounding juice available. Blood orange, cranberry, black cherry, apple soda, and... I pinch my brows together. This is a weird mix. I sip it again, trying to remember what else we poured in here. Fizzy grape? I can't remember. I wonder which flavour was the final straw.

I push out of the double doors and, naturally, it's chucking it down, so I skirt around the side of the building to stay as dry as possible. I scan the lot for Mitch's death truck but it's nowhere to be seen, and the streaks of rain on my glasses aren't helping visibility-wise. I duck back into the doorway to shield myself and I take another swig. Luckily the punch is kind of warming me up from the inside.

When fifteen minutes go by without Mitch arriving I head back into the building to go to the bathroom. The Halloween punch has gone right through me and I practically fall into the stall in my desperation to relieve myself. Has peeing always felt so orgasmic? I dry and flush and stumble to the sinks to wash my hands. I press the tap but for some reason it won't work. I press it again and again, until I'm about to try a different tap, but then a freshman girl says to me, "It's a twisty one."

I blink at her. She's sort of vibrating.

"Are you okay?"

I don't know if I just asked her or if she just asked me, so now we're both staring at each other in bewilderment.

"The tap," she repeats, "is a twisty one."

That makes a lot of sense. I twist the tap and the water gushes out so quickly that I start laughing. After I wash my hands I head back out to wait for Mitch feeling light and euphoric. The rain is hammering against my cheeks and it's such a lovely feeling that I take off my bag and my jacket, and I roll up my sleeves so that the rain can touch as much of body as possible.

I tip my head back and I feel the drops thrash against my neck. I slightly open up my mouth so that I can catch the streams on my tongue.

My glasses are so water-smeared that when the oncoming headlights beam my way I'm seeing kaleidoscopic refractions. I would recognise that dangerous black Ford truck anywhere, and right now I'm happy to see it. I'm fourteen again and quietly romantic. I'm also really stupid, so I decide to walk straight for the bumper as it approaches.

Tate slams the breaks instantaneously and jumps out of the truck. I can tell that if I started to run away right now he would chase me.

He says something loud, angry, and disappointed, but I

can't hear him over the sounds of the rain, the engine, and the common sense trickling out of my head. His tan skin is dripping with water already and I lean against the front of the car so that I can look at him from a broader angle.

This seems to confuse him and he shoves his hands self-consciously into the pockets of his jeans. I let my eyes wander to where his hands are now stuffed. Very interesting.

"Why is your stuff on the floor?" He's looking over at my jacket and my bag which I forgot to pick up and, before I even respond, he's collecting them in his arms and bringing them back to me. Only then does he look down and see that I'm drenched. "Did someone take them from you? Are you okay, River?"

He has that angry-concerned look in his eyes, like he's ready for a round with Caulder 2.0. I feel dizzy but I muster enough strength to claw my jacket out of his arms, even though I'm too warm to put it on.

"River?" he says slowly, like something's dawning on him.

Something's dawning on me too. Tate is hot as fuck and I can't remember why I started hating him.

"River, have you been drinking?"

My eyes scale up his torso and I drink in the breadth of his shoulders. He's wearing a black long-sleeve shirt, covering up those tattoos that I want to trace over with my nails.

What did he say again?

I find some words. "I'm waiting for Mitch," I breathe out, whilst simultaneously pulling my sweater vest over my head.

Tate's eyebrows shoot up and then he quickly starts steering me into the back. His warm hands are encasing my hips from behind as he asks me, "Who got you drunk, River? Tell me his name please."

His forearm wraps around my stomach as he uses his

other arm to open the door for me. I don't want his touch to leave me just yet so I subtly arch into him, enjoying the hard masculine press of his abs and groin. He sucks in a breath and for a moment I swear that the arm around my belly tightens, but after a few seconds I'm being pushed into the backseat and the door thuds closed behind me.

I assess the area as I pull myself from my hands and knees into an upright sitting position. There's a large metal handsaw on the floor in front of me, which would be concerning if Tate wasn't a joiner. He has a jacket on the passenger seat and I snatch it up before he enters the driver's side. I shrink down in the back and take a deep inhalation of the fabric. I think my eyes are rolling into the back of my head.

As soon as Tate gets behind the wheel and exits the lot I sit up on my knees and lean over his seat. His lips are rolled between his teeth.

"How come you never wanted to go to college or pursue those sports you were always doing?" I ask, sitting back again. "I guess you knew that you were always going to be a joiner like your daddy." I pause and eye him deviously. "*Our* daddy."

He breathes hard and flashes me a look in the rear-view mirror. Then he says, quiet and sober, "It was either that or the priesthood."

I swing his dangly Christian fish hanging above my window and test the words in my mouth. "Father Coleson. That's how I like to think of you anyway," I admit. "You would look so good in one of those little church prisons, on your knees. What do you call them again?"

"Confessionals," he replies patiently. He smells so good, like fresh rain and testosterone. I lean around further so that I can look at his little silver cross.

"Forgive me Father for I have sinned."

I smile as his hands tighten their grip on the wheel and he readjusts his lower body against the seat.

"Go on," I whisper teasingly, "say the bit that comes next."

He inhales slowly and his chest swells. His voice is low when he looks at me again. "What would you like to confess."

A thrill jolts through me. My eyes are burning a hole into his mirror and molten caramel is pooling in my belly. Why shouldn't a God-fearing motorbike-racing jock have a thing for the little librarian emo? I want to grab a handful of his soft chocolate hair and make him beg for me to forgive him. I want him to utilise every muscle on his body for the sole purpose of my pleasure. I think I'm accidentally telepathically transmitting these thoughts to him because he's running his hand down his face and swallowing like we're in the Sahara.

Where is my confidence coming from? I know better than to fight it, so I lean into it instead.

Bending forward again, my hands hesitate momentarily in front of his heaving shoulders and then I carefully wrap them around his throat. It's so hot and thick, and his sharp stubble scratches at the skin of my fingers. I'm so much colder than him that I cause his whole body to shudder, and a rumble sounds deep in his chest as he indicates to Mitch's street.

"It's your fault, you know," I whisper quietly, rocking when we hit a speed bump because, feeling *que cera cera*, I didn't strap myself in. "I thought you were my best friend, and you ruined it. And now I have to sleep in your bed and I can't get this itch off of me. I want this feeling to stop, but there's only one thing I can think of to solve it, and we... we can't do that."

We're parked up outside Mitch's house now and the warm porch light is on, but I don't think that anyone is home. I assume Tate is thinking the same thing because, whilst one hand is still on the wheel, the other is pressing firmly against the tent in his jeans.

"Why can't we do that?" he pleads, eyes imploring, veins cording.

I throw myself back against the seat and smack my skull against the rock-hard headrest. I rub the ache and a distant déjà vu flashes through me. I shake it away and narrow my eyes on him in a dare.

"Because priests are celibate," I conclude.

Suddenly he throws open the driver's door, slams it shut, and then I'm being yanked into the storm outside. His hands grip my waist and his eyes are aflame.

His voice is nothing more than a growl when he finally says, "Then it's a good thing I'm not a priest."

He tosses me over his shoulder and thunders into the house.

CHAPTER 14

Three Years Ago

Tate is at the door before my fist even meets the pane. He's grinning down at me with freshly-showered tousled hair and his eyes are all twinkly.

"Hey," he says, reaching for my bag strap so that he can pull me into the house. I see Madden leaning on the kitchen counter and he rolls his eyes when he looks over at me. He shuffles past, hands in his pockets, and mutters Tate a begrudging "see you" as he trudges out of the doorway.

Tate laughs and hauls me fully inside, unzipping my jacket pockets so that he can put his hands in them. I'm still a bit shaken by what happened with Hudson and I want to tell Tate about it, but I can smell the heady boy-soap scent exuding from the warmth of his skin and I don't want to spoil the moment. He rotates us one-eighty so that he can kick the door shut and then he walks me backwards to the kitchen stools.

"Homework time?" he asks as he pushes me down onto the chair. He unfastens my jacket and slips it off my shoulders after I disentangle myself from my bag. "Or can we just forget about the homework and go hang out in my room?"

He hangs my jacket over the chair and then drops to his knees, undoing the laces on my shoes before sliding them off my feet. He sits them neatly down next to me and gently cups my ankles, looking up from between my knees.

"My room?" he urges. "Before our moms come home?"

I deliberate for a few moments. Then I say, "That does seem like the most logical option."

Our fingers are entwined and suddenly we're rushing up the stairs. Once we're at his door Tate moves to stand behind me and we enter his room as one.

His room is much better than my room. He has a hand-carved wooden bed frame and a matching set of drawers that look artisanal in style. There are motorbike posters on the walls, sports trophies across his desk, and, most intriguingly, a glass jar filled with dollar bills, with a large label that reads *"TATTOO MONEY"*. The whole space looks lived in by someone with a full and exciting life.

"Okay, close your eyes," he says, moving us in front of the mirror so that he can check to see if I'm peeking.

I turn around, surprised. "But I just got here," I exclaim.

He laughs and presses a kiss to the top of my cheek. My eyes instinctively flutter shut and when he pulls back he whispers, "Just like that."

Once his body leaves mine I suddenly feel edgy and cold. I'm biting my lip to hide my nerves, and I wonder if being here is a bad idea. I want to know why Madden was here, and I *need* to know why the hell he's friends with Hudson. I have looked into Tate's bedroom window from the day that he moved in, but now that I'm inside of it everything feels too good to be true. Surely happiness can't be this simple to achieve.

"Are you ready?" he murmurs and I feel him set something sharp and cool into my hands. "Open your eyes."

If my hands weren't full I would have lifted them to my face in enchanted delight. I scrunch up my nose and my heart does a painful swell as I take in how unnecessarily thoughtful this was.

Saturate. We Are Not Alone. Dear Agony. Dark Before Dawn. Ember.

Every other studio album released by Breaking Benjamin.

I try to rub the flush from my cheeks onto my shoulder. "You must be pretty sick of *Phobia* by now, I guess," I joke, eyes down. I instantly decide to give him my *Phobia* album the next time we hang out together because this was so darn sweet. My irises have turned into little glowing love hearts, so I can't risk looking up into his right now.

It's no matter. Tate pulls me closer to his body and presses his forehead to mine.

I squeeze my eyes shut and I feel him take the CDs from my hands, tossing them onto his comforter. The water droplets that were running through his hair from the shower are now trickling down my cheeks.

"Never," he whispers. I can hear the gorgeous smile in his voice. "That CD is the best thing that ever happened to me." He presses himself closer. "Well, *you* are the best thing that ever happened to me."

His hands are rubbing up my arms - cupping, gripping, squeezing – until his palms meet my collarbones, and then his fingers begin firmly caressing my cool skin. His thumbs slip underneath the top button of my shirt and he pushes his torso flush against mine.

"River," he whispers, lips tickling over my cheek. "Can I kiss you, please?"

I open my eyes and shudder. His pupils have dialled out and his body is predatorily still. I tilt my face upwards and his body bows towards me.

"I need you to say yes or no, River," he urges, eyes

trained on my lips.

I'm drunk on the power that this moment is giving me over him. The ability to bestow or deprive, give or take. He's so desperate for my consent that it makes me feel luscious, wicked. My eyes flicker down and I see the cross pendant hanging over his t-shirt.

"What if I say no?" I whisper, sliding my hands up to his wrists.

His fingers press more firmly into the base of my throat. "Is that what you're going to say?"

We walk backwards until my body touches the hard surface of his door, and he quickly moves one hand to my head, cupping it protectively. He looks so wild. I want to toy with him for the rest of my life.

I shake my head and he groans.

"Please say it, River," he begs quietly, his soft hair tickling my forehead.

I can't restrain my little smug smile any longer and it makes him beam lovingly at me in return.

"Okay," I say. "Yes Tate, you can."

He smiles against my lips.

"Thank you," he says.

And then he kisses me.

His touch is so perfect that I choose to stay still, not wanting to disrupt the moment. He gently kisses his lips to mine and then he remains motionless, assessing my response so that he can decide what to do next. I have never been kissed before and he can probably tell. There's a hint of wetness between our mouths but I think that it might be his shower water dripping over us.

He pulls back after a few seconds and searches my eyes. His are dark and stormy.

"Was that okay?" he asks, forehead brushing against mine. His voice has never been this deep before.

"It was okay," I admit. It was kind of alien but, at the

same time, I don't want him to *not* do it again.

He breathes out a laugh and buries his face into my neck. "'*Okay*'," he repeats, his voice tormented. "I have to do better than that." He lifts back up and looks down into my eyes. "Have you ever been kissed before? In fact, don't answer that." He threads his fingers through my hair and gives me a devious smile. "*I* am your first kiss."

I laugh and he rubs his nose against mine.

"Can I do it again, River?" he whispers.

I nod.

And this time, it's different.

He presses his lips tenderly against mine but as soon as I kiss him back he begins to move. His mouth caresses me harder, with more urgency, and one of his hands fists and tugs in my hair. When I release a little gasp, his other hand slides around my throat, warm, domineering, protective. My heart is hammering faster than the downpour outside. He pushes the lower half of his body against mine and he lets out a satisfied grunt when he feels the pulse in my throat quicken beneath the firm press of his thumb. I slide my hands around the swollen curves of his biceps and rub my fingers up the solid muscle, making him relieve a long low groan. He moves his mouth to my neck and sucks until my chest is heaving.

"Can I take you out this Friday, River?" he asks, hands smoothing down my ribs. "I want to show you something, and I want to do this again - without a time limit." His teeth graze against my throat and then he delicately tugs at the skin.

I pull him back up to my mouth by entwining my fingers deep into his hair, so soft and wet from the shower. "Yes," I say, and I let him lean forward to kiss me again.

He inhales deeply as his hands envelop my hips, his fingers digging eagerly into my pliable softness. "I want to use my tongue next time," he whispers as he slots one of his knees between both of mine, and then he slowly lifts it up, up, *up-*

I jolt backwards and, having lost all of my brain cells, I bang my head hard against the door. I howl and laugh, but Tate quickly recomposes himself and pulls me flush against him.

"Sorry," he says, his fingers massaging soothing circles against my skull. "I shouldn't have done that, I'm sorry." He locks me into the cradle of his arms, his cheek pressed against the top of my head.

"It's okay," I say, laughing, but he's holding me so tightly I can tell that he doesn't think that it's okay. I can't even tip my head back to look at him because I'm compressed so hard against his chest. His whole body is rigid, including the long tense muscle pressing into my stomach.

I try to think of something to distract him.

"What tattoo are you going to get?" I ask, my voice trembling only a little.

"Your name, across my knuckles," he replies immediately.

I laugh again because I think that he's joking, but he isn't laughing with me.

I move my hands so that they are flat against his back and a shiver runs through his body. When he looks down at me he relaxes a bit. He leans forward and swipes a kiss across my forehead, before stroking my cheek with the backs of his fingers.

"Why did you have a shower?" I ask.

A small smile tugs at the corners of his mouth. "To calm my nerves," he answers patiently. "Not that it worked," he laughs, and then he dips his face into my neck again, sucking gently. "And I was going to get Madden to help me with something, but we didn't have enough time," he adds, before sinking his teeth into me.

I gasp – shocked, sensitised, and exhilarated – and he bites harder.

He runs his tongue over the area and his hands snake around my waist.

"I should go home, Tate," I whisper, in an attempt to throw some cold water over the fire in my belly.

I feel him smile against my throat. "You probably should," he agrees, and then he stands up to his full height, towering over me. He realigns my glasses on the bridge of my nose before quickly kissing the tip.

"I hope that you love the CDs," Tate says as he walks me across the street before my mom gets back from work, squeezing my hand in his.

I smile up at him before looking away and swallowing nervously.

I think that I might love more than just the CDs, Tate.

CHAPTER 15

Present

When we get inside the house Tate sets me down on the floor and spins me around by my shoulders. Mitch is standing in the kitchen with a bowl of freshly made popcorn and a startled expression on his face. I stand on my tippy-toes to check if there's any extras - M&M's or something - in the mix but it's unadulterated corn and salt for as far as the eye can see.

"That is a sad little bowl," I say to Mitch, looking pointedly at the corn in his hands.

"I think that her drink was spiked," Tate interrupts flatly, as if this explains why he's acting like a Neanderthal.

Mitch's eyes go crazy wide and he sets down the bowl. "Did you give her some water?" he asks Tate.

Tate's hands grip tighter. "I didn't have any," he replies, and I can hear regret lacing his tone. "Sorry," he adds, whether to Mitch or to me I do not know.

Mitch runs the tap into a glass and then he passes it to me. I gulp it down and he refills it again.

"Take her to bed," Mitch orders as he heads to the living room. Tate can feel that I'm about to burst out laughing so he cups his hand over my mouth to stifle the sound. When the wave passes he puts his hand back on my shoulder and he walks me up the stairs to his room.

My room.

Our room.

I realise once I'm over the threshold that I no longer have Tate's warm, grounding palms encasing my shoulders, so I turn around and see that he's gripping the top of the doorframe, head bowed and chest heaving. His hair has fallen all over his face and the tendons in his thick wrists are flexing.

The room is excessively dark, lit only by the faintest glow from the streetlamps outside, and the rainfall is thumping fast against the panes. The ambience is obviously quite distressing for Tate because he's breathing loud enough for me to hear from the other side of the attic.

"Are you waiting for an invitation?" I ask, still in that possessed nymphomaniac mind-frame that came over me in the car. "Get inside here now, you vampire."

Tate tilts his head up and I see a pained expression creasing his brow.

I open the bedside drawer and pull out my cleaning cloth so that I can wipe the rain smudges from my glasses, ignoring the desperation that I can feel radiating off Tate's body. When my glasses are clean I throw the cloth back in the drawer and storm over to the doorway.

"Get in or get out," I demand, only inches away from the hard planes of his expansive chest.

"Did you drink alcohol tonight, River? Or do you think that you were spiked? If you're under the influence I can't come in here with you."

That is so nice of him. I grab the soft cotton of his shirt and pull him inside anyway.

"River, I'm serious. I'm not doing anything that you're

not fully… lucid for."

I move around him to shut the door and twist the little lock, before I start pulling off my trousers. They are so rain-splattered that they keep sticking to my skin. I wriggle them off, fist them up, and then I throw them across the room like a shot-put. Slam dunk.

When I look up at Tate again his gaze has hardened and his jaw is set, which is unanticipated but also arousing. I start unbuttoning my shirt.

Tate grabs my hands, halting my progress, and he fixes me with an unyielding stare.

"Why do you keep saying that I ruined everything for us? How can you say that? I would have done anything for you." The timbre of his voice is sending shockwaves all the way down to my uterus. I rest my head against the door and my body pulses as I gaze into the dark depths of his glittering eyes.

I want to feel him, just once, and then I can let it go. What happened was so long ago, and he was so young, that it almost seems insignificant now, but it's still bad enough to make me know that I can never fully trust him again.

But I want one night to indulge myself before I shut him out forever.

Besides, why is it only men who can be casual with sex or wield it as a means of revenge? From the look on Tate's face right now I think that the idea of our bodies coming together will torture him for the rest of his life and he deserves nothing less.

I wriggle my wrists for him to release them, and then I run my hand up his sleeve to the bulge of his tattooed bicep. He instinctively encases my lower back in the warm press of his forearms, and he rests his forehead against mine, tickling my face with his soft hair, inky black in the darkness of the room.

"I want to start over," he whispers, his hard pecs heaving with each steadying inhalation.

I work my fingers up into his hair and tug at it hard. "I don't care," I whisper back.

He tilts his face back and looks down at me, my head coming to way beneath his chin. It's such a domineering angle that my stomach flips, and I give him a tiny *please don't hurt me* smile, although I guess it's too late for that really.

"You do care." His voice is low and scolding. I press my hips against his and he stirs agitatedly.

He *definitely* cares.

"I got over it a long time ago," I reply, blasé, although I feel kind of dizzy. "But I deserve a parting gift before I go to college, is all." His hands splay across my lower back, slowly inching their way down, and my thoughts short-circuit.

Just as his fingers dig into the round curves of my ass I push him off me. He stumbles back and swallows hard.

"I need water," I say matter-of-factly.

He runs his hand through his hair, breathing jagged, and then nods down at the floor. "I'll get that for you," he breathes out, and then he carefully steps around me and heads out of the door.

As soon as he leaves I throw myself onto the bed, moaning. Why the hell is he acting like this? And, more importantly, why the hell am *I*?

I think back to the Halloween dance and maybe Tate's right – maybe I was spiked – but a little shot of liquor in my system isn't the sole catalyst for these feelings. They have been festering since the moment I saw him again, as soon as I stepped foot in this room, as soon as I started sleeping in his sheets.

I pull off my uniform, leaving only my thermal vest, and I shuffle into my pyjama shorts. What the hell is wrong with me?

When Tate comes back into the room, he closes the door quietly behind him and holds out the glass of water for me. I go to take it but then he lifts it just out of my reach.

"I want a truce," he demands. He's using his low and commanding *what would you like to confess* voice that runs like a shot of whiskey down my naval.

"You're a jerk," I retort, but then I squeal because I feel something icy splash against my leg. He tipped a drop of the water on me and, when I get a good look at the glass in his hands, it's full of frozen ice cubes.

"Truce," he says again, expression unwavering.

I narrow my eyes on him. "Only if you give me what I want in return."

His eyebrows pinch in surprise but he quickly shakes it off. "You won't want that when you're sober," he replies. Then he yields, passing me the water and making me feel a little smug.

When he goes to exit the room I quietly ask him, "But what if I do?"

Tate's body stills, the large expanse of his back facing me for a few moments, and when he turns back around I can see that wild animalistic need has smothered all moral and rational thought. His body is thrumming with the want to satiate himself, and I am devoted to helping his plight.

I sit up onto my knees so that I'm closer to him, and he seals the space between us in one easy stride. He wraps his arms around my waist and pulls me to the edge of the bed so that our torsos are flush against each other. I cup his jaw in my hand and he leans into my touch, only tilting so that he can kiss the base of my thumb. I run my other hand up his abs until I meet his crucifix, and I grip it in my fist, causing him to release a deep strained breath.

"Will you do that for me, when I'm sober?" I whisper, euphoric at the realisation that – for some unbeknown reason, call it his conscience – Tate will do anything that he can to make amends. I grip the pendant a little tighter. *Thank you, God.*

He nods, his head ducking down so that our faces are at

a more equal height and his fingers holding me firmly in place.

I think for a moment. "And will you tell me what your tattoo says?" I ask, because why not.

"John 7:38," he murmurs immediately as he laces his fingers through the red ribbon at the front of my pyjama shorts. His breathing is so laboured that he's practically panting.

"Thank you," I say, making a mental note to check that out later. I watch him pinch the ribbon between his fingers and then he tugs it roughly. I make a small quivering sound and Tate's eyes flash upwards. His hand leaves my shorts and it moves around to the back of my neck, clamping it as if he's trying to squeeze more noises out of me. It works, and immediately his whole body is humming.

"One kiss," he whispers, and his eyes flicker down past my lips, to my throat. He lowers his mouth so that it's hovering over my pulse point and he murmurs, "Just here."

Once I give my small confirming nod he crushes his lips against my neck.

He laps at my skin, groaning at the taste, and then he sucks it hungrily into his mouth. One of his hands descends down my back, and when he reaches my behind he kneads the flesh desperately. His other hand climbs upwards until it reaches my chest, at first tracing gently around the curves and slopes, but then gradually pressing harder until he's palming me in frenzy. I lock my hands in his hair, holding him against me as he works my body into a grinding mess.

Suddenly I'm pushed backwards and I sink against the thick quilt, need coursing through me as I look up at Tate towering over me. He smoothes my wrists down against the bed, caressing the soft skin with his thumbs, and then he eases his groin between my hips. My body is thumping harder than the storm outside as he sinks his teeth back into my neck, the taut muscles of his back rolling effortlessly as he grinds against me, and his sharp stubble grazing at my sensitised skin.

I'm drowning in the pleasure of my willing surrender until I hear a gruff voice grit out, "You really are a piece of shit."

I gasp and startle, at first thinking that the words came from Tate, but in a second Mitch is hauling his son off my body and slamming him into the dresser.

Shit. I quickly look to the doorway to check for my mom but luckily no lights are on and I think that Mitch is here alone. I close my legs and try to balance myself on my elbows.

"Are you kidding me?" Mitch growls, his eyes boring into Tate. "This chick hates your guts, and the one time she has liquor in her system I find you pinning her to her bed and warming your dick between her thighs? Explain this, *now!*" The words are being spat out through clenched teeth, but his voice is hushed enough for me to realise that he has no intention of my mom finding out about this.

Tate rubs his head and looks down at the floor. "It's not like that," he replies.

"I am dating her *mom*, Tate – and if her *mom* finds out what you're trying to do, she will literally kill you. And then I'll have to break up with her, because I can't be in a relationship with the woman who murdered my son."

Mitch runs his hand over his face and turns around, but as soon as he remembers that I'm still here, he spins right back.

"She's not going to be here." Mitch jerks his thumb at me from over his shoulder. "She's going to go to college, and you know it."

Tate squares his shoulders, standing at an insane six-foot-four, and making himself an even match against Mitch. I feel evil and guilty realising how attractive they both look right now, so I squirm on the bed in shame.

"We don't even know that she wants that," Tate counters, folding his arms over his chest.

I quietly take a sip of my icy water.

Mitch makes a sort of unfunny laugh. "It doesn't matter what she wants. It doesn't matter what *you* want, and it doesn't matter what *I* want. If her mom wants her to do it, she'll do it. She has that kid in chains."

I shift uncomfortably because I don't like the fact that Mitch seems to sense how repressed my life has been. Introverted nerdy girls are not born this way. If it wasn't for all of the stolen moments that I had with Tate when I was younger, I wouldn't really have any childhood memories at *all*.

Tate clenches his jaw. "College or no college, I can make it work. I can do long distance."

Wait, what?

Mitch keels forward like he's about to rip his own brains out. "Tate!" he hisses incredulously. "The girl doesn't even *like* you, man! She broke your heart and she's going to do it *again*! When will you ever learn?"

Wait, *WHAT*?

"Whoa, whoa, whoa," I say, but when I try to stand I feel like I'm going to vomit a little, and I realise that I didn't eat dinner tonight. They both turn to look at me so I swallow and try to wet my mouth. "That's not what went down, Mitch," I say. I take off my glasses to blur out his hot angry face. "And you're right about my mom, I don't get a say. But I'm almost eighteen and... whatever we were doing here, my mom doesn't need to know."

Whatever I just said was definitely the wrong thing to say. Mitch is so furious that when he turns back to Tate he's practically aglow.

"Are you telling me," he grits out slowly, "that my almost-nineteen year old son was about to engage in sexual relations with a high school girl, and, to top it all off, she *isn't even eighteen yet*?"

Wow, I really did say the wrong thing.

The room is so silent it's vibrating. We both know what

Mitch is implying.

"This can't happen again," Mitch says in an *and that's final* tone. "I don't want to catch either of you trying this because there *will* be consequences – and I'm not talking about from me."

Mitch flashes me a distressed look and runs his hand over his hair. Then he claps Tate on the shoulder and nods for him to get out of the room.

Before he leaves Tate's eyes meet mine and there's a dark flame flickering beneath the surface. He's thinking about where his hands have just been, working, squeezing, rubbing, pressing. He's thinking about my softness splayed out before him, ready and willing to take his touch.

Mitch nudges him, irritated, but I see everything that I need to know.

Tate grips his belt with one hand and his crucifix with the other.

Tate is my penitent, and he's ready to confess.

CHAPTER 16

Three Years Ago

After the final bell on Friday I shrug on my waterproof, pulling up the hood to save myself from the torrential downpour, and I speed-walk to the bus stop just outside of the school grounds to wait for Tate. I'm glad that he wanted to hang out after school rather than on a weekend, because this way it will be easier to lie to my mom about my whereabouts. If we were going to go somewhere on a Saturday I would have had to make up a story about hanging out with Kit, which admittedly probably would hold solid seeing as my mom doesn't have Kit's home telephone number, but this way is easier. I can say that I stayed back at the library or that I was helping out with the Homecoming committee. Textbook excuses. Easy peasy.

When the bus stop comes into view I see that Tate is already there. A couple of his friends are hanging around him under the shelter but when he spots me he weaves his way out of the group and saunters towards me, with outstretched palms and a panty-dropping grin. I don't even have time to worry about the cheerleaders and football guys who are watching us disbelievingly because, as soon as I'm three feet away from him, Tate grabs me by my waist and presses his lips to mine. He's instantly drenched from the rain but he remains completely unfazed. He walks me backwards around to the side of the shelter so that no one can watch us, and my eyes flutter shut as he wraps his forearm around my lower back beneath my jacket and blazer, squeezing my body as close to his as possible. We haven't hung out or spoken in a couple of days so he's making it pretty clear that he's been missing me. My cheeks heat up at *how much* his body is proving that he's been missing me.

As if he can read my thoughts, Tate shifts his hips away from me and mumbles a "sorry" before he moves his mouth back to mine and then kisses his way down my neck.

"I'm so glad you're here," he murmurs and then he lifts his head so that he can look into my eyes. This is my second time ever being kissed so I've lost pretty much every ounce of sense from my brain in the past twenty seconds. I just stare up at him, nod, and try to calm my breathing. "Want me to tell you where we're going, or do you want a surprise?" he asks, smoothing his thumbs up and down my throat. If he keeps doing that I'm going to forget how to speak entirely.

"A surprise," I say breathlessly, and he gives me a dazzling grin.

"A surprise," he concurs, and then he wraps my hand up in his so that he can walk us back inside the bus shelter. Tate starts talking with his friends again, totally at ease, but I can sense some of the girls looking at me like I'm an extraterrestrial. I look at one of them from under my hood and she startles, surprised that she was caught in the act. I continue to stare at her until she looks away uncomfortably, her expression irked and embarrassed.

When the bus arrives only Tate and I get on it, probably

because this one is heading to the town's outskirts rather than the residential suburbs. He pulls his card out of his pants and tells me to go and sit at the back so that he can inform the driver of our stop without me hearing. The *back*? God, Tate Coleson really is a popular guy through and through.

I make my way up to the seating area at the back and, by the time I'm sat down, Tate is already almost by my side. He shakes the water from his hair, slides into the seat beside mine, and then he kisses me again, this time more fervently. The bus is empty and there's no one to catch us so he moves his hand to my hip and he scoots me so that I'm closer to him. As the bus pulls away from the stop Tate lifts his lips from mine and his eyes rake down my body. When they reach my legs, poking out from beneath the hem of my skirt in thin rain-soaked tights, he runs his hand over my knee until he's firmly clutching the sensitive underside. The sight of his large tan hand encompassing me so easily makes my breath stutter in my throat.

"It's gonna be about twenty minutes," he says, wrapping his other arm around my shoulders so that my head comes to rest against his chest. "You can nap if you want."

I almost laugh because how old does he think that I am? Five? But then I realise that, actually, it was less than a decade ago that I literally *was* five, and as school was tiring the best thing that I could do right now *would* be to refresh myself with a nap. I tuck myself tighter against his torso and he makes a low satisfied noise as I close my eyes.

He gives my thigh a little squeeze when we reach our stop. I open my eyes sleepily as he interlocks our fingers and starts walking us purposefully down the centre isle of the bus. Looking up at him I feel as though I've died and gone to Heaven. *Imagine waking up to Tate Coleson every morning.* My legs wobble at the thought.

Once we are completely out of the bus I realise that he has literally taken me to the back of Bumfuck, Nowhere.

There isn't even a pavement beside the bus sign. Instead, the road is encased by an arching alcove of evergreens, rainwater trickling heavily through the sparse gaps in the canopy, and a consistent pattering hammering against the leaves above us. There's a small location sign just behind us but Tate's grip on my hand doesn't loosen enough for me to be able to lean over and read it. He glances down at me before he attempts to wade through the dense forest which seemingly lines the road out of town, his expression cautious.

"We're only a minute away, I promise," he says, probably sensing my unease. I keep my face impassive but it doesn't convince him in the slightest. He pulls me away from the roadside, so that we're both shielded behind one of the bordering trees, and he gently rubs his thumbs up my jaw. My body traitorously melts a little, so I really hope that he isn't a serial killer. He leans down and presses his lips chastely to mine, to try and ease me up. The warmth from his mouth seeps into me and I shudder pleasurably at the feeling, not even minding the fat rain drops that are hitting against my forehead and exposed cheeks. He pulls away and says, "I wish that the weather was better, but I think that you'll still like it. It's my favourite place."

The vulnerability in his voice catches my interest but he turns away and starts leading us through the trees again before I have the chance to study it. *He's taking me to his favourite place?* My tiny ego shivers in delight.

It only takes another twenty seconds for the spot to come into view and I gasp when I see it. How have I lived here forever and never known about this place?

Hearing me, Tate turns his head and he gives me a small smile. "You like it?" he asks.

I *love* it. If anything, the onslaught of rain makes it even more atmospheric. As the thicket of trees becomes sparser we enter a secluded gravel clearing, encircling a gigantic lake. Its smooth silver surface is being pelted with shots of rain and it's creating a thunder of ear-bashing slaps, harmonised by the thud of pellets hitting the emerald leaves around us.

I look up at him, his teeth sinking into his lower lip as he watches me nervously, and I return his earlier shy smile. "This is so amazing," I say, still shimmering with the fact that Tate Coleson invited *me* into his secret sacred place. "Where even are we? We have, like, the *whole* place to ourselves."

His eyes roam down my body as he pulls me to his chest and he takes a long, deep inhalation, as if he's breathing in my scent. "Silver Lake," he mumbles, his hands rubbing up and down my arms. "And I'm glad you like it." When he lifts his eyes back to mine, they're dangerously sparkly.

He walks us backwards so that we stay under the sheltering canopy of leaves and then he shucks off his blazer and spreads it between a tree-nook, creating a sort of woodland throne. Somehow he manages to steadily sink us both to the ground, with me sitting on his blazer and him kneeling between my legs, his muscular thighs spread apart in a way that makes me blush. He dips down so that his head is level with mine, and then he takes my lips in his as he steadies himself, holding onto my hips.

He moves his hands so that he can pull down the zipper on my jacket and, once opened, he settles them gently on my waist. I have read a lot of romance books so I know that he's probably about to touch my chest, and I'm half-tempted to apologise in advance because there is really nothing there for him, but he catches me by surprise when his fingers trail to the lower half of my shirt, and he softly splays his palm out across my quivering stomach. My knees knock against the sides of his wide ribcage and it sends a jolt of electricity through both of our bodies. He pulls away, his breathing completely off the rails as he falls back onto his haunches. The way that he's sat is giving me the most explicit view of what lies between his thighs and I don't think that I have ever been so red in my life. He hasn't even used his tongue, although he said that he wanted to when we were in his bedroom the other day, but I can see that he has already stiffened drastically under the fabric of his pants.

He notices what I'm looking at and he instantly changes his position, getting to his feet and then coming to sit next to me. I'm half surprised that he doesn't take my eye out when he crouches down at my side before sprawling his long legs out. His dad must be a behemoth if this is what Tate looks like before he's even turned *sixteen*.

We sit in silence for a minute as we try to get our breathing to return to normal, and Tate leans his head back against the tree trunk, his Adam's apple rolling up and down his neck as he swallows. His caramel skin looks even more tan under the shade of the leaves and it's so beautiful that I don't want to look away from him. I fold my hands over where he touched me on my stomach and he tilts his head down to the side so that he can watch me.

"What's with the tummy thing?" I ask, kind of boldly, but I'm too curious not to mention it.

His eyes flash up to mine but he drops them back down to my stomach, a soft blush appearing and staining his cheekbones. "Uh..." he rubs one of his hands across the back of his neck, as if he's embarrassed or nervous and not sure if he should tell me. "I just... because it's where..." He breathes out a shaky exhale and shifts a bit, dropping his hand down again. "Not right now, of course, 'cause we're both young and all but... when we're older..."

I lean my head around so that I can meet his eyes and he runs his hand down his face, groaning a little.

"It's just... it's where you'll make babies is all," he finishes, and my eyebrows shoot up to my hairline. Whatever I expected him to say, it was not that. Tate wants babies? Why have I never thought about boys as wanting to have children? Honestly, I have never really thought about

babies, but the idea that Tate Coleson thinks about…
making them… it makes my breath catch.

"Okay," I say shakily and he laughs, dropping his head
into his hands.

"Sorry, that's so weird. I didn't mean to freak you out,"
he says, sitting straight again so that he can tentatively gauge
my reaction. Our gazes lock and we both laugh, ignoring
the loud current of excitement that hums between us with
the knowledge that *he wants to make a baby*, and he heavily
implied that *he wants to make it with me*.

Looking for a distraction I notice something on the
other side of the shore, so I ask, "What's that?" pointing to
the wooden structure to the East of the lake, the golden
wood turning a deeper, almost mahogany colour under its
blanketing of rain.

"I think it's-" Tate pauses for a moment and swallows
hard. His voice has gone so deep that I feel it reverberating
inside of me. He runs his hand through his hair, water
droplets cascading down his defined jaw and neck, and he
tries again. "I think it's an old chalet or a bungalow, but it's
been derelict for ages now. Super quaint and traditional."
He thinks for a moment. "I bet my dad and me would
know how to fix it up real good."

I look up at his face in surprise because I'm pretty sure
that this is the first time that Tate has ever mentioned his
dad. He moves his hand to mine and locks our fingers
together as if he can sense what I'm thinking.

"My dad recently moved back to town… and I'm kind
of hoping that my mom's going to let me go and live with
him, once he's got his business all set up and running again.
I want to start working with him as soon as possible," he
says. His eyes flash down to my mouth but then he quickly
looks away, and he tries to shield the large swell between his
thighs with his rigid fist. "He'd love you, just so you know,"
he adds, eyes still looking out over to the little wooden
chalet.

I look down at out connected fingers and ask, "Did he bring you here? Is that how you found this place?"

He nods, smiling, and a crimson blush delicately spreads over his cheekbones. "Yeah - I'm gonna sound like a wet-wipe but I guess it's sorta special to me, because of that," he answers, laughing as he shakes more rain from his hair. Tate Coleson is so cut that he's borderline Sasquatch, so the fact that he isn't afraid to admit his emotions lights up a flock of fireflies in my belly, and it makes me like him even more. "I haven't brought anyone here, ever. Not Madden. And *especially* not Huddy, even though we…" he sighs and rolls his shoulders, the large bones making intimidating cracking sounds. "We share everything," he finishes.

My stomach drops a little, but I don't say anything. At least Tate seems to be as uncomfortable about Hudson as I am - but then I have to wonder, why the hell does he stay friends with him?

I stroke my thumb up the long length of his pointer finger, falling rhythmically into the dips around his large knuckles, and his attention immediately snaps back to me. I avoid his gaze until I reach the tip of his finger and then I look up at him from underneath my lashes. The doe eyes seem to flick a switch in his brain because he hunches around me again, threading the fingers of his free hand into my hair.

"I wanted to bring you here so that I could ask you something," he says, bringing my face in closer to his. "And you don't have to say yes… or, if you already had plans…" He trails off for a moment, his eyes looking deep into my own, as if he's trying to read my mind before he follows through with the rest of his sentence. He braces himself – and I secretly brace *myself* – and then, with a deep, shoulder-heaving inhalation, he asks me, "River, will you go to Homecoming with me?"

My mouth pops open into a little *o*, because this is the second time in the past five minutes that he has completely knocked me for six. My eyes widen and he watches me carefully, as if he's tensely waiting for my response.

Never in my life did I expect *anyone* to ask me to go to Homecoming, let alone *Tate Coleson*. I'm all aquiver but no way am I going to let this moment pass me by.

"Tate," I whisper, blinking myself through my shock so that I can give him my tiny excited smile. "Of course, yes, I would love to."

His whole face breaks into the most gorgeous grin that I have ever seen, with twin creases setting deeply into the caramel skin of his cheeks. He stoops down so that he can kiss me again and I'm all but knocked out by the wave of testosterone that washes over me. Maybe it's the rain, but the air around us seems to be even more charged than usual, heavy with the dampness from the lake and our heady raging hormones.

Our entwined hands fall into my lap and I let out a gasp that has his chest stretching the cotton of his shirt. I move my other hand to his collar, tugging him into me, and his eyes flare.

"I would only ever want to go with you," I admit breathlessly, and his lips crash into mine.

The fingers that he had laced through my hair move down to my neck so that he can grip me steady, and then his thumb begins to move up and down the column of my throat.

"I can't wait to see you in your Homecoming dress," he whispers huskily against my mouth, before taking my bottom lip gently between his teeth. I make a small sound and it unlocks a deep rumble from within his chest. He drops his hand from my neck, spreading it protectively across my tummy, and just as he begins to firmly press, he slips his tongue inside my mouth.

"*Tate*," I exclaim quietly, and he pushes his palm against my stomach with more pressure, his fingers flexing as they grip into my softness.

He pulls away only so that he can ask, "Can I keep going?" and I nod ardently, his hair gently caressing my forehead as I lean back to look up at him.

He brings us back together and slowly slides his tongue all the way in, his low grunt hitting the back of my throat as he fully claims my mouth. I shift around on his blazer because I've got a fire going on in my privates and, from the loud sounds of his heavy inhalations, Tate can tell. He glides his tongue out in a lush, never-ending stroke before pushing it back in even deeper than before. He's wet and warm and so big everywhere that my body is growing limp beneath him.

He notices and pulls away, his dazzling eyes looking down at me urgently. The hand on my belly moves up to my jaw.

"Fuck," he murmurs, "I'm sorry, I'll stop, that was too much, wasn't it? I'm sorry, stay with me baby."

I lift my hand to my face and laugh as his fingers try to coax me back to full consciousness, my head shaking in embarrassment. "I'm the sorry one," I say, and then, trying to be light-hearted, I add, "if I borderline black-out from a kiss, imagine how I'll be when-" but Tate moves his hand up to my mouth, pressing his palm against my lips and preventing me from ending my sentence.

He swallows hard and then leads my eyes down to his crotch. I don't exactly know how it works with boys but I think that Tate has somehow grown even bigger than he was a few minutes ago, the long length of his arousal protruding even more obviously now against the sorry fabric of his pants.

"I think that it might be best if you don't finish that sentence," he says, in a voice that is painfully calm. He takes in my astonished expression, both lust-filled and terrified, and then adds a strained, "Please."

I nod my head, my lips brushing against his palm, and he pulls it away so that he can access my mouth again. He gives me a slow multitude of delicate pecks and then he helps me to my feet, bringing me in under the curve of one bicep, our hands still interlocked. He picks up his blazer and, without even dusting it off, he half-shrugs it over his other arm before we start silently traipsing back up the shoreline and into the thick greenery.

Tate doesn't let go of my hand for the entire ride home.

CHAPTER 17

Present

Kit and I have managed to submit our college applications before it's even hit Thanksgiving, to both the delight of my mom and the observing eyes of Mitch. I'm not sure what he is most afraid of but now I am the opposite of grounded, and he wants me as socially active as possible. This is kind of a challenge for an asthmatic introverted nerd but for the sake of him not telling my mom about my sordid agenda with Tate I'm holding up my end of the bargain.

I stay back at the library until the after-school sports practices end and then I go to the pool in town, to relax in the water for an hour. It's a low-lit and underused natatorium that mainly hosts aqua-aerobics for the elderly, so it suits my purposes of maintaining a low profile perfectly. I shrug into my swimsuit and, taking the side of the water that isn't being used by the pensioners, I wade through the streams unhurried.

I'm not the strongest swimmer, probably because I don't have the best lung capacity, but I love being in the water. It takes concentration and precision to keep myself afloat, and it helps to clear my mind when I want to rid myself of my creeping sinful thoughts.

After my swim I go to the shower room with all of the old ladies and wash the chlorine out of my hair in my little booth, using ten tonnes of conditioner to try and salvage my curls. Without the distractions that I had whilst controlling my paddle in the water, my mind is wandering down dark and dangerous lanes as I stand under the streams. I think about that night a few weeks ago with Tate and Mitch in the attic, and all of the confusing things that they said. They were right about a lot, but they were also wrong in parts too.

Mitch has banned Tate from coming upstairs and I have barely seen him what with spending so much time in the library, doing assignments, and finishing up my applications after school. We haven't spoken since that night and I can tell that it's eating him alive. I'm sadistically enjoying holding all of the cards so when I see him outside in the garage with his bike or hanging around in Mitch's kitchen I do a purposeful swish, and sashay away from the area.

I towel-dry my hair to the best of my ability, pull on my coat and hood, and then I walk down from the town square back to Mitch's house. It's so cold that it takes my breath away, especially with my damp hair and skin, so by the time I'm home my cheeks are pinched red and I'm almost gasping at the strong November chill. My lungs are officially dying for my inhaler.

When I open the door I see my mom, Mitch, and Tate all sat in the room at the back, which is weird because I'm pretty sure that they've never done that before, and even weirder because it's almost night, so Tate is usually gone by now.

I give a small wave to my mom, who does an unconvinced appraisal of my raincoat-winter-hat-and-clunky-school-shoes outfit before turning back to Mitch, so

118

after that I start ascending the stairs.

Ouch. It's just my uniform – why does she have to be so unforgiving?

I'm shocked out of my thoughts when I feel a pair of arms grip me around the middle and pick me up, carrying me hurriedly from the second floor landing up the last flight of stairs to my room in the attic.

Tate puts me down and slams the door shut.

"Where the hell have you been?" he thunders, his voice deep and rebuking. I'm guessing he thinks that, with my mom preoccupied with Mitch, his dad won't make a scene if Tate's only gone for a few minutes. He backs me up to the bed and when my legs hit the mattress I have to steady myself on his arm. I quickly let go of it and scowl up at him.

"I've been idling away the hours to give *you* enough time to get the hell out of here, that's where, and for some unbeknown reason *you're still here*," I hiss. I pull my hat off and throw it on the bed.

"I can tell what you've been doing, River," he growls. "You're still in your fucking uniform, and you come home at eight p.m. flushed in the face and panting."

I frown, confused, until he brushes two fingers across my neck and looks away, dismayed.

"You're literally sweating," he adds darkly.

And then I realise.

I dig my hand into my gym bag and pull out my rolled up swimsuit, slapping it into his chest with a cold wet smack.

"You're literally *insane*," I say and I push him away so that I can strip off my jacket.

He's blinking down at the swimsuit and his face is warming red.

"Get out," I hiss when I snatch the item back.

"River," he starts, but I push him in the chest to get him to back up. The size and rigidity under his shirt makes me suck in a breath and claw my fingers into him, and when I

119

try to pull my hands away he cuffs me and puts them back.

"Stop it," I say, struggling against his warm hold.

"I'm sorry," he says, "I shouldn't have assumed-"

"You're awful sorry about a lot it seems, and it's starting to really piss me off," I spit out.

His expression hardens. "How about I didn't want my father's hot little live-in screwing around whilst he gives her a roof to sleep under?"

I cock up an eyebrow antagonistically. "So this is in the name of the father, is it?" I ask, and then I look pointedly down at his crucifix. "Not, *the son*?"

Before he has a chance to retaliate there's an urgent banging on the door.

I give Tate a smug little smile and call out, "It's open."

His eyes go wide and he reluctantly releases my hands as Mitch storms into the room.

He's volcano-eruption red. "This better not be what I know it is," Mitch grits out.

I fold my arms across my chest and reply, "Don't take your tone with *me*. It's *him* that needs to be put on a leash." Then I turn around to Tate and whisper, "We can get you one to match your little clerical collar."

Tate smirks as Mitch grapples him out of the room, and seriously – what did Mitch think that Tate was going to do? Obviously he wasn't going to try and hate-fuck me because that's what *I* asked for, and he hasn't made any moves on that front in weeks. And in front of Mitch, too?

Actually, the thought of getting off whilst Tate and Mitch are both in the room is making me dizzy, so I better quickly swipe that thought under the rug.

"Don't worry," I say, brazen as they descend the attic staircase. "I'll be out of this stupid arrangement in no time, finishing high school and fucking off to college, and then you'll never have to see me again."

Mitch swings around. "Yeah, about that – you need to go to the living room because your mom wants to talk to you, now."

What? That's weird. My mom never wants to talk to me.

I wait a minute until Mitch and Tate are out of sight, taking two puffs on my inhaler when they are no longer in the hearing vicinity, and then I go downstairs to the living room at the back. My mom is looking at renovation photographs which I presume are from our house, but it looks so different in its bare state that it's virtually unrecognisable right now.

"Hey," I say as I tentatively sit down on the cushion next to her.

"Hey honey," she replies casually as she sweeps up the pictures and closes them into a folder. "So I have some news," she begins, and my stomach instantly drops. "First of all, I wanted to say that it's been great to see you getting on so well with Mitch these past months."

It really shows how much attention this woman pays me if she hasn't realised that my encounters with Mitch end with steam coming off his body. I look over to where he's standing across the room and I see that he's gnawing on the square edge of his thumb.

"And that's why I know that I can tell you this now," she continues, "because you've been so well behaved whilst we've been staying here."

Her elongated pause makes my heart start hammering at a dangerously fast pace.

"I know that I told you that our staying with Mitch during the renovations was a temporary situation, but really it's been a trial run - to see how well you mesh with him in the family. Mitch's work on *our* house is almost done and that means that, in a matter of weeks, I'm going to finally put it on the market – he's made it so saleable that it'll be off our hands in the flip of a switch, and then we'll be able to officially move… here. To Mitch's house. Permanently."

She gives me a little *ta-da!* smile and then pulls me into a tight squeeze before I can wipe the shock off my face.

What.
The.
Fuck.

*

When I wake up in my bed it's still pitch black outside. I roll over, face smushed against the dark pillow case, and I grapple for my phone so that I can see what the time is. *2:52am.*

I guess that's not so strange, but something that *is* strange is the fact that there is so much life coming from outside in Mitch's back yard right now. I sit upright, slipping on my glasses, and then I push off the bed. As quietly as I can, I open my door and tiptoe down the two flights of steps until I'm on the first floor landing. Then I turn around and start making my way to the back of the house so that I can look out of the windows overlooking the garden.

So that's why Tate was still here when I came home tonight. I don't even know if he knows that I'm going to be "permanently" moving into his room, at least until I enrol into college, and it technically wouldn't be of any consequence to him seeing as he lives in some unbeknown secret location, but it doesn't matter anyway – my "talk" with my mom is not the reason why he stayed here tonight.

Tate is hosting a pool party.

It's weird to see a pool party in November, especially when it's raining, but for all I know Mitch's new pool might be as equipped as a hot tub – and, judging from the steam clouding up from the surface, it is.

I haven't dared venture into the outdoor pool before, mainly because I never thought of Mitch's house as my home, but now that it sort of *is* I'm annoyed with myself. I don't want to get in there after all of the guys Tate hangs around with have washed their junk in it.

And I definitely don't want to get in there after all of the girls.

My stomach is rolling as I tentatively walk up to the window ledge to get a clearer look. I feel like I stepped out of bed and fell into a frat house, because Mitch's garden - lit up with yard lanterns and glowing cigarette ends - is perfectly illuminating a biker-chic college orgy for this one woman audience. It's dudes with tattoos and backwards caps (at *night-time* – in the *rain*) and girls with bleached hair and fitted stringy bikinis for as far as the eye can see. I try to ignore the fact that I love the song currently vibrating from the portable speakers.

When I see Tate I feel even worse. He's sitting on the edge of the pool, muscled legs spread wide with his calves half-dipped in the water, and his tanned abdomen fully on display. He's shirtless and his hair is mussed up, as if he's ran his hands through it fifty times in the last ten minutes.

Or as if someone else has.

There's a girl sat next to him talking animatedly and I think that she's trying to read what it says on his tattoo. I scowl. I wonder if she's the one who roughed up his hair.

When I look back at Tate I almost jump out of my skin because his eyes are dead straight burning into mine. I immediately falter backwards, bumping into the living room sofa like a pinball, but he's already shaking off the pool water and striding right for me. I put an armchair between us once he's inside the room.

"I wondered if you would show up," he says huskily as he shakes the rain from his tousled hair, momentarily entrancing me.

I fold my arms across my chest and flick my eyes outside again. The girl who was next to him is craning her neck to see where he's gone to. I hope that she can't see in here as well as he could.

"It's very loud out there," I observe, kind of hating how librariany I sound right now.

"I thought you'd like the music," he says, his mouth lifting slightly at the side.

"I do," I reply, "especially at three in the morning."

His dimples deepen. "You came down here to punish me?" he teases, stepping a little closer than before. I can smell the rain and the water radiating off his heated skin and it's... enticing. Once he's as close to me as the armchair will allow he tilts his head down and asks provocatively, "What exactly did you have in mind?"

I turn my head away and make a little dignified cough. "For all I know it could have been my mom and your dad out there," I lie.

He rests his hands on the back on the armchair and then grips into it as he takes a chest-swelling inhalation. "Yeah, I bet your mom loves Three Days Grace," he says, his eyes burning into mine.

I shake my head and move to exit the room but he pushes his body up and jumps stealthily over the armchair, regaining his stance instantly and then taking my shoulders in his hands.

"Don't you remember what day it is?" he asks, and even in the dimness of the room I can see the sadness etched into his brow.

What day it is? I blink, confused.

And then I realise.

It's funny how our minds retain certain information, even if the use has long-since expired. I kind of feel bad that I hadn't remembered sooner, but at the same time I'm high-fiving myself for almost forgetting it completely.

I look at the pendant resting in the severe dip between his pectorals and I wonder if the metal is cold from the night air, or if it's hot from his body temperature.

He stoops down a bit, eyes all sad and sparkly as they meet mine, and he locks our gaze together.

"My dad told me about you moving in here with your mom, and I'm sorry River. I know it makes you uncomfortable. I…" He looks away and swallows, then bites his lower lip into his mouth. When his eyes meet mine again, there's a flicker of something in them that I can't quite distinguish in the dark. "I wish it didn't," he finishes, and I realise that we are now almost flush together.

I don't even try to shove him away. I may no longer love his soul but I sure can enjoy his hot as hell body. I can't deny it, I love looking at him. In fact, I love looking *up* at him. I love tilting my neck all the way back just so that I can be met with his intimidating stare, made even darker because of the long curves of his lashes. I love breathing in the testosterone laden heat that oozes out of his pumped-up body. I may hate that I want to touch him but I love being held. Everything feels contradictory but, right now, I don't care.

I fist his pendant and lean my forehead into his hardened chest. God that feels good. He's been out in the rain all night and somehow his body is still volcanic. I think I mewl a little when he wraps his arms around my shoulders.

I want to cry but I don't let myself. Instead, before I drag myself out of his arms and force myself to climb *back into his bed*, I sigh and nestle in further. I run my free hand around the waistband of his shorts and I feel a twinkle in my chest when he shudders against me.

My voice is barely negligible but I know that he hears me. I tear myself away and straighten my glasses before I go.

"I wish it didn't, too," I whisper.

And then I'm gone.

CHAPTER 18

Three Years Ago

I'm nervously twiddling with the baby pink tulle puffed up around my thighs as I stand by the drawn drapes in the main hall, waiting for Kit to finish readying the playlist for tonight's Homecoming. I always knew that I was going to be coming, but I didn't always know that I would be *going*, and as the realisation fully dawns on me – I'm not just here because of the committee, but because Tate Coleson wants to be at the Homecoming Dance with *me* – happy butterflies nervously flit under the soft bodice of my dress.

Tate wanted me to come in the ride with him and his friends, so he didn't like it when I told him that I wasn't going to need picking up. Kit and I would be here from the final bell, setting up the hall with the rest of the committee. Admittedly, I *did* want to come with him – I wanted to see him suited up on my front porch, I wanted to hold his hand in the car, and I wanted to walk through the school's doors with him as my date – but I can also breathe a little easier this way. I didn't have to tell my mom that I have a date, let alone the fact that he's the boy across the street who I've been sorta-kinda secretly dating behind her back. Also, I didn't have to be in a confined space with Hudson, who no doubt would be coming with Tate and his friends. Hudson is a case of endless sideways glances and unnerving smirks, and I want to spend as little time with him as is possible, especially when I feel a little vulnerable in my outfit choice tonight.

I look down at my dress as I bite into my little coating of lip-gloss. It has a high-necked sleeveless bodice which puffs out into a small but full tutu skirt, all baby pink and shimmery. I think it's cute, but I know how weird the people at school get when someone who no-one thinks is cute *tries* to be cute. I try to block them out from my mind. Tate seems to like me and no-one else's opinion on the situation matters.

God, I hope that he thinks I look cute tonight.

Kit hits play on the playlist and the song instantly racks through the speakers, prompting the principle to open the door to the hall and admit all of the students who have been waiting in the foyer and outside. I immediately duck from my hiding place and skirt through one of the miniature side entrances, avoiding the rush as I go to find Tate.

I'm momentarily immobilised when I notice how much more grown up all of the other girls here look. Sure, I'm only a freshman and some of these are sophomores and juniors, but why do they look so much older than me? And how the *hell* did they grow *those*? I work my way around the foyer, sticking to the walls, until I come to the entrance and I glimpse outside.

It's dark out but it's mild, and Phoenix Falls' endless drizzle seems to have ceased for the moment. I study the vehicles that are idling in the lot until I come across the *I-eat-your-cars-for-breakfast* Wrangler and the group of students that are standing outside of it. It's Madden's car. I know this

127

because he drives it to school sometimes, having gotten his license as soon as he turned sixteen. No surprises that Count Dracula the Second is an October baby.

A nervous weight settles in my tummy as I take in the sight of their group. Two sophomore cheerleaders with dark sexy hair are leaning against the front of the Jeep, seemingly engrossed in a conversation with Hudson – they're beautiful, but obviously they are also sadly insane. And then to the side… a crowd of football guys from another car have met up with Madden and Tate, half-hidden behind another truck, and they're doing that minimal-contact hand-grasp-hug thing whilst nodding their heads to signal who their dates are.

I hold onto the side of the door with a shaky hand, shielding my body from view as I watch them shyly. I absolutely cannot go out there. This was such a bad idea. What am I even doing here? Oh God, oh God, oh *God*.

I turn around with the intention of speed-walking back to the hall to tell Kit that I'm leaving but the "queue"-cum-mosh-pit leading into the main room still hasn't dissipated. I shift nervously at the back of the crowd, tapping my foot agitatedly, desperate to disappear.

Suddenly I feel a rush of air as if someone has just ran up behind me and warmth immediately envelopes my back. I look down as I'm quickly encircled with two firm forearms, tan skin exposed from white rolled-up sleeves, and Tate leans down to rest his chin on my bare shoulder, his lips lightly kissing the side of my reddening cheek.

"Hey baby," he whispers and I drop my head, overcome with embarrassment, amazement, and pure, pure love. He leans slightly over my clavicle, peering down at my body, and I shrink a little under his scrutiny. I can feel his smile against my cheek. "I love your dress," he continues, and his thumbs stroke my ribcage gently, as if he knows just how out of my depth I feel right now. He kisses me again and then murmurs quietly, "I knew that my girl would be the sweetest little thing in here tonight."

I laugh, smitten, and I spin around, instantly drunk on the sight and the scent of him. He's wearing some sort of cocaine-laced cologne that's making my head crazy dizzy, and the picture of him in a half-buttoned white shirt and a pair of dress pants that barely contain his thighs is really not helping with the not-passing-out thing. His eyes sparkle as he looks down at me intoxicatingly, palms cupping my face as I tilt up to him like a sunflower.

"You look so good," I admit, and he flashes me a smug boyish grin that makes me laugh out loud.

"You wanna come meet the guys before I steal you away for the rest of the night? Or should I just steal you away right now?" he asks, leaning down like he's about to kiss me.

Steal me, I think. *Definitely steal me.*

But before his lips have the chance to graze mine a ruckus storms through the entryway and I instantly know that we've got company – by which I mean: the entire football team, the cheerleading squad, Madden, and-

"He's been sixteen for less than twenty-four hours and he's *already* getting his dick wet!" Hudson punches Tate hard on the back but miraculously Tate doesn't move an inch, otherwise I would have been pancaked underneath his concrete pecs.

Tate twists around, a vein that I've never seen before bulging furiously in his neck as he glares down at Hudson. "Watch it man, I could've knocked her," he grits out, and his hands move to compress me into his side.

Hudson cocks an eyebrow at him and then smirks at the guys around us. "I'm pretty sure that's exactly what you've *been* doing," he taunts. "Or at least, that's what you will be doing *tonight*." Hudson flicks his slits to me. "I'm sure you know what all guys do on their sixteenth, right?"

I blink up at him, my cheeks burning furiously at the attention, and his words settle uneasily into my brain.

Confused, I look from Hudson to Tate, and then back to Hudson.

Today is Tate's birthday?

There's a kind of awkward silence as the group around us looks shiftily between Hudson, Tate, and then me, but it's thankfully almost unnoticeable due to the noise coming from the hall. I'm not sure who needs to be deleted from this scene more to rectify the vibe: Hudson, me, or literally every single one of us. From the look that Madden is shooting him right now, I'm going to say Hudson.

Tate jerks his chin. "So where's *your* date, man?"

Hudson zones in on me like sniper. "Maybe I'm looking right at her."

I recoil at the same moment that Tate moves me to the side, and then he shoves his palms into the planes of Hudson's chest. Hudson stumbles and Tate grabs his collar, whispering something inaudible to him as he backs him out of earshot from the rest of the group. He keeps him away from us for about twenty seconds, before giving him another shove and then turning around, stalking back towards us with his hulking shoulders heaving. Funnily enough, the bizarre exchange seems to have sated the crowd of sexy popular sports people, and now they're looking at me with impressed curiosity. Tate grabs my hand and pulls me to him as he says, "'Scuse me," to the classmates who are in the crowd in front of us. Magically, everyone disperses to let him through.

Once we get into the hall Tate grabs me a drink and then spins me into the centre of the dance floor.

The past minute has confused me so much that all I can do is drink his offering and look up at him imploringly, the red lights which sheathe the hall making him glow like a dangerous angel.

He clutches my body to his and he murmurs into my hair, "Dance with me first. I'll explain everything later."

I tilt my head backwards and I notice that his eyes glint

as they linger on my mouth.

"I like that, by the way," he says, his eyes hooding slightly. I realise that he's talking about my lip-gloss so I give him a shy sparkly smile.

He smiles in return and then he presses a long, chaste kiss to my lips.

Then we sway.

*

Tate leads me from the hall, down the corridor which homes a lot of the staff offices, and then out of the exit near the science bay. He walks us around the side of the brick exterior until we are almost at the other side of the lot. Madden's Wrangler is in sight and we head towards it, the keys in Tate's hand.

Tate opens the passenger door and retrieves his suit jacket from the dash, immediately easing me into it to shield me from the wintry chill. Then he sits me down on the seat, my feet dangling above the blacktop, and he rubs his warm palms back and forth along my shoulders, ready to explain.

"There are... a few things," he admits quietly and my stomach twists nervously. His hesitance is scaring me. His eyes lock onto mine and he shakes his head, as if he's reading exactly what I'm thinking. "None of it has anything to do with you, I promise, you're the... you're the only good part of any of this."

He drops his head and takes a few moments to breathe deeply, calming down. I, on the other hand, am so anxious that I'm palpitating.

"It is my sixteenth today," he starts, "and I know that it's weird that I didn't tell you, but I didn't want you to think for a second about any of that shit that Huddy was insinuating. I don't want that. I mean, I do – you have to know how *much* I want that, but also how much I want to wait for you, until you're older." He pulls a pained

131

expression and looks away briefly. "I don't know if this is coming out right," he says, removing one of his hands so that he can grip at the back of his neck.

I nod up at him encouragingly and he relaxes a little. "I understand, it's okay, I… I'm sorry that I'm not-"

He shakes his head and uses both of his hands to cup my jaw. "Don't be sorry, please. I literally just turned sixteen, and I *want* to wait for you. I don't care how long that is. I want it to be with you, and *only* with you, okay?"

I swallow and make a little nod, hoping that he can't *actually* read my mind because something about Tate telling me how ardently he wants to wait for me is making me want to rip all my clothes off right here in Madden's car.

"Is that what was bothering you?" I ask. "Because it's honestly not a big-"

"I'm moving," he says.

I stop speaking and I instantly still. My feet are no longer happily waggling over the step beneath the doorframe.

"You're… moving?" I repeat, as if I didn't hear exactly what he just said.

"I promise it won't make a difference to anything, River, I promise. But I have to move because my mom and her boyfriend are getting married, so they found a bigger place outside of town for us all to fit in. I'm going to try and move in with my dad as soon as he's all set up and then I can transfer back so that we're still at school together, even though I won't be across the street from you anymore. I really, really wish that I didn't have to, and I'm so, so sorry. As soon as I can I'm gonna come back for you, River. I promise I'm gonna come back for you."

His eyes are shimmering and my chest is constricting tightly. I'm confused. I'm hurting. But I'm also awe-struck that, with all of the shit that is getting in our way right now, Tate Coleson still wants to be mine, and he still wants me to be his.

I'm only fourteen but he wants to wait for me for as long as it takes. His mom is moving him away and he's going to try and come back as soon as he can. As sad as I am, I can't help but feel lucky that this perfect boy is willing to fight anything to keep me in his life.

"Please say something," he says, pulling his hands back and pushing them into the pockets of his pants, visibly nervous as he assesses my silence.

I hop out of the Wrangler and wrap my arms, which are now enveloped in his suit jacket, around his neck. His hands instantly find my waist and he grips me tightly, pushing me slightly against the back door of the Jeep.

"I want to wait for you too," I whisper, and he lets out a strained relieved groan, dipping his forehead so that he can press it against mine.

"River," he moans, his palms running up to my shoulder blades. "I don't want to lose you. Ever. Please will you…" He takes a deep breath. "Please say that you'll be my girlfriend."

My heart stutters and my eyes widen in shock. He meets my gaze, irises glowing with a hunger that I don't quite understand yet, and I nod as if I'm under a spell. "Tate," I say, "of course I'll be your girlfriend. Yes – *yes* – of course."

I run my fingers through his soft hair and I stand up on my tip-toes, ready to show him just how much I mean it, but his lips catch mine first, to show me that he means it even more.

CHAPTER 19

Present

Kit getting detention has really messed with our end of term plans, but I'm going to make it work for us anyway. She hasn't told me *why* she got detention – only that some incident happened outside of class – but she's been exiled from lessons for the rest of the day and, even worse, she's been disqualified from racing in the track competition at the annual pre-Christmas sports evening tonight. I wasn't going to race, even though I'm Kit's running partner on every other occasion, but I was going to be up in the stands praying for her to win, and then jumping up and down with her when she destroyed the egos of everyone who shunned her from the athletics team.

She has to stay back for an extra hour after school, so I go to the library to wait it out for her, and then I promised her a girly evening, even though that means bringing her to Mitch's house for the first time and that makes me feel really nervous.

Seeing as it's the end of term I don't have any

assignments left to do, so I decide to freak myself out further by flicking through the college brochures for my chosen schools instead. The thought of starting work long-term in my mom's chosen field for me makes me feel nauseous – it will be like school all over again, and what if I hate the people? That's the crux of it: as someone who is not a people person anyway, the thought of working with people who I don't love for the rest of my life makes me… I sigh just thinking about it. It gives me very dark thoughts.

Kit finds me in the library after she's released from her imprisonment and she gives me a sad hug from behind as I put the catalogues back in the wall holders. I go to put my hand over hers but it feels weirdly hard so I look down at it and instantly scream. I spin around and see that I was being hugged by the life-size skeleton that we used as a decoration at the Halloween dance, only now it's wearing Kit's track tank and a floppy Santa hat.

"They were going to recycle it," Kit explains as she rests her chin on the skeleton's clavicle.

I try to bring my breathing back to normal and I nod as we exit the library. Even though that thing just gave me palpitations I say, "You did the right thing."

As we walk across the grounds outside I shield Kit's eyes so that she doesn't have to see the mascot, the cheer squad, and the banners being set up for the sports evening tonight, but I can tell that she's already in better spirits because she's shielding the skeleton's "eyes" too.

To make up for the absence of a sporting victory we're going to have a night full of sugary Christmassy distractions. In all honesty, I think that I might need the distractions more than Kit. Kit is so normal (okay, skeleton-kidnapping aside, she's sort of normal) that it makes me mad at myself for having such temperamental hormonal fluctuations.

When we get to Mitch's house I feel really anxious because Kit being here and seeing this as my new home makes it more real. She scopes it out as we ascend the porch with pursed lips.

"So does he live here then?" she asks.

I know who she's talking about. I shake my head. "No, but he works with his dad, so he is around quite a lot."

She squeezes her arms around her body and nods, and we drop the subject as we enter the house. I walk into the kitchen where we take off our bags and coats, wash our hands, and then I get milk out of the fridge so that I can warm it up for hot chocolates on the stove.

"Sugar cookies or brownies?" I ask, retrieving chocolate bars and the sugar icing box that I recently stashed in Mitch's boring protein-powder cupboard last week. I hold them up for Kit to decide.

Kit is emitting little pink hearts when she sees the sugar icing box. "Sugar cookies, please," she answers, and I think that she's fully over missing the track event now.

I grab the butter, sugar, flour, and eggs, and I set them on the table before pulling out the mixing bowl from one of the lower cabinets.

"This house is nice," she comments as she eyes up the kitchen, her aura still aglow with sugar cookie anticipation.

I twist my mouth to the side as I pour in the flour. "I know," I mutter quietly, and then I smash the blade of my knife into the shell of the egg, cracking it open.

She flicks her eyes back to me. Kit doesn't know exactly what happened all those years ago, but her female instincts inform her that it doesn't merit an apology. "You'll be out of here in less than a year," she says. I think she said it to console me, but my stomach tightens and I scrunch up my face even more.

Luckily, I have an egg to beat, so I start whisking it extra, extra hard.

I can sense her awaiting some sort of response from me, so after I pour in a little vanilla extract I begin. "I like Mitch and I like his stupid house, and being here makes me even like his stupid son. I'm so mad at myself because I'm a strong feminist, and yet whenever I see him my body is like *no you're not*. This is why it's so bad that I'm here – it's like *Lost*. You put a bunch of people on an island together and in two days they're falling in love. Only here, I already had feelings in the past so now they're rekindling with a vengeance, and he... he's acting..." I search for the most appropriate word, and the best that I come up with is, "Perfect. He's acting perfect. He's sixteen again and he's trying to give me the princess treatment, but I know that it must be an act, because how can someone perfect also be capable of doing something so terrible?"

In the time it has taken for me to finish my rant Kit has managed to eat seven pieces of chocolate from one of the bars that I left on the table, although she still manages to look attentive and thoughtful.

"Hmm," she says finally.

Okay, I take back the *"attentive and thoughtful"*.

"That's a lot to take in," she continues. She sets the bar down and folds the re-sealable tab, running her finger across it until it looks like it was never opened in the first place. "I think we're very hard on ourselves, as girls," she says slowly, as if she's choosing every word very carefully. I slow my mixing until I fully stop. "I think maybe you should allow yourself the right to be selfish, and maybe you should make some decisions that serve your needs right now, based on the circumstance that you've been forced into. Like I said," she reiterates, "you'll be at college soon, and the life your mom is making here doesn't have to be yours. But if you experiment as you please right now... I think it will be good to give yourself some options. You'll be able to literally run away from everything if you want to next Fall. Maybe you just need to-" And then she leans across the table, scooping sugar cookie mix onto her pinkie, and sticks it in her mouth. She swallows it down and gives me a small smile. "Indulge," she finishes.

I blink at her like I've just had a lesson in the ways of the Jedi. Kit Kenobi. Who would have thought.

And then we're both snapped out of our trance by the sound of a motorcycle revving up the driveway.

She gives me a look and I know exactly what it says.

It says *time to indulge.*

*

Tate remained in the garage until Kit went home. I set the tray in the oven, we watched a holiday movie, and then, under the glow of a couple black pillar candles, we "decorated" the cookies. For some reason all of Kit's cookies have smiley faces with little vampire fangs. Even the Christmas trees.

Once Kit is gone I put on a little music like I used to at my mom's house and start washing the bowls and utensils I'd been soaking. I'm not going to lie, it is not pretty music. It's an aggressive cover song by Three Days Grace, but I've got it on so quietly that you can't tell at first.

I hear him enter the room but I don't turn around. I'm very focused on scrubbing every millimetre of sugar cookie batter off the mixing spoon, even when I feel him settle against the counter behind me, eyes burning into the back of my head. My stupid, traitorous head.

"Do you want some help with that?" he asks quietly.

Darn it. We haven't been completely mute these past two weeks but I have been mainly keeping up the pretence of silent-treatmenting him. It's times like now where that comes to bite me in the butt.

He breathes a laugh and comes to stand right behind my back. I swear he secretes heat like an animal. He rests his left hand next to my torso beside the sink, so I deliberately get extra splashy with my rinsing.

"I wanted to tell you," he says, and my veins instantly tighten with nerves. *What the hell do you want to tell me, Tate?*

138

"Your mom is going away this next week, but she doesn't know about it because it's a Christmas gift from my dad. They're going to stay at a cabin at Pine Hills. I didn't know if he would have told you yet but I wanted to let you know because…"

He trails off and I feel the shift as he rubs at his neck or his shoulders with his right hand. It drops back so that it's next to my waist again and my stomach flutters at the proximity.

"It means that you'll have the house to yourself," he finishes.

This time when I slosh the water out of the sink it's not deliberate. It makes a huge wet patch on the front of my school trousers, causing me to jump backwards because the water is burning hot, and I smack right into the planes of Tate's chest. He steadies me, and then I reposition myself so that I'm facing him.

He's giving me a wary smile, like he's nervous about how I'm going to respond. He should be.

"*And?*" I practically shout the word. I really need to calm to fuck down. Regardless of what happened between us I need to start being more level-headed about everything. I can't change the past but I can change how I respond to it. "What are you implying?" I ask, cocking an eyebrow. "A bit presumptuous, don't you think?"

He drops his eyes to the floor between us and he shakes his head, his breathing unsteady. He mutters something that sounds a lot like "*not presumptuous, I've been praying*" but I don't think he was saying it for my ears. He keeps his head tilted down but he lifts his eyes to mine, and they're burning with the unspoken things that he's obviously dying to say. "My dad told me not to come over whilst they're gone," he explains, his voice deep and controlled. "And I won't." He pauses momentarily as his eyes search mine. Then he finishes, "Unless you want me to."

I'm angry with him for suggesting it, but I'm angrier

with myself for wanting it. Hell, *I* was the one who suggested it in the first place. Even though part of me wants to kick him out of the door and tell him to stay away from me until I leave for college, another side of me wants to get him to *lock* that door and forbid him from leaving until our parents return from their vacation.

Tate's behaviour right now doesn't align with the person I grew to hate – instead, it's completely in sync with the boy I was falling in love with. Can people change? Can they have moments that are so perverse and bad, but it's just a moment of insanity that they never slip back into? I have never believed that people change. Their behaviours only alter if there's something in it for them, which takes me back to the original thought that triggered my sadistic sex agenda: Tate wants my body, and my ability to provide or deprive it will be the screw in his neck.

But is that the case? Maybe I completely misunderstood *everything*. I hate second-guessing myself because it feels like I'm betraying my intuition, but not every thought that passes my mind is going to be right or true. Maybe Tate's motives weren't what they seemed at the time – and maybe, like Kit suggested, I can allow myself to indulge in his goodness whilst it's being offered up to me.

I scroll my eyes down the tan skin of his neck, over his tensed pectorals and stomach, and all the way down his denim-clad thighs until I'm looking at his huge black biker boots. *If this was three years ago…*

Just as I'm about to open my mouth Tate shifts slightly and lifts me out of my appraisal.

"Are those candles bleeding?" he asks, his eyebrows pinched together in… I'm going to say concern.

I look over at the black pillar candles which are flickering next to the draining board. I'd forgotten that I had lit my vampire's tears candles. Red wax is oozing over the tapered tip in a frightening, provocative way.

I move my eyes back to Tate with a nonchalant

expression on my face. "No," I say.

He breathes out a laugh and drops his eyes again, the toe of his boot now rubbing back and forth in the gap between us. "You're so weird," he murmurs, and then he straightens up and locks me in with his penetrating stare. "Do you want me to be here?" he finally asks, straight to the point.

I can see in my peripheral vision that his hands are gripped tightly around the leather of his belt and as I look up into his eyes my tummy does a sparkly flip.

I swallow a little and make my expression resolute. It's no more than a whisper but I choke it out before I can stop myself.

"Yes," I say.

Tate instantly closes the gap between us but, just as he does, the lights from Mitch's work truck flash up the driveway. Tate turns his head, groaning in frustration, and then he zones back in on me. He places his hands on my cheeks and I try not to shiver as his warmth seeps into me. I can feel it pooling in my belly and he's nowhere even near there.

Yet.

He dips his head to my throat and presses his mouth against me hard, quickly sucking at the soft skin before grazing it with his teeth. The sensation drips down my body like the molten wax on my candles and my stomach starts lapping with heat.

"As soon as they're gone, I'm yours," he murmurs quietly, the words warm and hushed against my neck. I shiver as he runs the tip of his tongue over the skin that he just claimed and his words press into my body with as much pressure as his hands.

I'm yours.

He really said that.

I. Am. Yours.

Before Mitch is out of the truck Tate pulls away and leaves the kitchen without a second glance.

I fall back against the sink and think about what the hell I just started.

CHAPTER 20

Three Years Ago

The last day before school closes for winter break also ends up being Tate's last day before he transfers. As soon as he told me that he was moving; he no longer let me keep up the pretence of not being with him at school, stealing me away to his table every lunch break and meeting up with me by the bleachers after the final bell, and I haven't minded one bit.

Okay, no-one around him can believe that he would pick me to be his girlfriend, but Tate is way too cut for them to argue with him about it. Even Hudson has shut his mouth, although I seem to be bumping into him in every corridor that I walk down and he really gives me the creeps. If only he was the one transferring schools.

It snowed last night so there's a sugar-icing dusting of it all across the sports ground, the grass blades sparkling with frost as I make my way across the yard to get to my next class. I spot the sophomores on the field doing their double Gym lesson so I stop to watch, knowing that Tate will be there. As it's the last day of term classes are basically all frees, so the girls have evidently taken it upon themselves to "observe" like I am, dressed in their gym clothes but sat on the bleachers to watch the boys.

On the field the guys are kitted out in their football shorts and jerseys, and they're currently split into two teams, huddling as they discuss their plans of attack. When they all stand back up, clapping their hands to pump each other up, I spot Tate on the farther side and I clutch my books tightly to my chest.

Wow. Even with that helmet on he looks to die for. And those shoulder pads? I want him to tackle *me*.

I push my glasses back up my flushed pink nose and start making my way to the door of the tech block when I hear a voice call out, "Hey!"

I turn my head, trying to squelch my smile as Tate comes bounding up the field, whipping off his helmet and heading in my direction. I step away from the door and walk tentatively towards the grass, stopping just as I breach the twinkling green border, brimming with both nerves and joy at Tate's display of attention. As soon as I'm within reach he wraps his arms around the back of my skirt and heaves me up, his fingers cupping my behind. I let out a surprised but delighted *oof* as he squishes me to his chest and bounces me up and down in his solid tan arms.

He grins up at me before lowering his eyes to my mouth and he gives me a light but long kiss, his lips frozen but soft as silk.

I giggle as he pulls back and he tilts his head to look up at me, his hands slowly slipping into dangerous territory.

"Hey quarterback," I tease and he gives me a cocky flash of perfect white teeth.

"Hey wife," he says, and he presses a firm kiss into my neck.

I bite back my startled gasp and I dig my teeth into my lower lip. He's never called me that before, but my body really, *really* likes it.

"I want you to stay back after school tonight, okay?" he asks, leaning back so that he can look into my eyes. "I'm staying out here with the team for the rest of the day, but I want you to meet me at the entryway after the bell so that I can give you your present."

My heart clenches. "My present?" I ask, eyebrows pinching in wonder.

He bounces me up again and I try to ignore the friction that's happening as the apex of my thighs meet the muscles beneath his jersey. "Yeah, your present. It's almost Christmas baby," he says, and then I realise, of *course* Tate makes a big deal about Christmas. My eyes fall to the chain just sticking up around his collar and I think of the pendant that is currently being nestled between his pecs. "You'll meet me?" he urges, bringing my mind back from the gutter.

I nod adamantly and, with another grin, he clasps the back of my neck so that he can bring my lips back down to his, slipping his tongue inside of my mouth and making a flurry of sparks jolt down my belly. He groans quietly as he slides himself over and around me, drinking me up as his hands start squeezing me gently.

"Coleson! Over here, *now!*"

I pull back, startled, embarrassed, and a thousand brain cells lighter, and I watch as his coach starts marching our way. Tate fluidly sets me down and he runs the backs of his fingers over my flushed cheek.

I take a step backwards, not wanting to get him in more trouble, but he pulls me into him again so that he can kiss me a couple hundred more times.

I laugh and push at his chest, hastily back-stepping before his coach can give us both a last-day-of-term detention. Tate does the same, that knowing smile playing on his lips as he watches me pull the door open to head back inside.

He watches me through the windows until I turn the corner and disappear from sight completely.

*

After the final bell rings I quickly run-walk to my locker, ready to shrug on my coat, stuff a term's worth of paperwork into my bag, and then go to meet Tate at the entrance. But as soon as I've almost emptied it I see one last thing laying on the metal base, as if it was just slipped in through the crack under the door.

I cock my head at it and slowly slide it to the front, aware that it could be something that fell out of my folders but, for some reason, I don't feel like it is.

I pick it up and feel a shock run down my spine.

It's another note.

This time it hasn't been typed in one of the computer labs – instead it's handwritten, a font more slanted and elaborately cursive than I was expecting, and it looks as though it was torn from a lined homework book. I immediately glance to the bottom of the page and see the name that I was hoping for. I relax a little and smile as I read the note.

Meet me at the changing rooms after final bell
I've got something for you baby ;)
Tate

I blink at the note and read over it a few times, a confusing anxious feeling settling into my gut. I turn the paper over to see if there's anything written on the other side, and then look back at the words again.

The main thing that makes me pause is the fact that he now wants to meet me at the changing rooms. I mean, for all I know, maybe that's what he actually meant when he said that he wanted us to meet at the entryway – maybe he wanted to meet at the entrance to the locker room. And he did say that he had something for me, and he *does* call me baby sometimes.

But for some reason, it just feels... off.

I fold the note into a few squares and then slowly close my locker, turning the key in a slightly numb haze. Why do I feel a bit uncomfortable? Maybe it's the winking face. Tate and I have never texted before, so maybe he's a winking face type of person, but it doesn't match the picture of him that I've been building in my head. It doesn't seem very... him.

I head down the stairs with the rest of the mass exodus, naturally overanalysing my own paranoia. Honestly, what is my problem? So what if he used a winking face? So what if his handwriting isn't as... buff as I expected it to be? For a reason unbeknown to me, a chill settles in my gut as I reach the bottom of the science block, and I pause.

If I continue going to the left, I'll reach the foyer and the main entrance in less than twenty seconds, give or take. If I go up and to the right, I'll be heading to the Gym and I'll be able to go to the changing rooms, which seems to be where Tate wants to see me now.

I stand at the wall of the corridor, glancing back and forth between the two directions.

I pull the note back out of my bag and read it one more time.

I'm being stupid. It definitely says the changing rooms, so obviously that's where I need to be.

I shove the note back into my bag and take the exit to the right, not knowing how wrong I was about to be.

CHAPTER 21

Present

When Mitch and my mom leave, I don't know what the protocol is going to be with Tate so I choose to go about my day as usual. It involves preparing food, eating food, and then reading until my next meal. After a while I realise that I'm behaving like a self-imposed inmate so I decide to do something that I haven't had the confidence to do on my own in a long time. I put my book down, slunk out of my quilt fortress, and I pull open a drawer. Once I have the necessary items, I change out of my in-the-house clothes and slip into the more fitted, purposeful pieces. I go downstairs, drink half a glass of water, and then head outside, locking the door and slipping the key into the pocket on the side of my leggings.

And then I start to run.

It's really more of a jog because I don't want to burden my lungs, but it's fast enough to get my heart-beat racing. I focus on the muscles in my legs and on controlling my inhalations and exhalations, trying to distract myself from the heavy burn that quickly settles in my chest. I count the houses on the street and then I count each truck that I run past, segmenting them in my mind by make.

The one thing that I didn't count on was deciding where to run to, but my feet seemed to find their way there all on their own.

I have been jogging for a while with a couple of walk breaks in between, and now I'm standing outside of my mom's soon-to-be-former home. *My* soon-to-be-former home. I can't see any of Mitch's changes from the outside so I walk up the driveway with the nervousness of an intruder and peer in through the window at the front. I feel a cold, sharp sensation spread across my chest, but it isn't anything serious – it's just because it looks different in there. It matches up to the photographs my mom had been leafing through the night that she told me that we would be moving in with Mitch. It looks nice in there, but it doesn't look like my home.

I don't know if it ever did really.

I walk down the driveway and I count how many steps it takes to get to the bottom of it from the porch. It's less than I expected. Then I stop my stalling and bite the bullet. I look up at Tate's former home.

It's basically the mirror of my mom's. They aren't big houses but they have all of the important bits. They look kind of quaint and it gives me a funny feeling near my heart. Nostalgia. I can't believe that, after three years of not seeing Tate, I am now feeling *nostalgia*. How can he still evoke these feelings in me? I thought that our bond had been severed.

It's after dinnertime when I dawdle back to Mitch's place, so the air is extra cold and it's getting dark enough for people to switch on their Christmas lights. I mull over what Tate must have done in the time between him leaving and then re-entering my life. Obviously he lived with his mom and step-dad for a bit. Then, at some point before he could legally live on his own, he lived with his dad. Where did he go to school? Technically, once he was back with Mitch, he could have come back to his former high school with me. Why didn't he?

I startle when I reach the curb in front of Mitch's driveway. Tate is sat on the step in front of the door just beneath the porch, with his elbows resting atop his knees, and he's looking down at his open palms. He's wearing denim jeans with a biker jacket and he has a large box packed in a white grocery bag on the floor to his left. On his right sits a small bouquet of roses.

He notices me when I'm halfway up the drive. His head snaps upright, and then he picks up the bag and the flowers as he stands, his eyes never leaving mine. I don't know what the protocol is for this moment because I don't even know what this moment *is*, so I walk up the porch until I'm right next to him – my shoulder to his chest – and I fish the key out of my pocket.

"I thought you had a key," I say as I slide my key into the lock, twist, and pull down the door handle. I open the door and step inside, and then I look back at Tate over my shoulder to silently invite him in. He has to walk in sideways to accommodate the box bagged up in his hand and – let's be honest – his giant shoulders.

"I didn't want to come inside whilst you weren't home. This place is more yours than mine," he replies. He closes the door with a backwards push from his deltoid and then he starts following me into the kitchen. I feel weirdly wired. I'm nervous because I don't really know what's going to happen whilst our parents aren't here, but I'm excited too, which makes me embarrassed for myself, because I'm not sure if I'm being strong and self-indulgent or simply weak-willed.

I also can't help the liquid heat that swirls in my stomach when I realise that Tate didn't deny still having access to a key. I kind of thought that Mitch might have confiscated it from him, so the knowledge that he can freely enter this house whenever he wants is alarming – but, for some sick and twisted reason, I like it.

Tate sets the bags on the table and he moves around me to flip the switches on the heating dashboard, then opening a cupboard and grabbing a vase. He walks to the sink and fills it with a quick, long spurt of water, before setting it in the centre of the table. He tears the cellophane off the roses and pours the feed sachet that falls from between the stems into the water. Once he pulls open a drawer he mass-snips the bottoms of the stems with a pair of medium-sized handheld shears, and then he places the roses in the water. He crumples the cellophane in his hands and takes it to the outside bin, not looking at me the entire time.

I swallow dryly and, in my brief reprieve from his presence, I take the opportunity to literally smell the roses. They are a dark wine red colour and the petals are still mainly tightly compacted together in puckered buds, having not yet blossomed. I feel a warm, slightly painful constriction in my chest as I think about Tate buying these for my benefit, for no other reason than the fact that roses are beautiful.

No, it's more than that. Roses are romantic.

"Are you running again?" Tate asks as he re-enters the kitchen. He's being suspiciously normal, which I find disturbing. He peels the bag down over the brown box and I have a sneaky feeling that whatever is inside it is there for me. That warm sensation in my chest from earlier does a resurge but I try to keep my expression neutral, so as not to transmit how shamefully deeply my body enjoys this affection. When I don't respond Tate continues talking. "I always thought that you would join the track team but you never did the try-outs, even though you had the stamina for it. I like your outfit by the way," he says, looking up at me from beneath long black lashes, and a dimple flashes on his cheek when he crooks me a small smile.

The micro-biomes in my tummy are flustering. It's hell in there. A fire has broken loose and every bit of my body is partaking in running, screaming chaos. I'm wearing leggings that are no doubt sucked six inches deep in my ass, and I have unzipped my waterproof jacket to unveil my halter-neck top that is damp with sweat, making it fit snug.

I cross my arms over my chest. I am deeply at war with myself right now. It's a cross-fire between *indulge* and *have some pride*. The irony is that whilst I'm beating myself down, for some reason it feels like Tate is the person lifting me back up.

Tate comes around to my side of the table and rests against it, spreading his legs apart and holding himself up with his palms flat on the surface behind him. If I take two steps forward I will be nestled right against the protruding muscle of his-

"Tell me what you're thinking, River."

I scramble for whatever was in my brain before I started thinking about his... body. I'm not going to lie, it takes a few seconds.

I think that maybe some female honesty will repulse him enough to high-tail and leave me to my sexual frustration in peace, so I say, "I don't know how to talk to you anymore. I don't really *want* to talk to you anymore. But when I do start talking to you, I feel like I'm talking to the old you, and that makes it easier. But then that makes it *harder*, because I shouldn't want to talk to you. You became a really unforgiveable person, and I don't know if I want to let that go, even if you were only sixteen."

To his credit, Tate looks as though he is trying to understand what I'm saying. His brow is downturned in contemplative irritation and his shoulders look a little tenser than they were a minute ago. He pushes off the table, somehow closing the little gap between our bodies with the sheer size of himself, and he gently clasps my shoulders in hot engulfing palms. He stoops a little so that I can look at him from a more even level. He speaks hushed but hoarse, and the words scrape down my sternum.

"What the hell are you talking about, River?"

I narrow my eyes on him. It's fascinating how things that are detrimental in one person's life can be completely forgotten in another's. Maybe he literally doesn't remember. To be honest, if he doesn't, I'm not going to remind him, so I shake my head to say *forget about it* but he isn't giving up that easy.

"Seriously, River, I don't know what you're talking about. If you think that I ever wanted to hurt you, there's been some misunderstanding. It fucked me up when things ended like they did. If I could go back and wipe that day out of our lives so that things could have stayed the way they were, I would. Trust me, I *would* River."

His death grip on my shoulders is now crushing me into his torso. He doesn't seem to mind my post-run sweat rubbing into his clean cotton shirt so I lean in further, and he instantly notices. His eyes hold a dark glint for one long moment and then he brushes my jacket from my shoulders, down my arms until it hits the floor. He doesn't let his eyes flick to my body – instead, they hold onto mine the entire time.

"I want to pick up where we left off," he finishes. His hands slide into mine and he tugs them so that my arms are wrapped around his waist. Then he moves his own back to my collarbones, slowly guiding them until they are wrapped around both sides of my neck.

"Will you strangle me if I say no?" I ask breathlessly.

His eyes widen momentarily and then he drops his head to my shoulder, letting out a gorgeous, exhilarating laugh. When he lifts his head back up, I'm dazzled by the playful yet obedient look in his eyes. "Out of the two of us, you know that it would be you doing the strangling," he teases, and I realise that he's backing me up out of the room. My heart drops to my stomach and starts racing too quickly.

Now? I think to myself. *Are we doing this now?*

He's walking me backwards up the stairs so it seems likely and I'm panicking. But worse than that, after everything that he just said, I think that *I* made a mistake – and I'm not talking about essentially asking him over to ravish me whilst I'm unsupervised. I'm talking about three years ago. I think that there's a huge gigantic missing puzzle piece that is spinning tauntingly on its sharp little edge, just out of reach. Then again, I'll never know if that's true, so it makes me think that I should never be able to trust him again. But I do. Maybe it's animal intuition, or maybe I'm just a moron. Maybe both. But I do trust him, and I hate myself for it.

My face must be betraying the secret nature of my inner thoughts because once we're on the second floor landing Tate asks me, "Why are you hyperventilating?" Then, just as he presses me into a wooden door panel and says, "The water should be hot in about five minutes," I blurt out at the exact same moment, "I'm not ready to have sex with you yet."

This is the moment when I realise that my back is up against the *bathroom* door and he has manoeuvred me here because he wants me to shower – i.e. he is *not* trying to fuck me in the first five minutes of our parents not being here.

He pins me with a look so startled that it borders on disturbed. "What did you say?" he asks, alarm managing to both raise and contort his brow. He looks shocked *and* distressed. Maybe he should be. I definitely am.

I quickly attempt to deflect. I languidly waft my hand in front of my face and make a woozy *oof* sound. "I think I feel a little bit faint. It must be my asthma." I do a light wobble.

His eyes are sharp but slightly hooded as he watches me. He can read my mind, and I know it. He's thinking about the fact that all *I* think about when I'm near him is the possibility of us getting it on. Or do I mean in? I don't know why this doesn't make him happy – I think it would for any other straight man with a librarian fetish. Instead he looks completely confused.

"Why are you trying to make this about sex?" he asks, his eyes glinting like knives.

"That's why you're here," I say, confused. The *duh* is implied.

His eyes narrow so severely that for a moment I feel a shiver of animal chill slithering down my spine. It's so much easier to enjoy him when he's like this because I can see the bad in him, and it helps me detach from all of his annoying *good*.

"That is *not* why I'm here," he replies gruffly. I feel the pane behind me give way, and I realise that he has opened the door and is crowding us into the bathroom. He yanks the bathroom cupboard open to grab a towel and he throws it on the counter above the sink. Then he leans us into the bath panel so that he can whip the tap around and get the hot water running. His eyes move back down to me where he does a quick sweep of my torso and then he turns me around and moves us to the centre of the room again, so that we're facing the vanity mirror.

He rests his chin on my exposed shoulder and I gasp when his stubble stabs into my skin. Our eyes are locked onto one another's reflections.

"You want to know how much that's not why I'm here?" he asks, snaking one forearm around my shoulders and the other around my stomach. He keeps still for a moment and then he suddenly grips my body to his so firmly that I almost pee myself. He drops his voice to a whisper and it runs down my neck like hot syrup. "I didn't bring any condoms," he murmurs. "And you better *not* have any condoms. So unless you want me to knock you up tonight, I'm going to need you to cut it out."

My eyes flick down to my stomach, where his arm is shielding me tight, and when I look back up I see that Tate is looking there too. I'm sizzling dangerously down below because, whether I like it or not, I *know* Tate. As in, I *know* what he likes. And I know more than anything that his deepest fantasy involves getting a nice girl to say *I do* by a church altar and then pumping her pregnant for the rest of her life.

"I'm taking you out tonight," he says, chin rubbing side to side, stubble grazing into my skin. "So you're going to shower, and then you're going to be ready for me at the door in an hour." His eyes lift to mine and his hands roam the sides of my stomach as he adds on, "If you want to."

I don't want to want to, but my common sense is being drowned out by the sound of blood rushing to all of my important parts. "Two hours," I say. Yes, I do hate myself.

"An hour and a half," he replies.

I scowl and try to push his hands off me even though that's the last thing that I really want, but it has the desired effect. He squeezes me tighter in his grip and relents with, "Okay, okay, two hours."

I'm evil and my insides are overflowing with the pleasure of getting princess treatment from Tate Coleson. This is what I've been missing for the past three years: someone to spoil me rotten.

"Is that okay? You're... you're going to come out with me in two hours?" he asks, eyes aglow with anticipation in the mirror. Three years of pining will do that to a man.

I huff, because I'm trying to think of a way to say yes without saying yes, and then I almost choke because in the past ten seconds the room has turned as opaque as a hot spring with all of the steam.

I take my glasses off because they've clouded over, and Tate removes them from my hand before I can even protest. I reach to get them back but he holds them far too high over his head, releasing a tidal wave of that heady cedar man smell. When I turn around I see a sliver of the dark happy trail running down his caramel abdomen and straight into the band of his jeans, so naturally I forget how to breathe, let alone how to put up a good fight.

"Hostages," he says teasingly, and the lenses glint down at me antagonistically.

"Fine," I mumble and then I push him out of the door, mainly just so that I can dig my pervy claws into his rigid abdominals. Delicious.

I slam the door, keeping up my *you're the enemy* pretence, but I feel my chest pick up the pace. Whether my brain likes it or not, in my biology Tate is ninety-nine percent forgiven – and for that, it wants its parting gift.

CHAPTER 22

Present

He's standing ninety-degrees to the door, his back pressed against the wall adjacent to it, with one leg kicked forward and the other arched up. When he senses me making my way down the stairs he immediately snaps his head towards me, jerks himself off the surface, and then plants his body at the foot of the stairs, a giant immovable barrier.

When I'm a few steps from the bottom and we're roughly the same height, his arms come to hover at my sides, and he looks into my eyes waiting for an invitation to let him touch me. I do the world's smallest nod and hell-born flames ignite behind his irises.

His hands instantly wrap around the backs of my thighs and he kneads me so roughly that I have to grab onto his shoulders to prevent myself from falling over. That's not exactly a hardship seeing as Tate has removed his jacket and now I am gripping into a body that spends more than twelve hours a day hauling wood. At least that's what I've been imagining him doing when I'm all alone in his former bedroom.

For some reason I was expecting him to work his way up to my ass, but instead I feel his palms press down until they're encasing the backs of my knees, and for some reason this feels even more explicit. Maybe it's because he had to bend a little and now his face is only a few inches away from my heat. He sees me palpitating and the corner of his mouth lifts a little. Then he heaves his body upwards, lifting me with him, and he quickly compresses me to the front of his torso. The way that I'm splaying against his shirt makes me fold my lips into my mouth to prevent myself from making any sounds that will betray my *I'm super aroused* hormonal tumult.

He's full on grinning because my pheromones have told him everything that he needs to know. *She wants you,* they are whispering. They are not wrong.

"You ready?" he asks as he repositions one of his hands to steady my back and he turns us around so that we're heading for the door. His hand slides into the pocket on the butt of my jeans, and he removes the case that I had slipped in there for my glasses, clicking the open-close button a couple of times and making me worry about him wearing out the function. He slips it back inside the pocket. How did he even know that it was there? Now I am also worrying that he has x-ray vision, as well as psionic abilities.

"You'll have to give me a yes or a no at some point," he jokes, but as soon as he says it my body stills and his eyes flash to mine, away from the light switch he was about to turn off. His shoulders swell and tense. Predator mode.

My eyes have traitorously expanded to five times their usual size in flashback-fear. Thank God I'm not wearing my glasses right now or they would look ten times their usual size. I swallow quickly and try to neutralise my face but he's not having any of it. There's only one reason why a person would react weirdly to someone asking for consent.

"You're going to have to explain that one to me, River,"

he commands, and it's in that moment that I become ninety-nine-point-nine percent sure that I have been wrong this whole time. The thing that happened that I thought Tate was the cause of? Tate doesn't know what happened. Maybe he had planned something, but what subsequently went down *isn't* what he had planned. No wonder he has been so confused.

The realisation makes my stomach sink with sickness, the anxiety about being so undeniably misled, but my brain clears as if a downpour has just washed away all of the shitty debris that had been festering for – I don't know – three years?

Silver linings, I think to myself.

"River," he prompts again, re-adjusting me against his chest.

I don't want to think about the past anymore. I don't *need* to think about the past anymore. This is a good moment and I'm so happy that I almost release a kind of exhilarated squeal.

I shake my head down at him with a smile breaking across my face, and I bury my nose in his hair. *Ugh.* It's so soft that I start breathing audibly and then I run one of my hands through it too, tugging at its thickness and length. We still haven't gone outside because Tate is now frozen in shock due to my one-eighty; it's too convoluted for me to care to explain it to him, so hopefully he will just accept my enlightenment as a godly miracle.

I hear him swallow as I continue inhaling him and he whispers, low and hoarse, "Is this a… a trick on me?" He threads one hand into my hair and lightly tugs it back so that he can see my face. Gauging his reaction I look like an addict mid-hit.

Eyes. Lips. Eyes. Lips. He's deciding whether to continue this conversation – albeit quite an important topic that I am dead-set on avoiding – or haul me upstairs and show me how much he's missed me. I would like to go with option number two.

"Tate," I whisper.

And that's all it takes.

I know that *he* knows that this is the first time that I have said his name in the three months that we have been trapped in this childhood-trauma sexual-frustration experiment, and before that it had been three *years*.

You would think that I just said his spy-operative activation trigger word because he somehow drops every single shield that he was holding whilst simultaneously expanding and hardening in every direction. The sound that leaves his chest is not human, and the way he pushes my hips down from his waist to press into his groin is not gentle. I'm higher than a hot air balloon and my little flame-pot just got a tug. Toot toot.

I'm now up against the wall that he was standing at as he waited for me, and there really is no place that I would rather be. He grips my jaw in one hand, forcing my face upwards, and his eyes – devilishly hungry – quickly scan mine. "Can I?" he asks gruffly, eyes on my lips.

Drunk on deviousness I taunt back, "Can you?"

And then he shows me that yes he can.

His hands are firm as they pin me in place, but his mouth is the softest thing that I have ever felt. He presses his lips to mine gently, only parted enough to breathe in my sighs as he caresses my skin, but his body is a different experience entirely. The hand that cupped my jaw has moved to grip the back of my neck, holding me in place for his mouth, whilst lacing his fingers through my hair and tugging forcibly. His other hand is bracing the wall for leverage as he rocks the metal zipper of his jeans roughly up my core. When he removes his hand from the wall he slides it over and down the centre of my ass until his fingers reach my heat, and he holds into me so securely that I have to pull away to gasp. He gives me about three seconds before drawing my face back to his and this time he slides the hot

161

length of his tongue into my mouth, gently filling me at first, and then gradually caressing until the strokes become relentless. The molten pool in my belly overflows as he parts my lips wider, and then he refills my mouth with his long wet muscle.

"I don't want to go out anymore," he says, his voice low and gravelly, lips mere millimetres from my own. I nip a tiny bite into his bottom lip and he groans. He runs both of his hands over the curves of my hips and then he rubs his hardened groin up my crotch, to show me exactly what he wants to do instead.

"You don't have any condoms," I whisper to him teasingly, and I stifle a quiet laugh when he drops his head into the crook of my neck, moaning in agony. I run my fingers through his hair, savouring how thick and silky it is. *Have you changed your mind, O moral one?*

Tate is so turned on that he's forgotten how to speak in proper sentences. His eyes are half-mast and his muscles are swollen and rippling. He keeps his mouth pressed against my throat as he mumbles something along the lines of, "*Need my girl tonight.*" I shiver in pleasure and he bucks against me, pushing my body into the wall again and again.

At that moment my stomach makes a sound and Tate lifts his head from my neck to look at me. He looks like he's mid-fuck, hair in complete disarray and his pupils so black that they have extinguished his irises. "You hungry?" he asks. I don't even know how he managed to choke the words out – his timbre has become so deep that I feel it more than I hear it.

I stare into his soul and nod, transmitting my innuendo-laden brainwaves. *I am sooooo hungry, Tate.*

Who needs subtlety?

He makes a gruff noise and bites into my neck, grazing and sucking as one of his hands finds my tummy. "Gonna feed you," he mumbles and then he walks me into the kitchen, mouth never leaving my skin. His hand reaches into my back pocket again, retrieves the glasses case, and he places it on the counter as he turns to leave.

"Wait," I protest, "I need that! And you still have my glasses - give me the hostages back."

He rubs his palm over my butt-cheek in the place that the glasses case had been, and then grips it as he swings open the front door. "You can't wear them right now, baby. I promise you'll have them back when we get home." As he locks the door from the outside he leans his head down to my ear and I clutch my arms around his neck a little tighter. He drops his voice to a whisper. "You know I'm gonna make you wear them when I fuck you."

I almost slip off of him as I startle. "Jeepers," I mutter, dazed, and he laughs as he deposits me on the ground. I have wobbly boat-legs from being carried like a koala and I almost trip over my own feet as I step around him.

Then I see it.

"Ohhh no," I say, backing up immediately, and therefore slamming right back into Tate's torso. He doesn't mind at all, and he wraps his arms around my middle, pulling me against the rigid planes of his chest.

"Why not?" he asks, his teeth finding their way into the side of my neck again. If Tate was a vampire, there would not be a single drop of blood left in my mortal vessel.

"My mom will kill me," I say, horror seeping into my blood-stream as I take in the sight.

"Your mom's not here," he replies, his voice husky.

"The spirits will send for her when they see this. She's probably already on her way."

Tate's gigantic motorbike is parked up on the drive. It's a blood-curdling monster and it's sexy as hell, but my mom will literally disown me if I so much as touch it with a stick.

I go to turn around but Tate has other ideas. The broken proximity barrier has unleashed three years worth of longing and his body has no intentions of leaving mine. He's rubbing circles on the side of my stomach with the arm that's wrapped tightly around my tummy, and his other hand is slowly travelling downwards, just about to push its way underneath my zipper-

"*Tate*," I hiss, and his hand magically moves to the other side of my stomach. "We are *outside*," I continue, and I can sense his smile pressed against my cheek. For some reason I can feel it pressing way further south. I scan the houses opposite Mitch's but I can't see anyone peering out of their windows, thank God.

"Open the box," he murmurs, and for the first time I notice that the box he had brought into the kitchen is sat next to the motorbike. There's no writing on the cardboard – it's simply a plain brown cube – but I can take a pretty good guess at what's inside.

I step away from Tate's body so that I don't arch my ass directly into his crotch as I lean forward to rip open the box. I pull the top folds open and then push back the boards tucked beneath. I stand upright and look down at it.

"Is it… baby pink?" I ask, cocking my head to the side.

Tate steps around me, suppressing a flushed self-satisfied smile, and he pulls the helmet out of the box. Very baby pink.

"Cute," I say. Then add, "Where's mine?"

He laughs and steps up to me, ready to place the helmet over my head. Hence the reason behind no glasses, I guess.

I step back but he keeps up with me. "You know I can't go on that bike. Why don't we just eat here?" I plead.

He shakes his head. "We can't eat here, because if we're *here* we won't be eating." His eyes scroll down my front and they linger over the top button of my jeans. "Well, *you* won't be eating," he adds quietly.

Crikey. I hop from foot to foot. "It'll have to be somewhere close by," I specify. "Like, a five minute drive." The thing is I actually really want Tate to take me out on his bike. I know that when my mom comes home the opportunity won't arise again so I don't want to miss it, but

I also don't want to be naïve and reckless. Okay, I don't want to be *too* naïve and reckless.

He runs a hand through his hair. "But then that means that I can only take you to the diner," he says, his voice a little disappointed.

"I'll take the diner," I concur and I step up to him so that he can put the helmet over my face. Before he does he leans over to peck a kiss on the top of my cheekbone. I squeeze my eyes shut as if that will help to quell the warmth that just spread across my chest.

"We have to get going before it rains," he says, slotting the helmet over me. It's really heavy and my curls are kind of in my eyes, but I can see Tate's mouth lifting slightly at the corners as he looks at me wearing it. He heads to the garage to pick up his own helmet, he shrugs his jacket on again, and then he walks over and lifts one thigh, settling into a straddle over the seat. He turns his face to me before he puts his gloves and helmet on. "Get behind me, Backpack," he teases, and I teeter for a few seconds before I move to him, placing my hands on the expanse of his shoulders as I fit myself against his back. I never realised how wide this seat would be and I now fear for exactly where the reverberations from the tyres are going to be hitting. As soon as I'm on, Tate grips my hands and pulls them tight around his middle. "Don't for one second think of letting go," he commands, and then he fits his own helmet on his head, and kicks the bike to life.

*

When Tate parks outside the diner in Phoenix Falls' town square I rise from the bike with all the grace of Ariel experiencing land for the first time. I feel like I've been rubbed raw. Tate unbuckles the strap under my helmet, pulls it off my head, and then laughs at my expression, which is reassuring.

He pulls me into the swell of his bicep and I gratefully melt into him as he walks us towards the diner doors. When we step inside, it's rammed. I didn't expect it to be, but I presume it's because it's the holidays. All of the red pleather booths seem to be full but there is one free stool in front of the counter, so Tate steers us towards it, and pushes me down so that I'm sat astride with my back to his torso. The lighting is low and shady-dive-bar red, so when I turn my head to look at Tate standing behind me I feel like I've fallen into one of my unhinged Tate Coleson sex fantasies.

His arms are blocking both sides of my body, fists clenched on the counter in front of me, and his chest is pressing into my back.

"Don't you want to sit?" I ask, even though I don't think that there is another free surface available in the entire restaurant.

"I'm good," he replies tersely, and his eyes stay on mine as he picks up a menu and slides it in front of me. His sudden mood-shift makes me anxious, because it makes me doubt the scepticism that I have been having about my*self*, but I try to put it off as him being hungry. I glance at the menu and I can tell from the mirror behind the counter that his eyes are still on me. My cheeks flush under his scrutiny but once I decide what I'm ordering I turn to him again and hold out the card.

He doesn't take it.

My panic is really mounting now. Maybe he took me here to murder me. Did he think that confiscating my glasses would debilitate my body entirely?

"Aren't you hungry?" I ask, my voice a little nervous, damn it.

He keeps his eyes on mine but they soften a bit as he shakes his head. "We're here for you, River. Get whatever you want, and then I'm taking you home." He leans further into me and suddenly I feel the stiffened length of his arousal digging into my back.

Relief sweeps over me. Thank God. The reason why he's rippling with tension is because he's about to bust a nut.

Contented, I turn back to the front and the waiter behind the desk nods at me.

"What can I get you?" he asks.

"Can we get a coke and large fries, please?" I hand him back the menu and he nods again. Tate takes out his wallet and scans a card on the reader, as the waiter puts the order in the kitchen and runs the coke nozzle into a cup.

The server sets the fries and the soda down in front of me, and I lean backwards into Tate, tipping my head back so that I'm looking up at him from below.

"Thanks," I say as I slip the straw into my mouth, sucking up the coke. He smiles down at me and, when I go to place the drink back on the counter, he picks it up and takes a sip, eyes glinting into mine. He's kissing me without kissing me. My cheeks flare pleather-seat red so I duck down to nibble my way through the fries. Every single time I take a drink, he immediately takes one afterwards, rubbing into me a little harder from behind. By the time I finish I'm wondering if I'll have a bruise.

Just as I turn to hop off the stool Tate is being pulled into one of those fist-gripping shoulder-knocking "hugs" that men do, and when I see who the other recipient is I am stunned into stillness. Black fluffy hair, and is that a lip ring? I stay immobile in the hopes of him not noticing me, but that becomes impossible when Tate slides me off the seat and crushes me into his side.

Madden's eyes cast down on me and narrow, a look that derives scepticism more so than contempt, but when they flick back up to Tate he immediately leans into his ear (annoyingly on the side of him that I am *not* standing against) and starts whispering. I can't hear a word because the diner is ablaze with rowdy booths and country music, but Tate's fingers never cease their caressing around my ribcage so I assume that it isn't too incriminating.

I never had an issue with Madden – from what I gathered he was (thankfully) Tate's favourite friend – but God knows what he knows… or worse, what he *thinks* he knows.

Suddenly we're walking outside and Tate is setting me by the side of his bike, positioning the helmet above my head. He speaks to me in a gentle, hushed tone. "Can you stay here for me for one minute, please? Madden's going to… I need his help with something," he finishes, his eyes briefly catching on Madden over my shoulder. I nod even though my nerve endings are flaring and he gives me a swift kiss before buckling me into the helmet.

I don't turn around to see where they're jogging to, but I hear the tinkle of a shop door as they enter, and once again when they leave. When he comes back, I can see that there's something stuffed in his jacket pocket but I don't comment, nor do I wiggle my hands into it as he ducks down to kiss the exposed skin at my neck. He settles onto the seat, I ease my body behind him, and then he kicks the bike into action, ready to ride.

CHAPTER 23

Present

I step off the bike onto the floor of the garage and Tate scoops his hand around the centre of my butt, hauling me up with one arm so that I can wrap my legs around his side. He buries his face into the warmth of my neck, veiled by my wind-swept curls, and he inhales deeply as he ducks us out of the garage, locking the door with his free arm, and walking us up the porch. He pulls away only to check which key to slot into the lock, opening it and stepping inside, and then he dips his face back to mine, planting hot chaste kisses down my cheek, making me shiver.

"What's in your pocket?" I ask – okay, I gasp – as he drags the fingers cupping my ass more roughly against my centre.

He makes a gruff sound behind my ear but I feel him dig into his pocket and pull out the cellophane-wrapped box. I turn my head so that I can see the item and he pushes it into my hand as he starts grazing his teeth up the other side of my neck.

I hold up the box and shudder involuntarily. I feel him breathe a laugh against my skin, his mouth lifting at the corners.

It's a twenty-four pack of condoms which sends jolts of both delight and fear up my spine. I can't help but wonder why he was with Madden when he bought them – was he being measured?

Tate pulls back, his eyes veiled with starry-night darkness, to study my reaction to the box. The movement inadvertently releases a warm surge of the heady pine-tree-fresh-wood-hot-skin scent that clings to his chest and I can taste it in my mouth. I try to shake off the dizziness as I pretend to read the packaging.

"'*Extra, extra, extra large*'," I say, eyes narrowed in deep concentration. He lets out a loud body-shaking laugh and his eyes twinkle in pleasure. I meet his gaze and make a little lip-biting hiss. "Ouch. Better not risk it, then."

He grabs the box from me, stuffing it into his pocket as he walks us into the kitchen. He feels around on the table and the next thing I know he's gently sliding my glasses back on my nose. He pulls off my trainers and kicks off his boots as I adjust my glasses to optimum comfy-ness, and then he pins me with a blazing all-pupil stare as he starts ascending the stairs. "I'll make it fit," he whispers darkly.

I'm bitten and squeezed until we reach the bedroom, where he closes the door gently behind us, locks it, and then sets my feet carefully onto the carpet. Tate's actions are so reassuringly tender that I start to doubt whether or not the condoms are for us to use, or if they are more of a prop to have on-hand just in case.

When he sinks to his knees I understand that we will be using them.

"Can I take these off?" he asks as he looks up at me from under his lashes, his head somewhere near the top of my ribcage. He really is very tall.

I realise that by this point I am supposed to answer

whatever it was that he said but instead my hands have found their way into his chocolatey hair and I'm tugging him harsher than I mean to. He doesn't seem to mind.

"What?" I ask back.

Tate smiles up at me and I notice that my top button and zipper have been released without my realising, and his fingers are skimming around my denim waistband.

"You want my jeans?" I ask. I don't know why I say it that way, but now it sounds like I'm offering him my jeans.

"Yes, for personal reasons," he says, his hands slipping between my skin and the fabric, and then he pushes them down to my ankles in one smooth swoop. He tucks a hand behind my knee, lifting me one leg at a time so that I can step out of my pants. Then he folds them and sets them aside, his hands gravitating to my hips like a magnet, and he encases both of my buttocks in the splay of his fingers, eagerly kneading them until I begin to gasp.

He spreads his thighs wider across the floor so that he can reach my lower half with more ease and he uses two fingers to minutely lift the hem of my shirt. He looks at my underwear with Pandora's Box infatuation. I still startle and jolt when he suddenly presses his face into the thin white cotton, covering my warmth with his mouth, and heaving shoulder-swelling breaths in through his nose. My stomach flutters as he grazes over the fabric and then he watches me with glinting eyes as he takes the gusset between his teeth and pulls it away from my skin. I suck in a breath, practically faint. The warmth I had encased between my legs is released from its underwear prison and Tate scents me like an animal, flames burning behind his eyes as he consumes my heat. Then he's on his feet and backing me up into the mattress.

Once my butt is on the comforter, one palm flat behind my back, I hold up the other hand and he pauses like he's had training. "You're fully clothed," I say.

The box of condoms is tossed onto the bed behind me

and his jacket is thrown somewhere near the door. He kicks off his socks and then reaches to the back neck of his t-shirt, pulling it over his body in one fluid swoop. The only thing left on his upper-body is his silver chain with the cross. I shiver and contract at the sight of the tan, meaty muscles rippling up his abdomen and the hard swell of his labour-pumped biceps. He drops the t-shirt next to me and I have to physically restrain myself from not smashing my face into it to smell his hot scent.

There must be a slight giveaway when my possessed crazy eyes dart between the severe shadows beneath Tate's pectorals and the black top crumpled next to me, because after a moment Tate picks up the t-shirt and holds it just under my chin. I don't know what he's thinking I want to do with it, but every thought that he is having is probably correct. I wrap my hands around his wrist and push my face into the cotton. It's Heaven. His smell is so male and delicious that I salivate. I inhale like an addict and when I pull back I'm high. Part of me expects him to laugh at me, but when I see his face he's not laughing. He's watching me intensely as I enjoy his offering, and he's unmoveable in his seriousness. This is not a joke to him… *I* am not a joke to him.

"Good?" he asks, his voice so low it vibrates.

I nod and he leans in to gently kiss me. He places the t-shirt in my lap and his fingers start unbuttoning my shirt. He un-loops the final button and smoothes the fabric off my shoulders without his lips ever leaving mine, but when he pulls back to look at me a deep grunt is ripped from between his bared teeth.

Did I slip into the baby pink push-up with black lace trim that gave him palpitations three months ago when I was getting dressed tonight? I'm a devious vixen. My usually petite chest is plumped up and heaving – soft, succulent, and tied with a little bow. The snug satin cups catch on the moonlight from the window, winking up at him and saying *unwrap me.*

Tate drops to his knees again, mouth open.

"You're fucking beautiful," he rumbles gruffly. Then he rasps, "Jesus Christ."

I look at his cross. *I'll say.*

Rough hands suddenly grip my ankles until they're hooked over the expansive breadth of his shoulders, and then Tate leans forwards and crushes his mouth into my flesh. He groans instantaneously as he sucks mouthfuls of softness between his lips, but when he slides his long wet tongue down the inside of the tight cup, brushing my nipple, I'm the one gasping. He uses one palm to plump me up and two fingers to slide the cup down, and then his mouth suctions around the little peak until I'm extended and squirming. He leans back, eyes dazed, and he watches my hips rub despairing little circles up his chest. He puts one hand on my hip, feeling my body buck, and his fingers dig into my skin, unyielding. When I make a noise to regain his attention he brings his face to mine and lets me tug at his bottom lip with a sharp little bite.

"Fuck," he grunts out as he unclasps my bra from behind. At least I know what he's thinking about. He pulls the bra from my chest and, as soon as I'm free, he massages my breasts in two rough palms. "That's my girl."

I slam backwards onto the bed and he rises to his feet.

The long leather strap of his belt slides through the buckle until it's slapping open against the loops in his jeans. He presses the button through the opening and drags down the zip before pushing the denim just below his hips. I take in the shadow he's casting through his boxers and lose a couple million brain cells. He looks like he's about to rough me up in a barn. Better yet, he looks like he's about to screw me in the workshop. Him in sawdust-covered denim, surrounded by his drills; me in fluffy bed socks, over a table he's just made.

I tell him that, and then his boxers come down too.

He pulls out the entire length of his hardened muscle, his fist gripped around the thickness near the coarse hair at the base, and he keeps it tightly clenched as he readjusts the heavy sac behind it. Then he rubs his thumb over the slick domed head, flushed dark in contrast to his abdomen, and I think I choke on my own spit. My eyes flash up to his.

For some reason I think that he's waiting for me to say something so I manage in a strangled voice, "Is that for me?"

He gives me a bashful smile, tan cheekbones glowing rose-red, and an ache spreads through my chest.

I sit up on my knees, wrap my arms around his neck and kiss him as sweetly as I can. I can feel the shy heat on his face and throat as I hold him. It makes me pull him in tighter, smoothing my softness into him until he's assured.

His hands are splayed across my back, covering me in his warmth. "I forgot to get lube, baby," he admits in a quiet voice, his brow taut with regret.

I rub my inner thighs together. "I think we'll manage," I say, and my breath hitches when he checks that I'm not lying.

He swallows heavily. "Wow."

I'm about to say "I know" but it turns out that his sentence wasn't finished.

"I'm going down on you," he says, in a voice so deep that my stomach clenches, and he sinks onto his haunches with his arousal on full display.

"I should get a shower first," I say, a little bit panicked as his thumb draws the gusset to the side. It's not as if he hasn't already smelled me but-

"But that defeats the whole point," he whispers, and then he presses his lips to my centre.

I'm gently eased backwards, arched, tilted, spread. Warm hands cuff and encase my ankles, then they move firmly behind my knees, and he eases his tongue into my most secret parts, lapping and sucking in tender adoration. My stomach is blazing and my heartbeat is embarrassingly loud. He makes a deep, worshipful sound and I stop breathing entirely.

"*Tate*," I whisper as quietly as possible, in an attempt to veil my whimper.

He makes a long groan that shoots straight up to my womb and he pushes his tongue harder against me. "Say my name again," he murmurs, but when the rough palm of his hand presses and rotates hard against my blushing nub I'm no longer capable of speech.

I dig my nails into his hair and try to drag him up my stomach, but all that seems to do is further the torture, as his long tousled fringe fluffs up and rubs over me.

"One more minute, baby," he mutters gently. "You're doing so well."

My thighs lift slightly, brushing each side of his soft brown hair, and he makes a low noise as he pushes in from a deeper angle. He raises his other arm up and uses it to hold down my stomach, restraining my bucking hips against the mattress as he gorges.

Suddenly he stands, lifting my legs by my ankles so that he can slip my underwear up and over my legs without me having to move an inch. He keeps the cotton clenched in his hand as he shucks off his pants and boxers.

"I'm keeping these," he says as the last of his clothes gets kicked aside.

I sit up on one elbow as he reaches for the lamp on the floor and switches on the low warm-tone bulb before getting back onto the bed. "Then do I get to keep yours?" I ask back.

He settles himself between my legs, biceps crowding up on either side of my head. He gently brushes my cheek with the backs of his fingers. "What do you want to do with them?" he replies, half-bemused, half-surprised.

I raise my eyebrow and his cheeks flush.

He gently places my underwear on the dresser and

presses a kiss to my throat as he leans down to pick up the box of condoms. "Only if you show me," he whispers, and now it's my turn to blush.

Tate sits back on his haunches, softly knocking my knees wider as he tears the cellophane off the box. His eyes stay locked on mine. It's like a staring competition, only we're both about to win. He digs his fingers into the cardboard to pierce the opening, but his shoulder ripples when the soft backs of my thighs rub up to caress his knees and the whole side rips open, half of the box of condoms splattering down on my stomach.

"Oh *fuck*," he curses hoarsely, before biting into his forearm, spinning his torso away from me, and squeezing his eyes shut.

My eyes flick between the packets spilled across my tummy and Tate's death-grip on his erection. He isn't moving it, he's more... restraining it. I quickly wipe the packets off of me and stuff them back into the broken box. Then I pick one back out and rest it just below my belly button.

When he turns back around his brow is pinched in agony, and when he sees the one foil packet he looks like he's about to cry. He picks it up and lowers his body back over me, his eyes meeting mine with a concerned, protecting look.

"Are you sure?" he asks, his eyes shimmering with worry.

I readjust my glasses and give him a little ready smile. I feel like I've just opened a test paper and the question at the top is exactly what I prepared for. "Yes," I say. Then I add, "Are you?"

The look in his eyes as he catches the foil edge in his mouth, rips the packet open, and then spits it out next to us answers my question before he does.

"You have no idea," he whispers, eyes glinting as he rolls the condom down his length.

Hmm, I have an inkling.

He drops his forehead to mine and moves himself between us, brushing me tentatively, and I have to bite back a little Chihuahua yelp.

Wow, I'm scared. What a time for it. Does this happen to everyone or is it only for people with PTSD?

Tate can sense it. I've stilled so completely that I can make out the fresh pattering of rain that has been unleashed from the inky black sky, and is now battering the window pane.

"Hey," he says in a gentle hushed voice. I blink back to him and I feel suddenly embarrassed – like, where did my clothes go? How did we get here? *Why am I letting him-*

When he slowly pulls back I realise why. Because this is Tate, the boy from across the street. It isn't someone else. He doesn't want to hurt me. He never wanted to hurt me.

I press my hands into his shoulder blades and give him an apologetic smile. My stomach rolls a bit. "Sorry," I say, wincing. "Did I just kill the mood?"

His eyes widen. "River, no. Please never apologise to me. What do you have to be sorry for? You're perfect – I'm pinching myself that you even let me in here." My heart throbs and I run my hands upwards, so that I can grip around the meaty muscles at the top of his back. He rolls into my touch and every part of him presses into me. "Do you still want to?" he asks quietly, his eyes searching my face for any hints of reluctance.

I nod and he leans down to kiss me long and slow.

Before I understand what's happening, Tate lightly lifts up my head and I feel him slip something over us and down my hair. When he releases me I feel a fine sensation around my clavicle and I look down between us. My eyes widen as I look at the cross that is now resting at the base of my neck. He frees my hair from the inside of the chain and watches me with wary eyes. "I didn't want it knocking you when I…" He trails off, swallowing hard and trying to gauge whether I'm going to recoil from it. Or maybe he's testing to see if I'll burst into flames. I'm fairly certain that Tate would baptise me himself if I would let him, and right now I don't think that I would even mind. I touch the pendant carefully as I look up at him. He's all twinkly with hope and it's so endearing that I lean up to give him a little kiss.

Tate carefully positions himself against me and I allow my body to sink further into the thick quilt and pillows. *His* thick quilt and pillows. I am entirely encompassed by him and I am truly happy about it. He uses one hand to push my thigh a little wider and I hum in nervous anticipation.

The bulging arm braced above my head is more rigid than steel and his voice is strained. "Should I… would you like me to…?" His breathing is erratic and his body is emitting heat like a volcano.

I pull one of my arms back to meet his hand situated tensely above me on the pillow. I gently unclench his fist and slide my fingers between his. "Yes and yes," I say. His eyes search mine for certainty and I give him a tiny smile.

He squeezes my fingers and slowly pushes in.

I make a small, quiet gasp and then I allow my eyes to close. I'm spellbound. Tate's hand above my head has slipped between the back of the black mattress and the headboard, gripping it for leverage as he fills me entirely. His other hand is wrapped around the back of my shoulder, holding me preciously against him so that I stay in place.

I feel one of his hands move and he lightly squeezes at the hollows of my cheeks, silently asking me to open my eyes, before sliding it back between my head and the pillow, tangling himself in my hair. I obey and flutter my eyes open. I'm enveloped in hard swollen muscles, his bicep brushing my curls, his chest almost touching my mouth. I tilt my head back so that I can look into his eyes and his face is rigid with tension as he waits for me.

"Baby, can I…" His sentence breaks off as a shiver runs through him, but he remains completely still as he desperately fights his own want. He inhales deeply and tries again, his voice more gruff than sandpaper. "Is it okay if I move?"

I'm mesmerised by his restraint. I nod and he groans, leans down, and sucks my neck in gratitude. He pulls out, long and lush, and then pushes back in.

"Like this?" he asks, his voice taut with need. He tries various alignments until my breathing hitches and then he rolls into the position with heavy determined thrusts. The storm is splashing harder outside and Tate's eyes are glinting like he's possessed. He shoves his body into mine again, and again, and again, and my nails try to find purchase in his inked and swollen biceps. He lowers his gaze down to my chest and he begins to thrust faster and harder as he watches me bounce up and down with his propulsion. "Tell me when you want me to pick up the pace," he breathes out, strained.

My mouth falls open. *What?* This is him going *slow?*

"*Tate,*" I whisper urgently. When his fierce eyes meet mine my question evaporates.

He dips down to slide his tongue against mine and then he asks hoarsely, "More?"

I have masochistic science-experiment curiosity so I bite my lip and nod, and within a second he increases the momentum to straight-up hammering. I'm held in place so that I don't crack my skull on the headboard. I feel like I'm being exorcised.

He's showing me what his hard-earned body was made for: pleasure-pain murder-salvation. His hands pull, press, rub, tease, and then he tilts his head down so that he can watch himself as he slips in and out of me.

The wet slapping grows louder as Tate thrusts us closer to the edge. He wraps his hand around the back of my leg and forces my thigh upwards so that he can see more. He grunts as he takes it in, and his shoulders undulate with strain. "I'm... I'm coated in you," he groans roughly, and suddenly, just as I grasp that I can't take any more, he splays the entire span of his warm rough palm across my stomach and he presses down *hard*.

"*Tate*," I whimper. I'm pleading with him, desperate for him to continue doing this to me for the rest of his life. The sound he makes in response is so obscene that I literally convulse beneath him.

He sucks my throat, palms my breasts, restrains my legs. He praises me for being a good girl, for being an angel, for taking him so well. He pushes through my tremors unrelenting as I blackout-collapse into his quilt and, though I'm approaching comatose, he doesn't stop. His body is anchored deep and he's plunging in and out so hard that his clenched muscles start vibrating with the need to release. He stills for a moment and then his hips begin jerking violently, over and over again, pounding against the softness of my thighs until his whole spend is pumped out and unloaded, angry grunts ripping from his throat.

He collapses on top of me, his heavy body keeping me pinned to the mattress as his hands slide into my hair and he buries his face into my neck. He repeats something a few times that I'm not coherent enough to decipher. I wrap my arms around his waist and I quickly fall asleep.

CHAPTER 24

Present

It's still dark outside when I wake up. There's an unusual purple tint to the blackness and it takes me a moment to place it. The splashing of the rain has turned to soft, almost inaudible thudding, and the whole neighbourhood is blanketed in quiet.

It's snowing.

I'm about to sit up to look outside when I feel a shift in the heavy weight wrapped around me. Both of Tate's arms are firmly encasing my waist, his hands are splayed protectively across my stomach, and his head is resting above mine on the pillow. I can feel that I'm wearing a t-shirt and my underwear from earlier, so Tate must have slipped me into them a few hours ago. The length of his arousal, stiff and protracted, digs into my back, and I arch into it subconsciously. The hands on my stomach instantly grip tighter and Tate takes a deep shock inhalation that makes me know that he's awake.

He moves carefully behind me, his hips lowering to

mine so that he can press himself against my behind, and he makes a deep guttural noise in the back of his throat.

"Jesus," he whispers, and he raises one hand to hold me by my clavicle so that he can push me back against his chest.

"Baby," he murmurs quietly, his voice a low bass in my ear. I shiver and he presses into me harder. "Are you awake?"

I smush my face into the pillow because I am only about five percent awake, but I nod anyway.

He makes an understanding noise. "Are you... too tired?" he asks, his tone hushed, deep, calm.

I think about it for a minute. I think about it for so long that I almost fall asleep again, and I can feel Tate breathe a soft laugh behind me. When I shake my head he swallows hard.

He presses himself over me so that his chest is pushing into my back, my tummy compressed against the bedding, and one of his hands gently pulls up my hip to meet the thick tent in his underwear. He's laden. A painful flame licks up my belly and I try to hold back a lustful purr. He slides my underwear down my legs and he eases the shirt that he was wearing last night up my back and over my head. His hands roam to my front, squeezing gently, and then he leans across my back to reach into the box on the nightstand. I hear the quiet tear of the packet as he pulls at it with his teeth, and he angles away from me slightly as he rolls it on.

"Is this okay?" he murmurs, his shoulders caging me in as he positions himself against me.

I tilt my head back to look at him and a vibration rolls down my spine, settling in my stomach. He's looking at me like I own him. His eyes are glinting with possessiveness as he awaits my permission, and my body clenches at the juxtaposition. I smooth one of my hands over his large fist, loosening his fingers from their death-grip on the pillow,

and he bends forward to kiss me softly on the lips.

"Be gentle, I'm sleepy," I whisper, and he makes a pained noise as he drops his face to my shoulder. He nods against my skin, his soft hair tickling my neck, as he pulls me higher and rubs himself up and down my centre.

"I'm gonna… I'm gonna take you so gentle," he rasps, his muscles straining as he crowds me, and then, with a long, painstakingly slow push, he guides himself inside.

*

After I shower I pull on simple red cotton underwear, a fluffy green sweater, and I check my phone, albeit blurrily as I wait for my glasses to de-steam. There are two texts from my mom, which is unusual but not a total shock considering that this is the first time maybe ever that I haven't been within arm's reach.

The first text is a photograph of Mitch standing outside a snowy cabin. He looks a bit put out, like he didn't want his picture taken in the first place, but he's being a good sport about it, one hand gripping the wooden railing and the other holding a flask. He's wearing layers of flannels and his baby blue jeans, making his tan obnoxiously dazzling. I still can't believe that this hunk is my *mom's*.

The second text is an actual message (*boooo*) and my stomach prickles a little as I read it.

Happy early Christmas to me! Arrived safe and enjoying Pine Hills. Did Mitch tell you about this? Anyway, do me a favour would you – hosting a house warming party when we get back, need some bits, listed them below. Can you grab them for us?

I instantly develop a minor migraine. I'm glad that my mom is enjoying her vacation but I hate the way that I'm starting to get tied to the Colesons. And it isn't because I don't *want* to be tied to the Colesons, it's because I don't want to be tied to them in *this* kind of way. As Mitch's step-daughter. Even worse, as Tate's step-sister. And a house warming party to officialise our move-in is only going to highlight my… role. I grimace and slide on my glasses as I walk down the stairs. This is gross.

I minutely decompress once I hop off the bottom step. Tate is cooking something in the kitchen as I approach, the broad expanse of his bare back exposed and his jeans hanging low on his hips. His hair is divinely messy and there are raised feline scratches marring his ribcage. Oops. I flush, squirm, and look away.

I must have released a little wave of oestrogen because Tate turns his head over his shoulder and looks down at me with a slightly surprised, pleased smile. He gives my outfit a once-over and his mouth lifts even more.

"Baby Grinch," he says affectionately, his eyes gently teasing.

I scowl and flash him my underwear.

He drops his spatula, curses, and then the oil in the pan spits at his skin.

"Red," he chokes out. Move over Keats. He turns down the gas behind him so that he can continue staring at the rosy cotton encasing my heat without risking another injury. God knows we've had enough of those in the past few months.

"To match my eyes," I say as he closes the distance between us and lifts me so that I'm sitting comfortably around his waist. He holds up the hem of my sweater so that he can observe the cotton pressed flush against his abs.

"I was thinking of something else," he murmurs and then he draws his eyes back to mine. He gives me a secret knowing smile and presses a kiss to my lips. Then another. A hum releases from his throat and his free hand moves beneath me so that he can readjust himself. He rubs his palm over my thigh and then gently hooks it around the back of my knee. His cheekbones are blushing when he pulls away. "Was... was last night okay?" he asks. His voice is quiet and husky. Hesitant. Shy.

I nod when he meets my eyes. "So was this morning," I say, and he inhales deeply, his whole body hardening with pleasure.

His gaze dips to my throat for a moment and he lightly tugs at the neck of my sweater. He peeks in and his smile widens. "You're still wearing it," he says, his rough fingers stroking the chain laced around my neck.

Now it's my turn to flush. Well, what was I supposed to do? If I'm going to enjoy my time here before I'm shipped off to college for a lifetime of academic flagellation, I may as well do it properly.

"Penance," I mutter, avoiding his eyes, and he laughs, pressing kisses to my cheeks in contented delight.

As if reading my mind he says, "Tell me you're not studying today. I want to spend the day with you."

I want to stay wrapped up in his arms for this whole week, forgetting about the past and *definitely* forgetting the future, but I also want to maintain my façade of indifference so that he doesn't know how horribly desperately I want this. I shuffle as if to dismount but he holds me steady. "I have presents to steal," I mutter and he buries his smile in my neck.

"Are you trying to kick me out?" he asks. His mouth is heavenly warm against my skin.

"Yes. No. Maybe." I cringe. I've turned into a magic eight ball.

"I actually have to do something for my mom," I say. "And your dad."

That gets his attention. He lifts his head, his jaw tensing slightly, but he squeezes his hand up my thigh for me to continue.

"My mom texted me this morning – maybe Mitch did the same to you, I don't know. They're having a house warming thing here when they get back and she wants me to grab, like, drinks and whatever." I shrug. I feel kind of shitty about it.

"The snow's too deep out there for you to walk in, and groceries like that are too heavy for someone who isn't driving." His eyes are a little narrowed and his muscles are becoming more rigid.

I feel a bit confused so I shift in discomfort. Why is he angry? I hate to ask but, naturally, I do it anyway. "Did I... do something wrong?" Oh how the tables have turned.

His body seems to swell protectively around me as he clutches me closer to his chest, and he starts walking us to the living room. He shakes his head and runs his hand through his hair. "River, of course you haven't done anything wrong. I'm... I'm not annoyed because of you." He sits down on the couch so that I'm straddling his lap, and he rubs his hands over the backs of my ankles. "I'll go. Just tell me what they want."

A little shiver of relief washes over me. I really do hate shopping in town, so I'm grateful for the aid. "I'll forward it to you," I say. "What's your number?" I distractedly unlock my phone to pull up the text, but Tate lightly grips my hand and pushes it back to the couch cushion.

He shakes his head. "That's okay, I'd rather you just tell me what they want," he says.

I can't help it. I pause instinctively as I feel my recently buried scepticism beginning to push its way up from beneath the surface, like mangled corpse bones breaching the dirt in a horror film. I look up at him and for a brief moment I'm scared that I'm about to see a little red flag waving behind his eyes.

Am I being crazy? I don't need his number, do I? He hasn't needed mine to contact me before, so I shouldn't be thinking that it's a big deal. In fact, I'm not sure that I've ever seen him use a cell phone at all. Does he have one? Does anyone?? Are cell phones even real???

He starts caressing my ankles. I shake off my insanity and recite the list.

"Okay," he says, "It might take a little while but I'll deal with it."

His hands have moved to the soft, warm skin behind my knees, and I don't want him to go anymore. I press my chest closer to his and the delicious heat from his pectorals plumes between us.

"I'll pick up their stuff after breakfast and take it back to mine. I'll be gone 'til around five." I let out an involuntary whimper and he grins. He's reverse psychologying me. He's giving me the space that I originally asked for and now I want to have all of his babies.

He gives me a light kiss as his hands move up the hem of my sweater and down the back of my underwear. "Then I'll come over and make you dinner. After we've eaten, I'll take you to bed. And then we'll do whatever you want. Wherever you want. However many times you want." His eyes are blazing dangerously. "I'm not wasting a single moment anymore, River. I've had so long without you and now we only have days until our parents are back. And after that you're going to go to a college that's as far away from me as possible. I need you for as long as you'll let me have you."

I wince because that's kind of exactly what I was thinking about *him*. I take a deep inhalation and stroke my palms up his biceps, then around his throat. He laces one of his hands through mine and holds us together over his pulse point.

I nod in agreement. He rewards me with another silken kiss.

*

It's dark out and I'm in the middle of swatting up on First Year History college syllabi when Tate knocks at the door.

And by 'in the middle' of it, I mean literally. I have every piece of History coursework that I have ever written surrounding me on the dining room table. I would have cleared it away so as not to flaunt it in front of Tate, particularly given the conversation we had before breakfast, but he's half an hour early.

"You're half an hour early," I say. He responds by ducking down to kiss me and he pushes us back in through the entryway, lightly kicking the door shut behind him. His face is flushed and rosy, and his skin is icy cold. He cups his frozen hands around the warm skin of my neck as he glides his tongue into my mouth and a waterfall of shivers cascade down my tummy.

He shucks the grocery bag that is hooked over his elbow onto the floor as he manoeuvres us into the dining room, but, as he pulls away to say something, his eyes flick to the table behind me and his hard breathing pauses. He straightens up a little, rolling his shoulders back, and he swallows. He doesn't move his hands from my throat. He simply glances at the papers littering the wood, not appearing to read anything but gathering the gist of the contents nonetheless, and then he looks back down at me with an unreadable expression. I kind of want to apologise and light my essays on fire, but I'm also glad that he thinks that I'm so indifferent. He strokes his thumbs up the centre of my neck and makes a contemplative humming sound.

I take a deep breath. "I was just about to clear up," I say, my voice traitorously a few octaves higher than normal.

A slight smile tugs at his lips. "Okay," he says, and, moving his palms to my shoulders, he turns me around. He wraps one arm over my collarbones and the other arm over my waist, squeezing me gently. The denim of his jeans is cold against my bare legs, and he dips his head to gently nip at the back of my neck. I'm rippling with shivers as he whispers, "Let me help you."

He leans us forward, bending over me, and he begins to

188

slowly pile up the documents. He slips his other hand from my waist up the hem of my sweater and then he rubs it over my bare tummy. I let out a little *oof* as he reaches over to collect the papers on the far side of the table and, on hearing me, he pushes us forward a little farther.

Two can play at that game.

I suck in a nice composing breath and ask him, "What did you do whilst you were gone today?"

He pauses, his palm hovering over the last couple of papers. I honestly refuse to look at the stacks he's made, knowing that they are not in date order. He presses his cool lips to my jaw, kissing me softly before grazing my neck. "I got the stuff for the house warming," he murmurs.

"Hmm, took you a while though. What else did you get up to?"

His chest swells against my back, hard muscles pressing me down towards the wooden surface. The hand on my belly slides upwards until it clutches the pendant hanging between the cups of my bra underneath the sweater. He tugs it lightly, his other hand leaving its perusal of the table to caress my hip. His voice is so deep that I feel it in my stomach when he replies, "I went to church."

I try to lift myself up with my palms flat on the wood but he's holding us tightly in place. "Did you feel the need to confess for your sins?" I ask, my tone a little bitter.

He's surprised. "What? No." He lifts up and guides me to turn and look at him. His brow is pinched together but his eyes are warm and kind. The rosiness staining his cheekbones is going to haunt me for the rest of my life. "We didn't do anything wrong, River. I don't want you to think that." He runs his hand through his hair and then cups it around the back of my neck. "I just went to pray," he says. "And to… light a candle."

I watch him wordlessly as he rubs himself over me. Fingers, palms, arms. I feel like I'm being marked, quietly but with intent. "And who was the candle in honour of?" I ask quietly, hoping that my prying comes off as cutely intrigued.

"The Patron Saint of Keeping Me On My Toes," he says, smiling and running one of my curls between two of his fingers.

"She sounds like a drag," I say, hopping up onto the cleared tabletop and hugging Tate's thighs between my legs. "You should move onto easier pastures."

He breathes a laugh, a pleased glow shimmering over him as I press his body against me, and he settles his hands on either side of my hips. He's warmed up exponentially. I can only assume why.

"I'm a sucker for pain," he whispers, eyes burning mischievously into mine.

I uncross my ankles, raising one leg back, and then I kick it hard into the butt of his jeans. He jolts forward in surprise, shoving himself on top of me, and he groans at the contact. His body heaves against mine and his eyes are sparkling, amazed, wild.

"River," he says. He's on fire and my name comes out like a warning.

I'm insatiable. I run my fingers up the sharp stubble of his jaw and a low growl rumbles from deep within his chest. How sweet that he goes about his life humouring this make-believe concept of docile domesticity, when in reality he's an animal, with primal violent need coursing through his loaded hulking frame.

He slips me off the table, takes one of my hands, and walks us back to the kitchen, picking up his grocery bag along the way. At least one of us has some self-control. I hop onto one of the counters as he unpacks the bag, filled with the items he's going to use to make our dinner. I'm being spoiled and it makes me waggle my feet like a child with delight. The last item that he pulls out is another twenty-four pack of condoms, and my face blushes darker than my rosy underwear.

"I like that you lit a candle for me," I say, watching him wipe down a surface with a dampened cloth.

He glances up at me, his eyes bright, and he smiles a little. "I do that a lot," he says.

He's so sweet it makes me ache. I can't believe that I've wasted so much time doubting him.

His thoughts must be on a similar path to mine because, as he diverts his eyes to start chopping up tomatoes, he says, "So have you decided." He waits a beat. "About college."

I wriggle like a little worm. If it was up to me, I wouldn't be going to college. Why are all of the smart girls told that they need to do that? In reality, my college outcome will be an embarrassing amount of debt and a low-salary job, only compensated by the fact that my mom will be happy that I'm officially her mini-me. I don't even *want* that kind job. All I want is to do something that I enjoy – maybe even to do multiple things that I enjoy – and overall to just be happy. I like that Tate knew what he wanted to do: he wanted to be with his dad, in an emotionally comfortable and financially stable space, working on stuff that comes so naturally to him. He has his friends, he has his father – and if I wasn't so anxious, maybe he would even have me.

I soften the blow by telling the truth. "It's never been my decision to make," I say.

He pauses the knife for a moment, head still bowed, and then he restarts his slicing as if he never stopped. He transfers the tomatoes from the chopping board to a ceramic plate. "Okay." He breathes audibly, as if he's trying to stay calm. "And what about after?" he asks.

I blink. "After?"

He picks out a pizza tray from the cupboard near the oven and uncaps a dark green bottle of olive oil. He tips the bottle and drizzles it over the tray, a quiet luxurious glugging sound escaping the neck as he pours the contents. He recaps the bottle and rubs the oil into the surface with his fingers, making his tan skin glossy and slick.

"After college," he clarifies.

"I'll get a job," I reply.

"Where?" His tone is sharper than before, demanding, inflexible.

I take a shaky breath. My mom and I have never actually spoken about that. All I know is that I'm going to be Professor Linton 2.0. "Um, I haven't really thought about it," I admit. This telling the truth thing is really addictive.

His muscles roll and he looks over to me, my body stilled on the counter beside him. There are lightning bolts flashing behind his eyes and I feel like he's trying to telepathically transmit something to me, but I can't quite reach it. He looks back down at the counter, picking up the box of rolling dough and avoiding my eyes as he prepares the sheet. His voice is quiet when he speaks.

"I'll only say this the one time, because I don't want you to get angry with me," he murmurs. "But there are other options for you. There are... other things that you can do." He swallows. "And people who want to take care of you."

I step down onto the floor and his eyes flash to mine. Intensity level: nuclear.

What other things can I do? And *who* other than my life-giving mother could possibly know what's best for me? I want to indulge myself in the fantasy but I know that we're too young to be serious. Adults say that kind of stuff about people like us all the time.

I frown up at him and put my hands on my hips. He slips his forearms between the triangular gaps that they make, locking his hands together behind me, and he presses into my back so that I crush forward into his torso. I can see what he was trying to transmit to me now. *I am right here. I want to take care of you.*

I feel lightheaded. This is impossible. I obviously have to listen to my mom, but there is nothing in the world that I want to do less than follow the orders she has given. I try to mask the molten yearning in my stomach by looking down at my toes, even as he pushes us together more roughly. "Is this what you prayed for when you lit a candle for me?" I ask quietly.

He breathes out a laugh and it's warm on my skin. He dips down so that his mouth is on my neck and he sucks the skin soothingly. "No," he says, and then I gasp when his teeth rake up my throat. "This is what I prayed for when I lit a candle for *me*."

CHAPTER 25

Present

Mitch stands in front of me in the kitchen, hands on hips, head bowed. It's Christmas Eve and he just got back from Pine Hills with my mom, so she's upstairs unpacking the suitcase he lugged to their room whilst I prepare for the Mitch Inquisition part iii. It's not such a chore when I can see the curl of his biceps through the stretched cotton of his white long-sleeve t-shirt, and he's wearing the same baby blue jeans that he had on in the photo my mom sent me. Does he only own the one pair?

He's rooted to the spot in silence for at least a whole minute, steam slowly seeping out of him like a volcano. When he looks up at me his expression is rigid but not aggressive. At least he isn't Cadillac red anymore.

He holds his hand up, palm facing out. I don't know if it's to prematurely subdue or silence me, but I remain both subdued and silenced as I wait for him to rip the bandage.

"It is none of my business, River, and I don't want to talk about this any more than you do."

If he's referring to me getting it on with his son - which I'm pretty sure he is - he may be surprised to know that I actually wouldn't mind talking to him about it. I mean, I have literally two friends, and his son is now sort of one of them, so I'm overdue a juicy indulgence about the mind-blowing sex I've been mercifully granted before my lifetime of sad academic servitude. Plus, Mitch is really attractive, so it wouldn't gross me out if he thought about me naked. I know I shouldn't be thinking it, but I am only human. If anything, it's going to be way more uncomfortable for *him* to discuss this than it is for me to discuss it.

Nevertheless, I don't say any of this, instead opting to silently observe him whilst he struggles. He's all hot and bothered. I wish I had some popcorn.

He shifts his weight from one foot to the other. "For the sake of your mom being my partner, and you being her daughter, and Tate being my son, there are a lot of people that I care about involved here, so I have to make sure that precautions are being put in place so that no-one gets hurt in the long run." His eyes burn into mine as he tries to determine whether or not I'm taking him seriously. I nod, relenting. I almost roll my eyes but I do value my life. "So," he says hesitantly. The muscles in his chest tense and he rolls his shoulders. I feel like he's a quarter-back, and I'm one wrong move away from him mowing me down. "Were you careful?"

I knew that this is what he was going to talk to me about, but for some reason, now that he *is* talking to me about it, I feel unprepared. My little gasp escapes me before I can stuff it back down my throat, so I try to detract from it by narrowing my eyes at him. There is no way for certain that he knows what happened whilst he was away, so I'm not about to hand him such prized information over on a silver platter.

I opt for innocent until proven guilty. "I cannot imagine what made you assume such a thing, Mitch," I say, my tone the perfect blend of distrustful teenager and scandalised step-daughter.

He narrows his eyes on me in return. "How about I rang my son's landline every day for the past week and he picked up a grand total of – how many times was it again? Oh, right. *No times.*"

I almost do a little pony snort but Mitch doesn't look like he's in a friendly mood. I give him my best perplexed look instead and say, "Very suspicious."

"River–"

"Yes." I blurt it out and he pauses like a VHS freeze-frame – stopped mid-motion but glitching a little. He's on the precipice of detonation so I choose to put him out of his misery. "I was careful. He was careful. It was all very nice and careful."

We stare at each other, gauging our reactions like we're not sure if we're on the same team or not. After a few seconds he realigns himself, standing to his full height and his chest engorging as he takes a deep breath. He nods once. Then he winces.

"I didn't need to know about the 'nice' bit," he mumbles, one rough tan hand scratching his scalp in irritation. I can't help the small laugh that bubbles out of me and it catches his attention. His expression is softer now, although I can see his discomfort in the lines twitching beside his eyes and mouth. He looks apologetic as he says the next part. "Obviously Tate is going to come round tomorrow, but I can't have you two being alone together at any point, okay? It'll be too obvious, and I want for you to know what's happening in your future before you let your mom in on this – if 'this' is still going on by the time that you've figured out what you're going to be doing. I know I sound callous and I'm sorry, but we need to be pragmatic about this."

Everything that he just said is totally logical and correct, but now all that I'm thinking about is Tate on Christmas

Day. Maybe I should have given him his cross back so that he could be feeling optimum holiness tomorrow, but I don't want to draw anyone's attention to it now, so I dismiss the thought.

He continues, "You might be able to find a moment at the house warming next week but, I'm telling you, strictly *nothing* inappropriate, River. If someone sees you and tells your mom you will be in deep shit."

Mitch swivels the ball of his foot back and forth, watching it like it's his soul's compass. He looks over to the entryway and then back to me, scratching the back of his neck contemplatively. "You know when you first met me and you said something like *I just want what's best for my mom*?" he asks. I tilt my head, puzzled, but I say yes anyway, not sure where he's going with this. "Yeah? Well, that's how I feel about Tate," he says, his voice tenacious yet kind. His hands are stuffed in his pants pockets, resolute. I nod in understanding, presuming that he's made his point, but then he adds, "And you."

My eyes flash up to his immediately, unsure if I just heard him correctly, and he holds my gaze.

"You're... family now. Whether through my son or through your mom, it doesn't matter. So that's how I feel about you, too."

I'm too shocked to speak so I just continue staring at him, the blood in my brain feeling as if it's coagulating, my muscles tense and immobile.

Mitch *cares* about me? It's impossible. Mitch *hates* me. I heard what he was saying to Tate in the attic that night. He thought that I was going to use his son and then leave without a trace, which – okay – is essentially true, but not in the sense that I have no feelings about it, because, annoyingly, I do. But Mitch doesn't know that. Right?

Finally he nods again and exits the room, leaving me alone and dumbstruck, with only the kitchen counter for support.

*

The housewarming party is tucked in perfectly between Boxing Day and New Year's Eve - that time of the holiday season when no-one wants the celebrations to end - so the Coleson's home is lit up like a middle-aged frat house tonight. Mitch's work buddies, who are all as thickset and sun-kissed as you could ever possibly imagine, are lounging in the living area near the back with their partners, reclining into the soft brown sofas with beer bottles swinging from lose fists. Tate's mom has even been invited here, but I'm pretty sure that she's going to politely decline coming round. Above the fireplace the mantle is lined with an evergreen garland, shiny red baubles intermittently dispersed through the leaves, and bowls of butter cookies and bottles of opened wine are set across the dining room table. The atmosphere is hazy with laughter, old Christmas songs, and cinnamon-bun scented candles.

Obviously I'm invited – I mean, technically *I* live here now – but I'm staying as out of the way as possible, although, for my mom's sake, I've made an effort to dress 'normally' just in case. I'm wearing my dark denim jeans as it's freezing outside, although the initial blanket of snow has disappeared for now, and for a touch of personality I'm wearing my cream long-sleeve top with a little Kewpie in the centre.

I've been in my room for the past hour, lying on my bed in the flickering candlelight and listening to a CD that I shouldn't be, but now I'm so hungry that I'm going to have to brave going to the kitchen. I pull on a pair of fuzzy socks and pad quietly out of my room until I reach the downstairs entryway. I turn right to the dining room and pluck two butter cookies from the bowl, biting into one as I head into the kitchen to put the kettle on. God, this is a really good cookie. It feels really bad to be enjoying it so much, but the

198

fact that Tate made them makes them even better. I can't wait for him to get here tonight. I don't know why but I need to see him. The cookie melts down my throat, creamy and sweet, and then I shove the second cookie into my mouth. I flip the kettle on after checking how much water is inside, whilst simultaneously retrieving a mug from the cupboard and a teaspoon from the drawer.

Then I hear it. The quiet shuffling sound behind me. It results in a prickling sensation at the back of my neck, seeping down my spine and into my muscles - a type of primitive paralysis keeping my body stilled.

What the hell?

I slowly lift my hand to the cupboard above my face and I open it to pick up a teabag. I'm moving like Frankenstein's monster, slow and unsteady, as I pour the water into the cup, staring straight ahead at the now-closed cupboard door, determined to stay as still as possible.

There are eyes boring into me, through my hair and to my skin, but there has been no shift in the air around me, implying that I am the only person in the room.

My spine flexes and a light shiver ripples over my shoulders as the realisation dawns on me. The kitchen window. It's right behind me and I'm almost one hundred percent certain that someone is staring at me through it.

I have a really bad feeling. On an animal level my body can sense the ill intent and it's making me lightheaded. The noise and cheer from the living room has descended to the underworld, throbbing in my ears as if I'm below a surface of water.

A slight movement catches my eye and suddenly I'm looking at the round silver doorknob on the cupboard in front of me. It's blurry and distorted but there is a blot of colour in the black smudge that depicts the window, like light catching on something pressed up against the pane-

I flip around and a flash of gold evaporates from view. There's someone out there who isn't meant to be. My heart is in my throat and I'm gripping the countertop behind me. Even if I didn't trust my eyes, I wouldn't be able to deny the whip-fast rustle of shoes on Mitch's gravel border. Now the only thing that I can see in the pane is my own terrified reflection, washed out in a watery silver tint against the blackness beyond the porch. Ten seconds, twenty seconds, thirty. I'm too panicked to be able to move. I want to run upstairs and hide under my bed. I want to get my inhaler and release the pain in my lungs.

I want to walk to the back of the house and tell Mitch that there's an intruder on his property.

I'm about to pry my frozen fingers off the counter behind me when the front door opens. The front door is *open*? We didn't even *lock* it? My eyes stretch wide and the blood runs from my face until Tate steps inside the entryway, fingers on the handle to close the door behind him. When he sees me his expression changes from warmth to shock to incensed concern. He looks angry as he rushes to me, leaving the door open, and he encases his fists around my elbows.

"River," he says. His brow is clenched, and his eyes are running all over my face. I feel weak. I'm glad he's gripping me so tightly because, if he wasn't, I think that I would be on the floor. "Tell me what happened."

My hands are shaking as I lift them to hold onto his forearms. I look down at them and my nails have turned purple. I'm icy cold as I think of what is happening. I know this reaction. My body knows this reaction more than my brain can comprehend right now, and all I can think about is the fact that I need to get as far away from here as possible.

"I need to go," I whisper. He doesn't hesitate. We don't check behind us to make sure that no one is watching as he pulls me from the kitchen, I slip into my shoes, and then he hauls us from the front door to his truck. I start shivering hard, and I'm not sure if it's because the temperature has dropped to frost level or because I know that someone is lurking out here in the dark. I don't look around me to see. I don't want to ever see it again.

What if I'm literally going crazy? There is no logical reason why I would have seen what I know I just saw. It doesn't make sense. It just *doesn't* make sense.

He unlocks the car and swiftly opens the passenger door, helping me lift up onto the step and practically pushing me inside. He strides to the driver's side and hunches in, locking it as soon as the doors are all shut.

He turns to me and grabs my face in both of his hands. They are so comforting and warm that it almost makes me cry. His fingers wind into the hair at the base of my skull and he rubs his thumbs firmly up my cheeks. It confuses me at first because his touch is so much rougher than it usually is, but then I realise that he isn't comforting me: he's trying to re-circulate my blood flow.

"Your lips are white," he murmurs disturbed. His face is twisted in pain as he starts pushing his thumbs into the padded halves of my bottom lip, pressing until I feel his warmth begin to seep inside of me.

"Tell me," he says again, and this time I want to obey.

"That day," I say, and I'm startled by my own voice. It comes out louder than I thought that it would and it reverberates around the car, making the silence even more penetrating. "You have to tell me what you thought was going to happen."

Tate blinks at me, as if confused, and I can see his mind trying to reach the place that mine is currently at. He isn't sure which day I'm talking about. There have been a lot of days, but only one day would merit this reaction.

As soon as he realises what I'm talking about his body tenses and stills. He isn't sure where I'm going with this and, to be honest, neither am I. But something doesn't feel right. Something has been amiss in our stories for too long, and I need to rectify it *now* or I'm going to go insane.

"The last day that we were in school together before Christmas?" he asks. His voice is low and quiet, unsure. I nod and he runs his hand down his face, then through his hair. "Um," he says heavily, "I thought... I thought we were going to meet up after the final bell. I was outside whilst you were in your classes, and I kept looking up at the windows to see you." He swallows and undulates his shoulders, his eyes diverted out of the window. He looks like he doesn't want to continue so I scoot closer to him and drop my hand to his thigh, which is widely spread and hardened under his jeans. I spot a slice in the denim above his knee and slip my hand into it. I'm instantly met with the searing heat of his skin, so extremely juxtaposed to the wintry tips of my fingers, and he makes a quiet groan. He rolls his head to face me and then he wraps one of his hands around the side of my throat.

"Do I have to continue?" he pleads, and I squeeze my hand around his naked thigh to encourage him. He groans again and this time pulls me by my neck so that he can reach my lips. He kisses me and a pained sound releases from his chest. He slants my mouth open so that he can kiss me more intimately, and he runs his other hand down my back, until he's gripping me forcefully from behind. I trail my unoccupied fingers up to his belt and he pulls my face back so that he can look down, a grunt of desire escaping him.

"Continue," I order and his distressed eyes flick back to mine. He removes both of his hands from my body and lifts his arms back so that he can grip the headrest behind him. The hot scent of his warm skin and cologne rushes over me.

"You weren't waiting for me where I asked you to, and then when I found you, you were so angry at me. You... hated me and you didn't want to see me again." His tone is slightly bitter, but I catch the glints of confusion and betrayal in his eyes, so I run the hand that I have inside his jeans as high up his thigh as the denim will allow. *"Fuck,"* he grits out.

He closes his eyes and his hands drop to his belt, slapping the tongue of leather through the metal buckle. His fingers hurriedly push his top button through the loop and the zip down his fly, and then he presses his hand in between the denim and his underwear. He palms himself with anguished strokes over the stretched cotton.

"Why are you asking me this?" he asks, his eyes still squeezed shut. As I watch his hand I momentarily forget everything else that has happened in the past five minutes, but then I feel the silent chill again and my body stiffens anxiously.

"The note," I say. "You forgot about the note you wrote me." *And without the note, none of this terrible stuff would ever have happened.* I have to know the truth. What were his intentions if they weren't for things to end up exactly as they did?

He opens his eyes and there is a new expression etched on his face. Defiance.

He lifts his arms up again so that he can grip the headrest the same way he did earlier. If he didn't, I'm not sure what his hands would be capable of right now.

"I never wrote you a note, River," he says, eyes staring intently into mine.

I feel the twist of a knife pressing in my gut. "Yes you did," I refute. "You did give me a note-"

"Yes," he replies, his voice straining with tension and a cacophony of emotion boiling beneath the surface. "I did *give* you a note, but I never *wrote* you a note. I *typed* you a note." He cocks his head, more confused than ever. Join the club Tate.

I press my temples roughly and then jolt my head straight. "You wrote me a note *and* you typed me a note," I say, agitated now. "The day that I'm talking about... that's the day that you wrote me a note." The minute details between these discrepancies is making my blood congeal.

He shakes his head, seeming less perplexed now but much more concerned. "River, there was no handwritten note. We had a plan that day. Why would I write you when we already knew what we were doing?"

A horribly logical thought. I brush it off, adamant in my refusal to be manipulated. "I literally showed it to you outside when I saw you, before I…" *Before I screamed horrible things at you. Before I clawed you, pushed you, shoved you. Before I absolutely lost it.*

He turns a full ninety degrees in his seat and his eyes are molten. "I thought that you wrote that."

I throw my head back against the headrest and it smacks hard. Tate immediately cups the back of my skull and laces his fingers into my hair so that I can't do that again. His jaw is entirely rigid.

"Why would I write a note and then sign it 'Tate'?" I ask. "You looked at it, you would've seen what it said," I argue. I'm losing my will to endure this fight – it seems so fruitless and I feel as though I can't trust my mind. What is happening to me?

His tone changes so that it's low and soothing as he rubs his thumbs up my jaw. "Baby, I didn't read it. I told you – I said something like 'if you want to say something to me, *say* it' because I didn't want to read a note. I glanced at it and I couldn't-"

He immediately stops and then glances around the car as if he's searching for the rest of his sentence. *Why wouldn't he have read it?* He changes paths completely.

"I thought that you were mad at me for leaving or you wanted someone else, and that's why you were so angry. I thought that you didn't want to, like, long-distance with me because we were crazy-young. And I got that – I didn't agree with it, but I understood it. I was going to stay with my mom and my step-dad until I could move into this house with my dad, and then I was going to transfer back to school. When you didn't want us to be a thing anymore I still moved here because I didn't want to be at home with my step-dad and…" He shakes his head. "My dad let me do online schooling until I graduated. It was easier. It helped with… certain things." He sighs and dips his forehead to mine. My eyes have grown wide but he's so lost in his past that he hasn't noticed.

He lifts his head and his eyes are on my mouth. He presses his lips against mine and another soft anguished sound comes out of him. He shifts in his seat and grips his hands on me tighter, one lacing its way up into my hair and the other rubbing its way down around my throat. I'm too startled to react. My eyes are open as he parts my lips and gently slides his tongue against mine. I feel it deep in my stomach and I stir at the heat that's sliding down my belly.

Tate pulls back and looks into my eyes, understanding that something that night went seriously amiss, and now he wants answers too.

I'm desperate for clarity – I need to be one hundred percent sure – and Tate can tell. A pained look crosses his face, as if he didn't want it to come to this, and he presses his forehead against my shoulder. I hear him inhale deeply and his broad shoulders swell. I run my hands across his muscles and squeeze them in my palms.

It takes him a few moments to gather himself and then he lifts his determined face to mine. "Baby, the reason why I typed you a message that time instead of writing it… the reason why I didn't want to read the note that day…" He looks away from me briefly, wincing slightly, and then draws his eyes back to mine. "I'm dyslexic," he says. "I have dyslexia. It's not a big deal but when I was in school it was… hard. Some people handle it better and with good tutorage they can improve, but I was kind of stubborn back then so I just threw myself into sports, and biking, and the stuff with my dad instead. Don't get me wrong, I can read, but at that time – especially with handwritten text – it was… it would take me just a *lot* longer than the typical kid to read something really fucking basic. That's why I was so angry and, to be honest, embarrassed when you showed me that note. I didn't want you to see me like that, especially since I thought you were breaking up with me." His brow is contorted as he studies me for a reaction. "I'm really sorry River."

My heart hitches in my chest as the pieces of the puzzle slowly fall into place.

Tate never wrote me a note.

Tate never wrote me a note.

Tate's dyslexia… it's in everything. Everything he's said or done that I didn't quite understand at the time. It's been right in front of my face and I didn't even see it.

Tate never wrote that note, and Tate has no idea.

He's waiting for me to respond so I do the only thing that I can think of to convey all of the emotions that I'm feeling right now. I wrap my arms around his neck and kiss him *so freaking hard*. He groans as I crush myself against him and I feel the relief from his lungs pour inside of me. His chest is heaving. I run my hands all over him – around his throat, up his jaw, into his hair – and I part my lips so that he can slide inside.

Why on earth did he apologise to me just now? I hate that he felt like he should say that. I have never been so relieved in my life.

I pull away from him so that I can slip off my glasses and I place them down on the dash before I move over to settle in his lap. His pants are still unzipped, exposing the cotton of his boxer briefs, and the pressure from my groin makes his head fall back in pleasure. He spreads his thighs wider, stretching my knees out until I gasp, and then he slides down in his seat so that his face is closer to mine. He uses the hand around the back of my neck to bring me to him so that he can kiss me again, and his other hand slides between us. He deftly rips my jeans open from simply pulling the denim alone and he slips his fingers down the front of my underwear, grunting in pleasure as he feels how soft I am. When I try to do the same to him he eases me back.

"Wait, baby, we need to-" He restrains my wrists in his hands and I struggle pettily against his hold. "You need to finish this. You need to tell me what happened."

I roll my eyes and sigh exasperatedly. *Seriously?* "I don't want to. It's over now."

He shakes his head. "Uh-uh. You need to tell me what caused you to feel like this for so long."

I stare at him with narrowed aggravated eyes and he strokes my wrists consolingly, coaxing me with princess treatment. I huff and throw my head back. He grabs it in his palm before I can do any more damage, like smashing it into the windshield.

"You're not gonna like it," I warn. God knows I definitely fucking didn't.

He nods. "I know. If this is anywhere near half as bad as what I'm thinking, I'm about to get arrested."

A little flame of delight licks up my sternum. In the dark of the car with only the neighbours' Christmas decorations to light up his face, Tate glitters down at me like an angel. I press a chaste kiss to the pad of his bottom lip and his chest enlarges protectively.

"Tell me," he says finally.

So I do.

CHAPTER 26

Three Years Ago

It's weird. The building that houses the Gym looks completely deserted, evidently because all of the other students are leaving by the entrance in the front foyer, ushered by teachers saying their goodbyes as we leave for winter break. Maybe that's why Tate wanted us to meet up at the changing rooms – because there would be no-one else here – but that kind of makes me confused because he has been so openly affectionate with me these past few weeks. I look around the empty yard once more, and then I pull open the doors to enter the Gym.

The entryway is freezing cold and the smell of rubber equipment and aerosol spray lingers in the air. Plus, Tate isn't standing in the main entrance, which confounds me even further. Naturally upon seeing no-one my eyes subsequently move to the two doors directly in front of me - the girls' changing room on the left and the boys' changing room on the right. I glance around at my surroundings again, the building so chilled that my breath mists opaquely in front of my face, and I feel really uneasy now. Why would Tate bring me here?

Tate definitely wouldn't go into the girls' changing room, that much I *am* sure, so I hesitantly take a step closer to the boys' changing room instead. I haven't ever been inside of the boys' locker room. Obviously no-one is going to be in there except for Tate so it should be fine, but I can't help the uneasy sloshing feeling gurgling around in my gut. I take a long, slow breath of the sharp December air and then I pull open the door to the boys' room.

The first thing that I notice is that the automatic light is still on, which means that someone is still in here, so I relax a little. I think that the boys' room is a little bigger than the girls', bending around a corner where more benches and lockers sit, cleared out for the holidays. I hesitantly round the corner, and I see a Gym bag resting alone on the bench in the centre of the room. I squint at it, assuming that it must be Tate's, but I swear that I have never seen him wearing it before. Seeing that it's still unzipped I make my way over to it, wondering if my present is in there and if this is some sort of slightly unnerving treasure hunt, but all that I see is a crumpled football kit, a pair of long-abused trainers, a can of men's deodorant, and an opened box of-

I immediately spin around and Hudson clamps his hand down on my mouth, his palm so cold that it sends needles prickling across my cheeks. I stare, horrified, into his upturned glinting eyes. I dart my eyes around the room to see if Tate is standing nearby and I try to hold back the wetness that seems to be about to spill down my cheeks. *What the hell is going on?*

"I'm so glad that you could join us, *baby*," Hudson taunts, his mouth grimacing in some sort of satisfied sneer. My eyes shoot back to him and he seems to read the fact that I'm looking for Tate. If this is a joke, I am not getting it. Not at all. "He's not in here," Hudson comments, and then he adds, "he's waiting outside so that I can give you your present alone."

My eyebrows pinch upwards and then Hudson grips his fingers into my cheeks more tightly, making a pained shriek involuntarily escape my throat and muffle against his palm. So stunned by the turn of events I didn't notice at what point he had clasped my elbows behind me with his other arm, making my shoulder blades strain and ache from the distorted position.

"I'm going to take my hand off of your mouth River but don't even think about screaming. I swear, if you even try it-" He digs his nails into my cheeks and I nod my head fiercely, tears now spilling over my skin and onto his fingers, promising him that I won't scream. I want him to get his hands off my face. I hate the fact that my lips are touching him right now. *Why the hell does Tate want me to be here with Hudson?*

Contented, Hudson takes his hand away from my mouth and immediately he shoves me backwards, the backsides of my knees bashing into the wood behind me and I fall down on my ass, onto the bench next to his bag.

"What's going on?" I say, my voice shaking slightly. "I'm meeting Tate-"

Hudson laughs and crosses his arms over his chest, smirking down at me. "First of all, shut up for a minute, I'm doing the talking." My eyes widen as I stare up at him but I keep my mouth shut. The longer he's talking, the longer he's not going to try and... and... "You know how Tate is – so religious and all – and he can't bear the thought of doing anything to dirty you up." He looks me up and down, from the top of my jacket zip to the hem of my skirt. "Fuck knows why, you really aren't anything special. The point is, you really disappointed him at Homecoming on his birthday, so I'm here to give you both a gift and rectify your problem."

My brow creases together significantly and I glance back towards the bend in the room which leads to the exit, desperate for Tate to come in here and tell me that this was a weird joke. I look up at Hudson and shake my head. "I don't understand what you're talking about-"

His hand whips across my cheek and my head snaps to the side, my skin instantly aflame with icy pins and needles, burning their way to the surface of my flesh. My glasses imbed painfully into the side of my nose, but if anything I'm just thankful that they didn't go flying across the room. I readjust them and will myself to stop the flow of tears. I wish that I wasn't crying in front of him, but at least my sobs are silent.

"Shut up," he says again. "Tate won't do anything with you unless I fix your issue first, so you should be feeling fucking grateful right now."

I shake my head but I don't say anything because I don't want him to hit me again.

The next thing that I feel is Hudson grabbing my head and smashing his face into mine. It's one of the most painful things that I have ever experienced, and I have literally just been whacked across the face. His mouth is so hard that it makes me squeeze my eyes shut to try and relieve the suction. He bites his teeth into my top lip and I think that I'm going to scream from the pain piercing through my nerves.

He pulls back and looks at my face, crumpled in confusion and agony. I want to cry out to Tate but then I remember that he *wanted* me here, so really what I need to do is escape, quickly, and as soon as possible.

Is this really what Tate wanted? Is this what he expected to happen right now?

"Why are you being so weird?" Hudson says, a disgruntled look on his face as he hitches up a pale eyebrow.

I literally can't believe what is happening so I just continue to stare at him as I try to think of how I can remove myself from Hudson's grasp and flee the building before he catches me. Hudson takes his hands off my face, making me almost shudder with relief, and he puts them on his hips instead. I look at his wavy blond hair and golden eyes and I consider how, were he a completely different person, Hudson could have been a beautiful boy. But the reality is that I can see the thoughts leaking out of his brain and seeping into every crevice of his face, the actuality of who he is unable to stay truly hidden. He's like one of those jump-scare portraits that people decorate their houses with at Halloween – from one angle it's a reputable gentleman, but from the other it's a hideous zombie with evil eyes and a blood-smothered grin. There is no disintegrating portrait hidden in Hudson's attic. I can see the cracks just fine from here.

"It's what *he* wants, *River*," Hudson says, bringing me back to the present. "Surely you're not so selfish as to deprive him of that before he *leaves*."

He raises his eyebrows as if prompting me to respond so, shuffling back a little, I say quietly, "Tate wouldn't want this," although now I'm not so sure. Everything is adding up.

I wish that it wasn't.

Hudson blows out a breath as if exasperated, shooting it upwards and making a few of his blond tendrils flutter above his forehead. "This is exactly what he wants. He wants me to help you, and by doing this you're helping him, so stop being a bitch about it. It's what was always going to happen. Me and Tate... we share everything."

And just like that, the last dime drops.

We share everything.

The exact same words that Tate said to me not that long ago, almost as if it were a blood-pact motto. Tate hadn't sounded so happy about it at the time, but then what do I really know about Tate? What do I really know about *anything*? So what if I've been pining for him from my bedroom window since the day that he first moved in? That doesn't mean jack shit. Obviously boys lie, and they're damn good at doing it.

I've been played, and I need to exit this game *now*.

But before I can rise to my feet Hudson shoves his hand into my clavicle and my head smashes down against the bench underneath me, whacking with a horrible loud thudding sound. The back of my head is throbbing, and my blood is pumping so wildly that I can hear it in my ears.

I lift up onto my elbows but it's too late because Hudson has already ripped a gash in the fabric of my tights and his hand is now clawing at the material around my crotch.

My entire face blanches of any colour as I lift one hand to my mouth, shaking uncontrollably at the sight of what he's about to do, what he is doing, what he has done-

I feel one finger push into my body and I squeeze my eyes shut at the burn and the sting. *What the fuck, what the fuck, what the fuck, no, no, no-*

No good feeling comes from the intrusion, and instead I feel sore, dry, and then totally numb. It doesn't feel like how I expected, and it is *nothing* like what they say in the books that I have read. I think about the steamy dark romances that I have stacked up in my bedroom and how I'm going to bin every single one of them as soon as I get home. There is no joy in this moment. There is no desire, there is no lust. All that I feel is dead inside.

I'm paralysed in shock and fear for an immeasurable amount of moments before my brain starts to re-register what is happening to me.

I risk a glance at Hudson's hand and clamp my mouth down to stifle my sob.

No more. *No. More.*

I look to the side to see if there's something that I can smash against Hudson's temple and my eyes instantly land on his canister deodorant. Thank God.

I grab the can and immediately spray it in the direction

of his face, aiming for his eyes or his mouth but my own vision is too blurry right now to make the situation out clearly.

Hudson instantly jerks away, cursing wildly as he covers his eyes, and I raise my feet up, shoving him hard in the ribs and sending him toppling backwards. I pelt the can at his body like a shot-put and lunge off the bench, streaking around the corner and crashing myself straight into the door. As soon as I breach the exit of the boys' changing rooms I thunder towards the doors marking the entrance to the Gym, suddenly overwhelmed with gratitude for always running track with Kit.

I push through the entrance and almost topple over the tiny step that I've never really noticed before, but I manage to keep my footing and I sprint across the yard, leaving the Gym building behind me and heading directly for the now deserted car park.

A sweat that I don't remember releasing is making the hairs around my face stick to my temples and my forehead. I swipe at it with my shaking hands and the icy air laps at the tear-streaks completely covering my cheeks. I hurtle towards the end of the emptied lot, desperate to get out of here as quickly as I can.

I should never have believed him, I think to myself. *I knew that this was too good to be true.*

My trust.

My faith.

My fault.

As soon as I turn the corner I crash into the solid planes of Tate's chest.

At first he smiles down at me, a wondrous look in his eyes, but then his face quickly drops and his forehead contorts into confusion, fear, pain.

I instantly stumble backwards, refusing to become trapped in his arms, and I meet his eyes with some confusion, fear, and pain of my own.

But also rage. Mainly rage.

"River," he says, in a hushed but urgent tone, his hands reaching for me. "What's wrong? Baby, what happened? Where have you been?"

He's distractedly running his eyes all over me, perhaps checking for clues that what almost just happened actually did happen, so I take the opportunity to throw back my arm and smack him across the face.

His eyes widen momentarily but he takes the hit, a soft pink glow instantly spreading across his cheekbone and jaw. He meets my eyes, seeming even more desperate than before, and clasps my shoulders in both of his hands.

"*Ugh!*" I groan disgustedly and I shove at his chest, trying to get him off me, but he holds me firm. "Get away from me, Tate! Get your hands off me right now!"

He doesn't take his hands off me. Instead he dips his head down to mine so that our eyes are level and he gazes at me with a worried look on his face. "What happened, baby? I've been waiting for you. Tell me what I need to do."

Rifling through my bag I slap the note from my locker into the centre of his chest and he catches it in the splay of his palm so that it doesn't fall onto the frosted concrete.

"You've done enough," I spit out, and I wriggle myself free from his grasp on my shoulder.

Tate brings the paper between us so that he can look down at it and his eyebrows pinch together. His eyes don't even run over the lines, and why should they? He wrote them. They more swirl around the page, his desperation and frustration increasing by the second, until he shoots his eyes back to me, then back to the page, and up to me again. Is he shocked that I'm calling him out? Is he experiencing some form of delayed guilt? I don't know and, right now, I don't care. He inhales deeply, like he has the audacity to be hurt and irritated, and he crumples up the note, tossing it to the gutter as he reaches for me again.

"If you want to say something to me, I don't want it in a letter, I want you to say it to my face," he says, momentarily confusing me. I can't help the startled laugh that bursts out of me because technically I wish that that had been *my* line, but my laughter seems to anger him further. "River, please tell me what's going on."

"Tell *you* what's going on?" I shriek, my whole body quivering with shock and cold and hate. "If only you had told *me* what was going on. That… that *shit* with Hudson? Unforgiveable," I say and I go to move past him, absolutely done with this, but he blocks me. I slash my nails across his bicep, attempting to claw him out of the way, but he's actually backing me into the side of the wall now.

"This has something to do with Hudson?" he asks, his tone so low that I almost don't hear it.

"This has *everything* to do with Hudson!" I growl. "You're a monster and I can't believe that I *trusted* you! I should *never* have trusted you!" My eyes overflow as my mind suddenly fills with the image of my mom, the wants that she tried to instil into me for my whole life. I went along with her but I never truly *agreed* with her, obviously thinking that I had some deeper, more enlightened understanding of the twenty-first century than she did. *Why can't I date a handsome jock? Why do I have to pick a 'sensible' job?*

Now I know. If I had just listened to her, this would never have happened to me.

Tate's eyes are shimmering and I choke up a half-laugh half-sob. Did he think that I would have been okay with this? With him and Hudson *sharing* me? I don't care about whatever dumb-ass bro-code they have together, I want absolutely *nothing* to do with it.

"River, please," he whispers, his voice stifled and thick in his throat. "I can be better, I can do more. I thought that you wanted me too." He shakes his head as he tries to lace his fingers into my hair. With my back pressed against the wall, all that I can do is turn my head away from his mouth, endless streams of tears flowing silently from my eyes. He buries his nose into my neck, inhaling deeply as his chest shakes against me. "River, I'm in lo-"

I pull my elbows up and ram them as hard as I can into his chest. Although the force of it doesn't make him move, he gets the hint and backs up, pushing one hand into his pocket as he rubs his other wrist across his dampened cheeks. I notice that the crucifix chain that he always wears is wrapped around his fist instead of hanging on his neck, and I wonder why he took it off. Then he puts that hand into his other pocket.

My voice is flat and cold when I speak again. "You're nothing to me, Tate. This? This was all nothing. You're the biggest fraud that I've ever met and I never want to see you again, ever. I thank *God* that you're not going to be living anywhere near me anymore, and I hope that you never do again."

Without a second glance I turn and bolt, my tears gushing noisily now as they fall down my face and neck. My throat feels tight and strangled, and my lungs are aching with the pressure of my heaving cries. I would fumble in my bag for my inhaler, but I can barely feel my fingers anymore.

As I run through the school gate I feel the wintry air gust up my legs, piercing the now bare area underneath my skirt where my tights were pulled and torn. I cry anew as I recall what just happened and I pull my skirt down as far as I can, to ensure that my legs are as invisible as possible.

My feet pound the pavement and I look down at my tights, a long ladder stretching all the way down from the inside of my thigh, trailing off into a snake's-tail point just below my knee.

I look back up and swallow painfully, my chest so tight that I think I could die.

No more skirts, I think to myself as I round the next corner, clutching onto my bag for dear life. *No more skirts.*

CHAPTER 27

Present

I had climbed off of Tate's lap before I told him what had happened and now I'm watching him nervously as his hands clench and unclench around the steering wheel. His whole body has gone rigid and I can tell from the way that he's staring out of the front window that there's only one thought in his mind right now.

He punches on the engine and grabs the gear stick.

"Tate, no!" I shriek. "You can't drive like this!" I wrap my hand over his and his head snaps to face me. In the darkness of the car his eyes are burning red. He shoves the car back into Park and pulls me back on top of him.

"I thought that you... all this time I've thought that you..." He folds his lips into his mouth and takes a few scarily deep breaths, the rise and fall of his chest so extreme that my eyelids start fluttering. He surveys me up and down, his rigid jaw clenched, and a shiver runs through me. "I want to kill him, River. I really want to kill him."

I hide my face in his neck, nodding gently before

nuzzling into his warm skin.

"I don't even know if I should touch you right now," he admits quietly, his voice rough. I don't know if he means that he shouldn't touch me because I just told him about being sexually assaulted, or because he's so angry that he doesn't know what he's capable of, but I have had years to come to terms with being touched by Hudson, and now the only thing that I want is for Tate to wipe the memory of him out of my brain forever. I lean forward, pressing my lips to his, and I make the decision for him.

He moans when I stroke my way up his shirt, his hard abs flexing beneath my fingers, and he gently fills my mouth with the length of his tongue. His hands knead me from behind and he slowly rocks his hips upwards, rhythmically sensitising me until I'm panting.

"I'm going to take you to my place right now," he murmurs, moving his mouth from mine. "We can't do this out here. No one else gets to see you like this."

He runs one of his hands over the dip in my waist and then he reaches up to my chest, where he splays out his palm and squeezes, massaging me gently until I'm gripping my fingers into his sides.

"*Tate*," I whisper warningly.

"One more minute, baby," he murmurs, and his lips trail down the centre of my neck.

I close my eyes and sigh. In one more minute I'll be comatose.

My stomach is swarming with butterflies. I rub my body against Tate's, thinking about how I'm not sure if we're going to be able to make it to his house. I have no idea where he lives and I want to see what it looks like. I love that he wants to take me there and have me inside of his secret space. I love everything about right now.

I love it so much that I open my eyes as Tate kisses along my collarbone, but instead of looking down to watch his mouth sucking my skin and his hand softly teasing my breast, my eyes lock onto the face grinning at me straight through the window.

I scream and immediately roll off of Tate's lap, hiding my body behind his side. "*Shit!*" I shriek, panicked. Ice drops straight through my stomach and, if I wasn't about to pass out, I think I would be sick. It takes Tate a moment to recalibrate but as soon as he sees what I'm seeing he pushes me to the other side of the car and whips the shirt hanging over the shoulder of his chair on top of me. He's out of the car before I even blink.

Hudson is backing away from him but his mouth is still spread into a sly smile. I knew that I saw him. What the *fuck* is he doing here? How did he know where we were?

My blood runs cold. Does he know that I live here?

Hudson puts the bed of the truck between his body and Tate's, and they both grip the sides as they stare at each other - Hudson gleeful, Tate murderous. My hands are shaking as I fumble to pull the shirt up my arms and I numbly click the truck door open, ready to grab Tate and get the hell out of here.

"Tight for a little slut isn't she?" Hudson snickers as I come into view, wrapping my hands around Tate's tensed forearm and futilely trying to pull him back inside the car.

Tate moves his head from side to side, cracking his neck and rolling his shoulders, and then he murmurs quietly so that only I can hear him, "Let go for one minute baby."

"What was that?" Hudson shouts over, cupping a hand to his ear. His cockiness makes him drift back around to us, seemingly underestimating the muscle mass that Tate keeps hidden under his unassuming clothes. Tate's body is vibrating under my fingers. The last thing that I want to do is let go of him because I know that, if I do, he will immediately begin pulverising Hudson, and as much as I too have fantasised about strapping Hudson down and cutting him into long meaty ribbons, I don't want the repercussions of public assault to come back to Tate.

"Tate, let's go," I whisper, my eyes pleading up at him.

He stares down at me and I almost shiver at how intimidating he looks. His body is rock solid and I can feel the pheromones radiating from him as he eyes me up and down, his breathing heavy. "Get back in the car," he tells me. "I need to take care of this, and then, after that, I'll…" He inhales deeply as he drags his eyes away from my lips, up to my eyes. I can read his mind. I know exactly what he's thinking.

And then, after that, I'll take care of you.

I nod and slowly let go, but as soon as my fingertips leave Tate's arm I hear the sharp *smack* of skin on skin.

My eyes flash in shock to Hudson's fist, which only two seconds ago was meeting Tate's jaw. Unflinching, Tate hasn't moved a millimetre. His eyebrow arches as his hand goes up to stroke his cheek and a bemused look crosses his face as his eyes finally flick back down to Hudson.

And then he smiles.

In the next moment Hudson is shoved down and pinned to the blacktop, with one of Tate's hands wrapped around his throat and both of his thighs straddling his waist. His other hand is squeezing Hudson's wrists together, unfazed by his attempts to free himself, as he grits out to him, "You touched her? You touched my girl, huh? And now you're waiting outside my truck as if I'm not about to fuck you up?"

Hudson spits blood out of his mouth, as if he's badly bitten his tongue from when his head hit the road, and with a hint of smugness in his voice he rasps out, "You know that you can't do shit to me."

This time Tate laughs. "Oh yeah?" he asks, and then, letting go of Hudson's wrists, he pounds his fist into his cheek. Hudson's head smacks sideways into the road, both sides of his face split and swollen when he twists back around to Tate.

Hudson makes a low pained sound but he keeps his

hoarse voice neutral. "You know, I didn't expect you to bring a girlfriend to your dad's housewarming, so things must be pretty serious there." He spits again, and then loudly whispers, "But just remember, *I got there first.*"

Hudson's head is yanked forward and then Tate slams it back against the road. Tate stands up, hovering over him with his hands clutching the loop-holes of his jeans and, for one moment, from looking at Tate's face, I think that he's about to piss on him.

But then new lights and noises appear from Mitch's house and three people come running out. The first person looks so much like Mitch that I realise he must be the uncle – Jason – who I hadn't got around to meeting. His brow is sterner and his stubble is darker, making him appear formidable as he storms towards us. Then behind him-

Oh *no. No, no, no.*

Behind Jason is Mitch and my mom, holding hands as they run over to us.

"Jason heard you through the fucking *double-glazing*, Tate," Mitch thunders, and they all abruptly stop, seeing Hudson tentatively trying to sit himself upright against the curb. Mitch's eyes are wide. "What the hell is going on?"

I'm thinking the exact same question. *Why the fuck is Hudson here?*

Tate's eyes flick from Hudson to his dad, but just as he opens his mouth to speak a completely unexpected voice rings out.

"Why are your pants open, River?"

My mom has stepped away from Mitch, and she cocks her head to the side as her eyes linger on my crotch. I look down at myself as if I'm not about to see my fly wide open but, sure enough, my jeans are exactly as they were five minutes ago, when my mom's boyfriend's son was one minute away from fucking me in his truck.

As my head snaps up to try and explain this to my mom, her eyes have already made their way across to Tate, whose clothing is in similar disarray, his open belt swinging rigidly down the long length of his groin.

Her hands shoot up to her mouth and she stifles her gasp. Her eyes meet mine and she's disbelievingly shaking her head. Her voice is garbled behind her hand but I can hear her loud and clear. "Oh you *stupid* girl," she whispers. I cringe as her words slice through me.

Tate moves his body in front of mine and I take the reprieve from their eyes to fasten my pants. I want to grab onto Tate's shirt and press myself into him but now isn't the time.

Will I ever have the chance to do that again?

As if he can read my mind, Tate moves his right hand so that it's resting palm-out against his lower back, and he flexes it in invitation. I don't know who needs the comfort more right now but I immediately envelop his hand in mine, and I wrap the other tightly around his wrist.

Hudson heaves himself up from the ground and he makes a spluttering laugh, despite the lopsided stance that he is currently sporting. He makes a vague gesture between me and my mom and then says, directly to Tate, "Wait. Are you... No way. Are you two, like, step-siblings?" His eyes are glinting so brightly they look radioactive. He coughs wetly after another laugh and then he says with unabashed glee, "Please tell me that that's her mom."

My mom speaks up. I can't see her from behind the protective muscle-shield in front of me but, from her tone, I can tell that she's talking to Tate. "Are you serious? Is this a joke to you?" I hear her step closer. "You know how smart she is, right? You know that she's going to be leaving for college."

Tate's shoulders bristle and I immediately have a new-found understanding for why he's been so cautious around me whenever he saw my pre-college work and applications.

Aware that this might be a sensitive subject for Tate, especially considering what he told me tonight, Mitch steps in.

"Come on, they're just kids," Mitch says, his tone placating. Then it turns stern. "I'm more concerned about why *my son* is beating up the kid of a *cop*."

I pause. Hudson's dad is a *cop*?

Tate rolls the muscles in his back and says, low and gruff, "Self-defence. He threw the first punch."

My mind rewinds back to Tate's predatory patience with Hudson, and I marvel up at the smooth caramel skin above the neckline of his shirt. So that's why he was waiting him out – so that when he *did* hit him back, he wouldn't be obliged to stop. A warm sparkle spreads through my chest and I feel a primal sense of belonging, almost enough to make me smile, even in this hideous situation. But just as quickly as the little swarm of butterflies flutter in my stomach, a cold chill of premonition begins to still me, trickling slowly down my body.

How does Mitch know who Hudson's dad is?

Worse still, how does Mitch know who *Hudson* is?

I don't have time to process this information as my mom incredulously spins to Mitch, a dry laugh choking out of her. "'*They're just kids*'?" she repeats, her voice deadly calm. "Maybe your son is *just a kid*, but *my daughter* is anything fucking but."

I squeeze Tate's hand in mine as his arm grows rigid with tension, and he manages the tiniest little press in response. I peer around his shoulder to look up at his beautiful face and its intentional blankness makes my heart constrict painfully.

My mom whips around to face me as soon as I come back into view. "Please tell me that I'm wrong about this," she demands, her brow raised into a venomous arch.

I have no intention of saying anything in front of Hudson so the only word I say is, "Mom."

She's shaking her head. It's worse than disbelief – it's disappointment.

Why is the one thing that I want the most, the thing that my mom wants for me the least?

Mitch exchanges an unspoken dialogue with his brother, and Jason retreats up the driveway, heading to the garage. Mitch looks between my mom and me, his authoritative big-dick calm apparently here to save the day. "Look, I didn't mean it like that. River's a great kid, very smart, I know. I meant that they're young and they have a history-"

"A *history*?" My mom's eyes are electrocuting. Mitch flinches and looks away from her, his hands shoved in his pockets. She spins back to me. "What the hell does he mean, 'a *history*'?"

Hudson stifles a guffaw and suddenly I wish that Tate *had* urinated on him.

My mom turns back to Mitch, her voice far too controlled. "Why are you so calm about this?" she asks. Mitch looks down at her narrowed, searching eyes and his responding gaze is hard. She tilts her head as if she's navigating her way through his brain and then she crosses her arms, her brow softening. "Tell me you didn't know about this," she says, her tone so unnervingly gentle that even I wince. "Tell me that you weren't aware about what your son was doing to her."

Doing *to her*? I recoil. The irony of my mom demonising Tate, especially when he's stood right in front of Hudson, is not lost on me.

"It's not like that," I say, no longer in control of the words coming out of my mouth.

"Don't talk," my mom snaps.

"Hey," Mitch barks and he moves to stand in front of her. If Tate wasn't so tall, Mitch would be blocking my mom's view of both Tate and me completely. "Enough, alright? They aren't doing a damn thing wrong. There's no need for you to be going in on her like this, because these are two trustworthy kids-"

"You want to talk about trust?" she replies, her voice

cold.

The silence grows and grows until I'm suddenly aware of how freaking freezing it is out here. I look at my hands wrapped around Tate and I'm ghostly. When I exhale through my mouth a dove-grey wisp billows and evaporates into the clear black night.

My mom steps to the side so that she can see me behind my wall of Coleson men. Her eyes are disappointed but I know that there is a maternal sentiment in there. "Get inside and pack your things," she tells me. "We're going back to ours for a little while."

My breathing pauses. We are literally at the housewarming party for her and her boyfriend, and she wants us to move back into her old house *now*?!

Tate's hand is suddenly a vice and I'm not sure that I could pry myself away from him even if I wanted to.

"*Now*," she shouts, with more severity this time.

"You should let go of her Tate," Hudson burrs, dawdling along the curb so that he can catch my eyes. I absolutely refuse to look at him, and I inch further behind Tate. "Don't want me calling my dad out here, do we?"

The threat would seem embarrassing for a nineteen year old to be throwing around if I hadn't just become aware that Hudson's dad is a cop, but something about the insinuation behind his words has the dip between my shoulder blades prickling. Why did he say it like that?

My mom twists her head to appraise Hudson and she cocks an eyebrow. "Exactly who are you?"

Hudson grins at her and then looks back at Tate. "Yeah, Tate. Who *exactly* am I?"

Mitch folds his arms across his pecs and glowers over to Hudson. "Shut up."

Hudson looks at my mom again and I want to shove my fist down his throat. "Tate and I go *way* back. We're, like-" he stares pointedly at Tate "-*really* close."

Tate flexes his free hand, itching to put it to work, and

he grits out, "Not by choice."

There's an uncomfortable palpable tension in the air and my earlier fears are resurfacing. What is not being said right now? What else don't I know?

Hudson jerks his chin at me and it causes me to instinctively glance at him. I know he's speaking to me but I look away anyway. "Wanna know how I came to be here tonight?" he taunts. "Albeit, I actually didn't know that *you* would be here. But word got back to me from town that you'd been together at the diner, so I thought, seeing as there was a party going on, it was the perfect opportunity to come and see. And lo and behold…" he trails off, a triumphant smile on his face. It looks sinister when juxtaposed to the blood drying on his cheeks.

I'm still standing behind Tate but my eyes are locked in with Mitch. He's got that apprehensive worried-for-me look on his face that makes my intestines constrict. My face is so ashen you would think that I was dead.

How did Hudson know about the party at Mitch's house tonight?

Sensing the secret dialogue happening between Mitch and me, Hudson turns to Mitch with renewed vigour. "Thanks for the invite by the way. Obviously Pam wasn't gonna come, but it was real gentlemanly of you to ask."

Pam?

Hudson's eyes hone in on Tate, and I feel his entire form swell. My mom is looking between the two of them, unaware of the significance of the exchange but suspicious about the mounting testosterone levels. Mitch keeps his eyes on me the whole time, shaking his head slowly as the realisation finally punches through the surface.

The reason why Mitch knows Hudson. The reason why Mitch knows Hudson's *dad*.

The reason why Tate and Hudson had to be friends at school. The reason why they shared *everything*.

The reason why Hudson left school at the exact same

time that Tate did, when Tate was moving house with his mom.

I stumble one step backwards as it all falls into place.

Pamela is the name of Tate's mom, and she just so happened to be dating a guy who was a cop three years ago.

It can only mean one thing.

Hudson is Tate's step-brother.

CHAPTER 28

Present

The amount of information that has come to light in the darkness outside of Mitch's house is too much, too quickly, and I'm struggling to process all of it. There's a deadly tension mounting between Tate, Hudson, and Mitch, and even my mom can sense it, although she doesn't quite have all of the pieces of this puzzle to facilitate her in understanding the significance of what Hudson just revealed.

If Hudson is Tate's step-brother then that means that he is going to be in his life *forever*. And of all of the people in the world, Hudson is the last person who I ever, ever, *ever* want to be in the vicinity of again.

If I want to have Tate in my life, then I have to have Hudson in my life too.

And that is something that is simply impossible.

The driver's door of Tate's truck is still ajar from when he jumped out barely ten minutes ago, so I release Tate's hand from my mine and turn around so that I can climb up on the step, kneel over his seat, and collect my glasses from the dashboard. I slip them on as I dismount from the car, my movements burdened with weightlessness as the paralysis of my distress spreads through my veins. When I get my feet back on the road Tate has turned one-eighty to look at me, but I don't meet his eyes, too scared of my own reaction. I one hundred percent refuse to cry in front of Hudson – I did it back then but I won't be doing it now – so I can't risk looking at Tate's face.

I glance in the direction of my mom and fiddle with my frames as I say, "I just need one minute. I'll be back… I just need…"

I clamp my lips together, turn on my heel, and then I begin to walk quickly down the street, crossing to the pavement on the other side of the road, eager to put as much distance between this whole situation and myself as possible.

I hear my mom shouting something about how dangerous it is to be out alone like this at night, but I keep on walking with no intentions of stopping. Little does she know that the biggest danger to me in this neighbourhood is standing right next to her.

By the time that I round the street corner I break into a full on run. It shoots a rush of adrenaline straight to the centre of my chest and in the next second three years' worth of tears are gushing out of me. It's ugly. I'm sobbing so hard that my sternum is burning and a rusty ache is scraping at the back of my throat. I wish I had my inhaler with me because I don't know how long I can run like this without external aid to my lungs. My legs are shaking, but my horror-induced adrenaline is propelling me forward, hands swiping at my soaked cheeks and wet lashes leaving salty dots across my glasses lenses. An involuntary sob escapes my throat and I wish that I could just shut the fuck up. What if someone hears? I hope that no one sees me because this is the most embarrassing and heart-breaking moment of my life.

I only register the footsteps behind me when they're one second away, but as I spin around, expecting whoever is there to try and stop me or bring me back, I'm met with Tate's warm chest. He scoops me into his arms, enveloping me in his body, and he aids my escape without a word. His jacket is hanging over his forearm and he tries to drape it around me as he jogs us further away from Mitch's house. My tears are still audible and I cringe into his neck as I think about how weak I look right now. But then again, if a life with Tate is now impossible, it shouldn't matter if he thinks that I'm lame, because he won't have to be around me for much longer anyway.

The thought makes me cry harder.

I don't know where he's taking me but the even confidence of his strides tells me that he does. I pull away slightly from his neck so that I can try and look up at him but the hand that was cradling my back strokes upwards, and he presses my head to his body again. My tears are silent now and I feel a little bit less pathetic knowing that he can't hear them. I rub my fingertips around the thick base of his neck and press my cold nose against his skin, inhaling. His scent is masculine, comforting, warm. His entire ribcage swells sharply against my body, as if he felt a palpable physical extraction by my breathing him in.

He slows to a walk but I don't move to see where we are. I quickly rub at my face to remove any further evidence of tears, and the tracks sting icily as the night air touches them.

I feel my back press up against something hard and Tate slowly lowers me to my feet. I can't bear what I'm about to do so I quickly reach up to his neck, entwining my fingers into his soft hair, and drag his mouth down to mine. My haste elicits a groan from his chest and he doesn't fight me like I expected him to. He never denies me. My eyes sting because I'm going to have to give him up when I only just got him back.

His hands move to my shoulders, re-securing his jacket carefully over them, before allowing himself to give in completely. He holds my face to his with the expansive grip of his hand, keeping me in place, before sliding his palm down the column of my throat. He holds me more firmly than he ever has before and the unyielding domination makes my body grow limp, sweet liquid heat swirling around low in my belly. His other hand dips under the back of my t-shirt and roams upwards until he's between my shoulder blades. Then he uses his forearm to press into me, making my cold skin blaze with heat, and he pushes me flush into his solid torso.

I pull away slightly so that I can begin to say what needs to be said but he forces my mouth back to his. He knows what's coming and he's determined to prevent it. I mumble his name against his lips but it only makes him press against me harder. My eyes flutter as he unleashes all of the strength that he usually keeps under such tight reins against my body, so much smaller than his and therefore so much easier to control. He slides his tongue into my mouth, filling me so deeply that I feel the movements in my womb, and his hands work together to restrain, control, and reward the involuntary movements of my body. I know what he's doing and it's so achingly unfair. He's reminding me of who he is and what only he is capable of.

He's showing me what I'm going to miss when I let him go.

And I don't *want* to let him go, that's the tragedy here. What *I* want is for Tate to go get his truck, drag me inside, then take me to his secret home and never let me leave. I want to give him all of his fantasies because, somewhere along the way, they became *my* fantasies too. I want to play his spoilt little girlfriend and then become his ravished little wife, watching him obsess over me as I make him his beautiful tousle-haired babies. I don't want to go back to

Mitch's house, pack up my belongings, and then head to my mom's, wherein I'll spend my days studying until I finish high school, and then get shipped off to college to fulfil *her* dream for me.

But that's what I have to do.

"*Tate*," I moan, pushing with all of the strength that I can muster at his chest. It doesn't move him an inch. His head is buried under my hair at the sensitive curve of my neck and he's inhaling me so deeply that I now understand his earlier reaction. I *can* feel it, the magnetic pull between my soul and his, as he consumes my pheromones that are inviting, taunting, and begging for him to do whatever he wants. His body is rippling as he decodes the message and sounds that are more animal than human rumble gruffly in his chest.

"Tate, please, we have to talk about this," I implore, but my voice is weakened in my lust. "You know that I-"

"I know," he says, his face suddenly looking down at mine. The timbre of his voice is so low that I whimper, and his eyes become half-mast upon hearing the noise. He swallows hard and leans back down so that he can give me kiss after kiss after kiss. "I know," he whispers, cupping my cheeks in his hands.

As if a faucet has been turned my tears begin to fall again and Tate wipes at them with his thumbs as his lips try to chastely console me. His brow is contorted and his eyes sparkle, as tears of his own glass over the surface. It has always been like this, this abnormal connection that sometimes doesn't even come *once* in a person's lifetime. My pain is his pain. *He's hurting because I'm hurting.*

I have been blessed to know Tate Coleson but my time is now up. Nothing this good ever comes without a price, and God knows that I have had my fair share of pain to balance against his goodness.

I wish I could stop crying. My eyes are too blurry and I can't see him properly which makes me cry even harder, because this is the last time that I'm going to see him and I *can't even see him*. I wipe my fingers over my cheeks and under my nose. It's not pretty. All of the happiness that I have had as a result of Tate is bleeding out of me in every form of liquid that my body can conjure up. It's so painful that I rub my chest, worried that this agony will never end and my heart will be permanently severed. I've read stories about people dying from broken hearts, old couples leaving the world only days apart, because it's like their body knows – it knows that the best part is over now and there is no longer any reason to stay. And that's how it feels. Leaving Tate feels like the best part is over... and there is no longer any reason to stay.

"Baby," he whispers, "I'm so sorry."

My tears continue to run down my face and down my neck until they are deep into my cleavage, anointing Tate's silver cross. I pull out the pendant and we both look down at it as it glistens with my tears. He can sense that I'm about to pull it over my head and give it back to him because he grips it in his hand and slides it back into my top, wrenching my chest to his so that his necklace rests finally between us. He presses his cheek against the top of my head and tightens his arms around my waist.

It's a long time before either of us moves again.

CHAPTER 29

Present

It's only when I look up to see Mitch's truck pulling around the corner that I realise where we are. My back is pressed up against the stone walls of Tate's church. I'm supposing that he was looking for a little divine intervention tonight, but even as I stand with a tear-soaked cross digging into my chest I'm not so sure that that's how it works.

Tate turns his head towards the familiar rumble of the engine and I can see that he's scoping the cab interior, to ensure that Mitch is alone. Satisfied, he dips his head back down to mine, pressing a light kiss to the tip of my cheek as he hauls me up and around his waist. He walks us over to the truck and he opens the door to the backseat before setting me down and guiding me in by my hips. Once Tate closes the door he pulls me onto his lap and then straps us both under the belt. Mitch turns one-eighty so that he can get a look at us in the seat behind him. His eyes flick between us for a few seconds and then they finally settle on me.

"He's gone, just so you know," he says, and I let out a low whistle of relief, despite Tate growing tense beneath me. I don't ever want to see Hudson again so I'm grateful that he's gone - but the remembrance that he will forever be an eternal fixture in the life of Tate's mom, and by extension the life of *Tate*, makes the situation bittersweet — heavy on the bitter.

"This shit with your mom…" Mitch continues, running his hand anxiously through his hair. "Because you aren't eighteen yet you don't have much leeway in terms of independent choice. Your mom's so livid that she wants you wholly moved out by tomorrow morning."

Tate's arms, which are wrapped firmly across my chest and stomach, tighten significantly. I feel like a child's favourite toy as it's being taken away from them, when their parents believe that it's time to grow up.

"Not happening," Tate bites, and his hands begin to clutch at places that are frankly inappropriate to have Mitch's attention drawn to.

Mitch's eyes flash to mine as if he's thinking the exact same thing that I am, and he inhales sharply, turning around so that he doesn't have to watch. He props one elbow on his doorframe as he wipes his other hand down his face. After a moment of torn contemplation Mitch twists the key in the ignition and kicks the car into gear.

Tate claps his palm over his dad's shoulder rest and husks out in a gravelly voice, "I want you to take the long way home."

Mitch snorts. "Ha. If you think that I'm gonna chauffeur you around so that you have enough time to get it inside of her then you've got *another* thing coming." He's shaking his head but I swear that he takes a wrong turn on the road from the church.

"Then let me help her pack up her room," Tate says.

Mitch breathes out another laugh. "Real subtle, Tate. You think that her mom isn't going to be able to hear you cracking my walls when you're ramming her headboard into them a mile a minute? Not to mention my house full of *guests*." He makes an anguished sound as he rubs his forehead. "If you're looking for a place to carry out your goodbye sex then you're gonna have to think up something real crafty, 'cause her mom isn't gonna let you *any*where near that girl. Like, I'm serious. You go over to their house and she's gonna slash your tyres. She told me."

Tate's breathing is so irregular that I'm actually worried for him. I turn my head so that I can look at him and his eyes have gone glassy. As soon as my mouth is in his proximity he takes my chin and lifts my lips to his, the hand in my lap suddenly stroking harder. The pained look on his face is splitting my heart irreparably. When he pulls away he holds my cheek against his chest and I can feel the quick thudding of his heartbeat as he mutters, "It's not goodbye sex. I'm keeping her."

A constricting ache grips at my temples and I push my forehead into his shirt.

Tate laces his fingers through my hair as he whispers, "I just got her back."

Mitch lets out a loud exhalation through his nose as he drives down the street adjacent to his own, and I listen to the sound of him impatiently rapping his fingers against the steering wheel. Just before he reaches the corner he pulls up onto the curb and stops the truck.

Mitch clears his throat. "You all decent back there?"

It is all decent back here, which is surprising considering the thick slope that I can feel digging into my backside. As if he can read my mind Tate shifts beneath me, gripping his fingers into my hips, and then he rubs his way up and down my core. The spike in Tate's adrenaline levels has made him rough and sloppy tonight, so much more out of control than he usually allows himself to be, and my body is burning up for it. I cover my mouth with my hand, too overwhelmed and confused to take arousal on top of all of my other emotions right now, and Tate buries his face into my hair with a groan.

Mitch gives us a few seconds and then he turns around. Whatever my expression is showing, he doesn't comment. Instead he looks at me calmly and asks in a kind paternal voice, "What happened outside of my house tonight?"

Although we are all rampant with anxiety and high from the fight, the energy in Mitch's truck - with the little orange interior light turned on and the merciful mist of heating coming through - is so warm and comforting that I can't help but spill it all out to him. Tate's heavenly temperate radiates from his chest into my back as his palms stroke up and down my arms. Mitch keeps one hand pressed over his mouth as I recount how Tate and I met, what subsequently happened with Hudson, and how we were both mislead by the fine points of the situation, only now having the reality of that day come to light. I'm surrounded by the undivided attention of the Coleson men and I have never felt so safe in my entire life.

When I finish Mitch interlocks the fingers of both of his hands and holds them palm-out to his forehead. He lets out a quiet gush of air and shakes his head, looking out of the side window as he gathers his thoughts.

It takes him a minute before he returns his gaze to mine. "Does she know?" he asks.

I blink. Too much has happened for me to know exactly what he's talking about.

He spells it out for me. "It's been a shit night, for you especially, but forget about your mom not wanting you to date outside of the Ivy League for a minute. Does she know about what happened with Hudson?"

I stare at him until he gathers my answer from the ringing silence.

He nods and then sighs. "If she doesn't... you should tell her."

Telling my mom the depth of my feelings for Tate *and*

about my horrible past with Hudson won't change the fact that a life with Tate also now means a life with his step-brother. Tate presses a kiss to the side of my neck and I hug his arms more firmly around me. "It won't change anything," I say.

Mitch gives me a sympathetic look. "You never know. It might change everything."

He turns back around and we sit in silence for a minute, my body growing more and more weary as the weight of the night settles down on me. I recline sleepily into Tate's chest, mentally and physically exhausted, and he silently kisses his way up my cheek. I'm embarrassed that even after seeing Hudson, who I would personally like to dismember, and after feeling the emotional severance with my mom, after her realising that I'm nothing more than a red-blooded teenager, I still want Tate. Part of me doesn't care that I would have to endure Hudson for the rest of my life. I just want Tate.

As if he can sense the little flame rekindling in his backseat Mitch points his finger at Tate and then jerks his thumb over his shoulder. "Gotta get out, kid."

Tate moves his fingers to my chin and tips my head towards him. The tenderness in his eyes makes me ache. "Just 'til you're eighteen, right? Then I can come and get you."

I duck my head down as the tears overspill. I feel his chest shake under my touch and that's it. I'm falling into the most anguished pain that I have ever felt.

Mitch's door opens with a click and, before he slams it shut, he says quietly, "Y'all have one minute and then she's got to go, okay?"

I look up at Tate, glittery-eyed. "I have to think of my mom, Tate. And it's not just that – it's Hudson now, too. Now that he knows, he's going to be everywhere. He'll make my life hell, and I don't want to go through that again." I'm trying not to sound like I'm sobbing but it's hard to keep it under control anymore.

Tate is shaking his head as he rubs the tears from my cheeks with the heels of his hands. "Stop thinking about everyone else, River - no one else matters. I want it to be you and me. If you move in with me after you graduate he'll never know where you are. I'll never let him near you again."

"You can't promise that," I argue. "He's in your mom's life for good, and she doesn't owe me anything."

"If I told her what he did she would never let him in her house again."

I shake my head. "If she loves his dad then this won't change her mind."

Tate's grip on my face becomes more desperate as he tilts my head further back. "Forget about him. Tell me you'll come back to me." I try to hide my face but he isn't having any of it, pressing his lips against mine and kissing me deeply. I pull away and shove at his heaving chest. He grabs my hand as I move to unfasten the seatbelt and he practically embeds it over his heart. "Goddammit River, tell me that you aren't giving up on us."

I don't reply. He squeezes his eyes shut and pinches the bridge of his nose, letting out a loud groan that's as pained as it is angry.

He opens his eyes and cups his hands under my jaw. "Are you fucking serious?" he asks, his gentle voice contradicting the rage and the heartache in his words. His searing eyes search mine frantically. "I've wanted you for my entire life. I've been in *love* with you for my entire life. Can't you see this? Can't you see what we have? We won't ever find this with another person – I know that I won't. It's only going to *ever* be like this with you, River." I bite down hard on my lip as he presses his forehead to mine, and a lone tear runs down his cheek. "Only with you."

I hold onto him for the remainder of our minute, but as soon as Mitch opens the door I wipe away my tears and leave.

CHAPTER 30

Five Months Later

I stare at the dress on my bed in contemplation as the late May glow shimmers in through the window. On the one side of my bed lies a white shirt – my usual uniform shirt – folded over a pair of black dress pants. It's boring, because this is what I wear all the time, and it's alternative in a way that doesn't even match up to my personality. Either way it's not what I want.

Yet looking at the pants option doesn't make me feel like I'm about to vomit up my intestines, much unlike the dress. Whereas my Homecoming dress from three years ago was sweet, with its baby pink bodice and clouds of tulle, this dress is demure and sophisticated. It's a full waterfall of black satin, starting right under my neck and draping all the way to the floor, with bare arms to expose my skin and a sweeping cowl back to… well, I suppose to do the exact same thing there, too. Don't get me wrong, it's not flashy – I'll be utterly blend-in-able if I choose this dress – and it matches the Old Hollywood theme for our senior prom perfectly. But still, I can't help the anxious flutter I feel in my stomach when I look down at it, nor the flashbacks that resurface.

No more skirts.

I pick up the hem and run the smooth material over my fingers. It's so glossy that it almost glitters in the early evening sunlight streaming into my room from over the roof of Tate's former home. The warm summer scents of sweet-pea blossom and coconut suntan lotion drift in from outside, and I drop the dress from my hand as I fold my arms and look out across the street. My room is bigger than it used to be after the reno that Mitch's guys did, but other than the extra space, it's still pretty much exactly the same as it was before. The memories sure as hell have hung tight. The all-consuming tension in my chest dulled down after the first month, but it never seemed to fully go away. Once I get my exam results and I subsequently know whether or not I'll be admitted to my college choices the pain will have to go. I'll move away and I'll move on. I'll be so busy with school - a whole *lifetime* of school – that I won't have time to dwell on my desires. My mom will be happy. I won't have to worry about Hudson.

But I won't have Tate.

I suppose he will have already moved on, and I can't blame him. If I was him, I would have moved on too. Why spend your time pining over somebody like me, someone who is too shocked to even say *I love you* back, when you could have someone fun, beautiful, normal? I think that I may have pushed him away too hard this time.

And it's not as if he didn't try, for months, repeatedly. He *did* come round to try and talk to my mom and she *did* warn him that she would slash his tyres if he didn't get the hell away from her property. She didn't need to confiscate my phone from me because I never had his number to begin with, but she has made an effort to fit me into her schedule more, mainly so that she can pick me up after school and ensure that I haven't been whisked off my feet by the knight in denim jeans and a motorcycle jacket.

She has slowly been reintroducing Mitch back into her own life – they took a break for the first month and then started to see each other once every few weeks, whether as friends or partners I do not know, but he hasn't been around here at all. She told me that Mitch wants to see me but she told *him* that he shouldn't hold his breath.

Overall, I feel very Bella Swan spinning-round-on-her-chair empty.

But at least my mom is happy.

There's a knock on my door and I instantly check the time on my phone. It flashes 18:35. Doors open to our prom at seven so I need to get going soon. I promised Kit that I would be there, and it would be nice to see all of our efforts – making posters and banners and menus and playlists – having their moment after all.

"Yes?" I ask, and my mom opens the door. She's been out all afternoon, which is weird because she wasn't working today, and she looks a bit flushed, like maybe she caught the sun.

Or like maybe she's been crying.

"You should just go like this," she jokes, jerking her chin to gesture at my attire. I'm wearing plaid pyjama pants and a baby pink tank top, but my hair is floofed up out of its usual scrunchie prison, and I've applied some mascara and lip-gloss.

I nod in agreement, although my arms tighten across my chest. "It would be very me," I admit.

"Kit would do something like that," she remarks, but I don't comment. I feel like I have a right to be slightly bitter. *What do you know about my personal life, mom?*

When she takes a step inside my room I know that something is up. I move closer to the window so that I can take in some deeper inhalations of the fresh May air, and I watch her cautiously as she moves to stand in front of my prom outfit choices, her hand pressed against her cheek. She rolls her lips into her mouth so that it becomes a tense flat line, and then she sighs as she lets it go.

"I met up with Mitch today," she says.

My stomach instantly drops. Is she baiting me? This feels like a trick conversation starter, so I stare back at her in silence.

She rubs her palm up her forehead and then gestures down to an empty spot on my bed. "Can we sit?"

She can sense my suspicions from the waves of tension rolling off my body and she holds her hands up to me in surrender. My stomach drops further. "We had a conversation," she continues, and her voice is a little shakier now. She takes a seat at the edge of my bed and nods her head for me to do the same. Immobilised, I ignore her and grip onto the window ledge for dear life. "About you," she finishes.

I turn around and drop my elbows onto the window sill, gripping my hair in my fingers and willing myself not to ruin my amazing spidery mascara. *Don't cry, River. Do. Not. Cry.*

"He told me that you had told him something – on that night... the night of the world's most ironic housewarming party – and that it was really important that I asked you about it. It had something to do with his son and something to do with that boy who was there, too."

She pauses for a minute, expecting me to turn around, but I don't. I look up and stare across the street, right into the room that used to belong to Tate. How long will he haunt me? When will this feeling end?

"I'm going to admit this to you right now," she says, matter-of-factly. "I absolutely forced him to tell me everything. I mean, I know that – gentleman that he is – he undeniably spared specific details for your sake, but I couldn't risk you *not* telling me something that even *he* believed to be highly significant. I'm really sorry that I did this behind your back, but I'm not sorry that I now know the truth." She pauses again and a whole minute goes by without us saying a single word. For a moment, I think that I can hear her crying. "I can't believe that this happened to you, and that you were so afraid of what *I* may think that you didn't tell me. I wish it had never happened to you... and I wish that I had been there to help you through it."

I shake my head but I actually feel a weight lift from my shoulders. Maybe Mitch was right – a problem shared is a problem halved. I feel powerful to be seen in the light of such naked truth.

I guess a guy with shoulders like Mitch's would know a thing or two about carrying a heavy burden.

"I don't want pity," I say finally, turning back to her. My eyes are, to my own amazement, dry.

"I know, River. You're a strong girl. I *wanted* you to be a strong girl, which is why I guess that you didn't tell me. But, honey, I think that you were almost *too* strong. And then, on top of all of that, having *me* make you feel guilty about falling in love with Mitch's son?" She puts her head in her hand for a moment, as if ashamed, and then looks up at me with pinched brows and a set jaw. "Who am *I* to dictate to you? I'm a *single mom*, River. And, honestly, I have never seen a boy so dead-set on breaking a girl out of her house. You have no idea the amount of nights that I had to kick him off our front drive."

Actually I do. I could hear them outside every single night, and I made a note in my journal every single time. No words needed. Just a little heart.

"It doesn't matter," I say, moving to pick up my shirt and pants, hoping that she'll get the message and clear the hell out. "His mom's step-son kind of raped me, so I am officially not going to ever be involved with their family."

She stands up and places herself in front of me. "That's why we were out so long today, River. Giving up on Tate because of some pseudo-connection to... *Hudson*..." She eyes me warily for a second and then she lets out a rush of air, as if she's diving into the deep end whether I like it or not. "I told Hudson's father. Declan King, he's a cop. And his son's badness isn't... hereditary. Declan was mortified, and he won't *ever* let Hudson be around you again. I mean, I'm sure it's not from a place of total innocence on his dad's part – Pamela was absolutely disgusted, and you could press charges – but it's a start. Don't let one asshole get in the way of you doing whatever it is that you want. And I mean *whatever* you want. Not what I want." She straightens her spine. "You want a gap year to figure out what you want? Take it. You want to say *fuck college* and live like a nomad? Do it." She steps closer and gives me a look that travels past my irises and into my soul. "You want to date Mitch's son and start a future with him? Then that's exactly what you should do. I have been absent, stifling, dictatorial, and I am *so ashamed*. You let go of the good, but now it's time to let go of the bad. I will be making this up to you forever River, starting now, but most importantly I want you to know that you have options."

Tears are burning in my eyes but not because of what she just said. I'm emotional because moments like this always come too late. Tate won't be waiting for me anymore, I have no idea what to do if I *don't* go to college, and I'm about to be late to my prom. Triple fuck.

There isn't enough time for me fully digest my mom's words and she thankfully makes no move to embrace me in my overwhelmed state, but a palpable sensation squeezes between us in silent promise. *You. Have. Options.*

The sun burns a little brighter on my back as I drop the shirt and pants onto the floor, and lean across the quilt to pick up my dress.

CHAPTER 31

Present

I hand the driver a twenty, giving her a quick *thanks* before I step out of the cab onto the gravel. I close the door and she peels away, kicking up a little dust cloud in her wake as I take a step backwards to look up at the exterior of the hotel. Dammit Kit. I could get a little teary eyed thinking about how brilliant my best friend in the whole wide world is.

The white pillars which stand tall above the porch steps are wrapped up in black chiffon and twinkling yellow fairy lights, switched on despite the evening sun still glowing. A little red carpet is spread in front of the open wooden doors and inside I see the huge cardboard Hollywood sign that Kit and I spent two weeks of lunch breaks at school perfecting. The black and white film posters that I designed are hung in black baroque frames, and my little fake cinema tickets are strewn across every table, mantle, and desk.

There are a few older boys smoking and milling around by the entrance, presumably the band that we hired, but I don't bother looking at them as I take my first steps inside.

I can hear loud instrumental filler music playing from a stereo, and I walk directly ahead to follow the noise. Just before I round the corner to the right to step inside of the main hall, Kit barrels out like a tornado and throws herself into my arms. For some reason, my throat constricts and my eyes prickle as if I'm about to cry.

"This is awesome," I croak out. My voice is hoarse and whispery, and when she pulls back I can see how round and glassy her eyes have become too. Neither of us knows what our precarious futures will hold, but what we *do* know is how few high school friends stay close post-graduation. She gives me a soft half-smile and it sends us both fully over the edge.

I choke out a little sob but I will the tears to stay in my eyes. I did not spend five whole minutes applying mascara to cry it off in ten seconds.

"*This* is awesome," Kit replies, prodding me roughly in my bony chest. I concave and whine, tears forgotten as I jab her back in the fleshy bit under her arm. She laughs and takes my hand, half-dragging me into the main room. It's all draped velvet curtains and obscene crystal chandeliers glinting in the late evening glow. Our classmates are sat and stood around tables, taking group photos and willing each other to dance. It's not really me but I guess it's kind of... nice.

"Sort of sexy, right?" Kit asks, glancing at me from beneath thick black lashes. Her long onyx hair is spilling over her shoulders, and her bright pink cheeks give her a Snow White flush.

I nod, leaning down to pick up a handful of the fake hundred-dollar bills that I made, and then I shower them like confetti into the air above us. A bright flash to our left momentarily blinds me, and I glance over to see a guy in a loosened tux holding a bulky camera up to his face. I blink at him and then become even more confused as I notice that, stood beside him, is evidently the person who is the actual photographer. He lowers the camera and my eyes widen exponentially.

Madden is grinning down at us, a guitar pick clenched between his teeth and his eyes glinting like knives. He hands the camera back to the photographer, who rolls her eyes as she walks away from him, and then, with his hands in his pockets, Madden steps languorously closer to us. He gives Kit a thorough once-over and I can't help but blush at the obvious insinuation of his stare. She's watching him with a bored expression, one eyebrow cocked, and her arms folded neatly over her suit jacket. His lip-ring sparkles under the crystal refractions from the chandelier and, after removing the pick from his mouth, he rolls the ring steadily with the tip of his tongue.

"River, this is Madden," Kit says, sighing. "He's one of the guys in the band, and he's really annoying. Madden, this is River – she's my best friend, and she's off-limits."

My eyebrows practically hit my hairline as I watch their stare-off. I feel anxious seeing Madden but I'm not really sure why. Maybe it's because he makes me think about Tate, and Tate is more than likely using his finally found freedom to fuck his way around this town with his God of Thunder body.

Good for him.

I try to unclench my teeth.

Good. For. Him.

Madden tosses the guitar pick into the air, re-catching it over and over again with long deft fingers. *Ooookay.*

"Don't need to tell *me* that she's off-limits," he says finally, his eyes flicking to me with razor sharpness. Jesus. I can only imagine what goes on in that head of his for his gaze to be so cutting. "I've known that for a *loooooong* time," he finishes, and he flashes us his perfect white teeth.

I cross my arms over my chest, mirroring Kit. We must look like the two most hostile girls in the entire State, let alone in this room. "Actually-" I begin, but he holds up two fingers, his pick wedged between them like a cigarette.

"Yeah, I'm sure," he says, and then he jerks his head to the stage. "Got some things to do," he drawls and then, with one last look at Kit, he turns on his heel and stalks back to where he came from.

What the fuck?

I spin to look at Kit for some sort of explanation but she's already giving me her *don't even ask* eye-roll and head-shake. I glance over to the stage and see that the other guys from outside have joined Madden, retuning their probably already perfectly tuned guitars, and turning down the track on the stereo so that they can resume their role.

"A drink?" Kit says, and then she hauls me by the arm to the long table at the right side of the room without waiting for a response.

Nice try, but I am not one to be distracted. I stare open-mouthed at Madden as he runs his fingers up and down the neck of the guitar, his eyes trained on me like a laser-pointer, with a knowing and expectant expression quirking up the corner of his mouth. Should I be unsettled? My brain says yes, but my intuition isn't sensing a danger. I narrow my eyes on him as he makes a test-strum. He taps his nose to tease *I've got a secret.*

"Here," Kit shoves a tumbler of something carbonated and sparkling into my chest but, unaware, I jolt and it sloshes down my front.

"*Shit*," I hiss and her cheeks flush crimson. Why is everyone so on edge today? I look around for a paper napkin but I don't see any, so I squeeze the hem of her sleeve reassuringly as I shout over the mounting volume of the band's guitars, "I'm gonna run to the bathroom, I'll be right back."

As I weave back through the groups and tables to the entrance of the room, the curtains are drawn and all of the lights dim as the music explodes from the stage. I'm almost at the doors which have since been pulled shut when the song finally registers in my body. Heavy chords from the guitar slam down, emphasised by the drummer who is battering the tom with the force of Thor's fucking hammer, and a shiver runs down my spine as I prepare for the lyrics that I know I'm about to hear.

This isn't what we put on our suggested playlist.

But I know this song all too well.

I turn around and see that everyone has crowded into the pseudo mosh-pit area in front of the stage, teachers guarding the perimeters, but I don't focus on them. My eyes are locked in with Madden, who only occasionally looks away from me so that he can glance down at his fingers as they flex over the strings. The vocalist next to him wraps his hand around the mic and, even though my body knows what is coming, my mouth drops agape when I hear the lyrics.

I'm angry and he can tell, but Madden's expression remains unflinching. I storm from the back of the room with the intentions of worming my way to the front of the crowd but, given the compactness of the swarm, there's no way that I can get my hands on him. God knows what I'll be capable of when I *do*.

Could he possibly know? Did Tate tell him? *Until The End* was my favourite song on the Phobia album that I gave to Tate when I was fourteen, the one that I know he still keeps in his Ford, and as the band rocks through the song, the lyrics start to hit a little harder than they used to.

What is he saying? This song is about post-desolation hope, so I'm pretty clear on the symbolism, but if this is Madden's attempt at a joke then he's about to meet a very unhappy ending, starting with my fist and ending with his face. Sensing eyes on me, I stand on my tip-toes and look over to the far right of the crowd. I catch Kit signalling me with a *what the frick is going on* expression regarding the band's playlist mutiny, her arms raised in confusion. I mirror her with a head shake that says *me and you both, sister*.

I flick my gaze back to Madden and his face has subsequently twisted, as if he's trying to hide a smile. His steel eyes watch me mockingly from beneath his veil of spiky black hair and, newly recharged with vengeance, I draw my thumb across my throat to let him know that he's a dead guitarist walking.

When he strikes the last note I shove my way through the tide of bodies, newly loosened as they air-punch and holler, and I don't stop until I'm eight feet below his cocky little grin. Everyone is too distracted to notice us – bar the guy whose foot I just impaled with my ice-pick stiletto – as I scream up at him, "What the *hell* was that?!"

He grips the mic stand from in front of his band mate and tilts it towards his smug up-turned lips. He murmurs into it, "River, your ride out front is blocking the road, if you would be so kind as to move it."

I'm half-tempted to lob my shoe at him. "I don't *have* a ride out front," I grit out.

He cocks an eyebrow at me and then drops down so that he's squatting in front of my face. The band behind him begins plucking up the intro to a new song, keeping the crowd satiated, but Madden leans forward and whispers to me, "You sure about that?"

He rises up and mouths at me *go*, before turning around and walking to the other side of the stage so that he doesn't have to deal with me anymore. I narrow my eyes on him for a few seconds and then spin around, pushing my way back through the throng, ready to find out what this asshole has up his sleeve.

I push through the wooden doors and I'm momentarily disorientated. It's so much darker than it was fifteen minutes ago. The deep twilight hues are bleeding in through the floor-to-ceiling windows and it takes me a few seconds to remember which way I came from. I turn left towards the entrance and I start walking at as quick a pace as I can manage. I shove my glasses back up my nose as I make it to the front of the foyer, stabbing through the plush red carpet, and then descending the wide porch steps with Cinderella haste.

And then I freeze.

He steps around from the side of the truck, uncrossing his arms from the front of his white button-down shirt, and I stare at him in shock, my mouth popped into an open *o*.

Tate looks up at me.

I shakily make my way down the last two steps, my fingers holding up the black satin so that it doesn't slip under my stilettos, and I try to gulp in enough oxygen to keep up with the frantic jack-hammering of my heartbeat.

When my feet reach the gravel I look up at him with a pinched brow, chewing my lips out of sheer nervousness. He takes a cautious step forward and, when I don't retreat, he takes another. He stops when he's about six feet away from me and my heart is in my throat for him to close that distance. I'm the sorry one now. I'm the one in the wrong.

"What are you…" I begin, but my voice is quiet and small. I do a little cough and try again. "What are you doing here?"

He watches me carefully, his chest rising and falling under his suit shirt. I can't believe what I'm seeing right now. Tate Coleson, no nonsense jeans-and-a-t-shirt Tate Coleson, is dressed for prom. His shirt is crisp and pressed, and I'm fairly sure that the reason why the top buttons remain unfastened is because they simply can't stretch any further across the expanse of his chest. His black pants show off an anatomical level of bulging thigh muscles, and my heart swells when I see that he's wearing his dark brown leather belt through the loops. *Just so Tate.*

He takes another step forward and this time I do too. I don't feel as though he's here to reprimand me, punish me, or gloat. I can still feel every ounce of the sincerity and promise that he has always bestowed on me, radiating between us into the warm May air. My erratically pumping pulse and the buzzing summer mosquitoes are the only sounds to fill the stillness of the dawning-night.

"Two reasons," he says, and the deep timbre of his voice jolts straight down my spine. On instinct I take another step forward – a big one – and he does the same. We're barely two steps apart now. I'm practically shivering with longing, fear, anticipation. "Something happened with your mom today." He moves one hand to scratch the back of his neck and my eyes roam over the swell of his bicep. My yearning is unhinged and Tate's arm flexes under my gaze, as responsive to it as if I had physically touched him. "She came round with my dad and she wanted to talk – to apologise. It was surreal," he states, and then he takes another step closer. "But I'm taking it."

I'm ready to fall into his arms but I keep the tangible inches of air pressed between us. The evening has grown so balmy that I can taste it on my tongue.

"What's the second reason?" I ask, my hush-puppy eyes sparkling up at him, alight with tears that I refuse to shed as I clench my jaw to stop the wobble.

He remains silent for five, ten, twenty seconds, as if he's gauging what's going on inside my brain, and then he takes the final step forward. Our bodies remain un-touching, but if I was to lift up my pinkie finger I would be able to graze the black fabric enveloping his thigh.

"Because you turned eighteen yesterday, baby," he says softly, "so I had to come and get my girl."

I jump into his hold just as he wraps his hands around my hips, lifting me in a swoop so that he can meet my lips with his. A light sound, somewhere between agony and relief, releases from my chest at the feel of him holding me again, and Tate replies with a deep protective growl. I grip my arms around his neck, tangling my fingers into my hair, as he holds me tight and kisses me sweet. I melt against the solid crests of his chest as he turns us around so that he can walk us back to his car. When my calves meet the door he sets me down and pulls away so that he can look at me. His warm hands find their way into the open back of my dress, sliding firmly up the sides of my rib-cage until his thumbs brush against my nipples, and I make a little gasp.

His eyes are trained on my mouth.

"Lip gloss," I say thickly.

His eyes are hooding a little. "Haven't seen you in that since Homecoming," he murmurs quietly, and I roll my lips together, feeling self-conscious. He removes one of his hands from the front of my dress, making a shudder rip through my nerve-endings, and he plies my bottom lip out with his thumb, before rubbing the pad of it over the rosy swell. "Looks good on you," he finishes. Then he dips back down to take it with his own.

"I'm sorry," I whisper as he spoils me with kisses, up my cheeks and down my neck. "I shouldn't have given up like that. I should have fought harder." My voice is hoarse.

He shakes his head and then presses his forehead to mine. "You went through so much. *I'm* sorry, baby. But I'm here now, and I'll be here always. Whatever you want, you're going to get."

I bite into my lip, my earlier worries resurfacing. "But college- now that my mom's set me free I don't know what I want to do about it all. I'm so fucked," I say, tears threatening to fall.

He grips my jaw in his hands. Heat shoots in my belly. "We'll talk about it, baby. We'll figure it out. *I'll* figure it out. 'Til then I wanna take you to my place and..." He looks deep into my eyes. "And I'm gonna take care of you now. For as long as you'll let me."

He crowds my body against the passenger door before he leans down to kiss me again, one hand entangling in my blown-out curls and the other fisted on the hood of the truck.

I pull back, gasping, as another brain cell resurfaces. At this point, it's one of few. "The song- and the band- did you get Madden to play-"

He shuts me up by pressing his mouth firmly to mine, a low growl rumbling in his chest. Okay, I guess the answer to that is pretty obvious, plus I can quiz him as much as I want tomorrow morning when I wake up in *his bed*.

And not the one in Mitch's house – I'm talking about finally going to *Tate's* house, wherever the hell that is. I run my hands up over his shoulders and then move one of them to meet his fingers cupping the back of my neck.

He makes a quiet startled sound and pulls away slightly, his eyes moving to our hands. I look up at him surprised – did I scratch him or something? – but then he looks down bashfully and shakes his head as if to clear it.

"Uh," he starts, and he swallows thickly. "So this is a *I'm taking you back* kinda moment, right?" he asks, his cheekbones glowing sunset-red.

I blink up at him confused but nod anyway. "Yeah, obviously," I say, trying to pull his face back down to mine.

He laughs shyly and then nods. "Thank God for that," he says, and then he moves the hand from my hair so that it's resting over his chest.

My eyes instantly move to his hand and my mouth drops open. I read the letters freshly inked into his knuckles in neatly scripted capitals.

RIVER.

Just like he always said he would.

My fingers fly up to my face and I burst into tears. He breathes out a laugh as he pulls me into his chest, cradling my head against the open collar of his shirt, his beautiful strong scent filling the air around me.

"The only word I never fuck up," he jokes, but it only makes me sob harder. The most faithful person that I have ever met has branded his inhumanely incredible body with my name, *permanently*.

How did I get so lucky?

I lean my head back so that I can look up at him, taking

257

off my smudged glasses so that I can get a clearer view, and he wipes the mascara tracks from my cheeks with the rough pad of his thumb. His eyes glitter against the setting blaze of the sun and they are the most beautiful colour that I have ever seen. Molten. Sparkling. *Mine.*

I have to say the words clearly because you only have one try at saying it for the first time, so I swallow hard and take a few deep breaths before I go in. I run my hands up his neck and lock my fingers into his hair. I didn't say it before but there's no way anyone could stop me from saying it now. We have both waited long enough.

"Tate," I say, all hoarse and quiet because my emotions are insane right now.

He's smiling down at me, jerking his chin to say *yes* before he settles his forehead down against mine again.

I clench his hair tighter as I pray for the strength to get this out right. I pull back so that I can look at his perfect face, and his eyes meet mine with patience, adoration, and trust.

"I love you."

Those three words are all that I have the time to get out before Tate crashes his lips back down to mine and he shows me how much he loves me too.

EPILOGUE

One Year Later – December

The blinding morning light streams in through the open curtains, pulled back from the patio doors that lead from the bedroom to the porch. I blink at the whiteness all around me – white pillow, white walls, white duvet – before scrunching my eyes shut again and wiggling backwards into Tate's warm body. One of his arms lies under my waist so that his thumb can rub up and down my stomach, and his other hand – the hand which reads my name – is holding my hip, tracing gentle patterns onto my skin with the hypnotising tips of his fingers.

After taking a year out to reapply to different courses and different colleges from my first time around, whilst working as Mitch's sole PR and design assistant to amount a little cash to go towards my college fund, I started college in October as a Literature major. Tate came over at literally every moment that Mitch didn't have him working, but now that it's my first winter break I'm going to be staying at his house over Christmas.

Well, it's not so much a house really. The little wooden chalet which overlooks Silver Lake has the cosy warmth of a cabin to it, but with no other residents anywhere in the vicinity.

Tate drove across to my campus yesterday to come and pick me up, and we arrived back to his place just as the night dawned. We talked whilst he was driving but once we got to the lake house there were other things that we wanted to spend our time doing.

I turn around and look up at him. He's laying contentedly, eyes shut, with a steadily heaving chest that lets me know that he's awake. I scoot closer to him so that I can press a kiss to the cavern between his pecs, and a satisfied groan quietly escapes his throat.

His hands roam until they are holding me just beneath my armpits, and he lifts my torso so that my head is resting at the same height as his on the pillow. Then he manoeuvres himself so that he can roll his body on top of me, hitching my knees up around his waist, as he settles between my legs and presses his lips into my neck.

"Hey angel," he murmurs, his morning voice deep and consuming. I shudder beneath his bodyweight and I wrap myself tighter around him. I should probably mention that, although I'm wearing his t-shirt and soft boxer briefs, he is top-to-bottom naked.

He laughs quietly and tries to angle his hips away from me. Not so easy when you're borderline centaur. When he lifts himself up onto his flattened palms there are still inches of hardened muscle dragging across my thigh.

I reach down to touch him and he restrains my hands, a secretive smile playing across his lips. Even half-asleep he has more strength than his tiny nymphomaniac girlfriend. "Baby, no," he chuckles.

Um, baby *yes*. I lift one calf so that it's resting against his shoulder and I pull the shirt up over my head. He sucks in a breath as he looks down at me but he unclenches his jaw and reconfigures my limbs like a Rubik's cube.

I look up at him with a sad little expression and he presses chaste kisses up and down my cheeks.

"There's something I want to do first," he whispers, and then he pulls us upright so that we can look out of the windows.

I'm instantly dazzled as my eyes meet the shimmering blanket of snow carpeting the porch just beyond the bedroom, all the way down to the gravel and sand, right up to the edge of the lake's smooth surface. It really is called Silver Lake for a reason. I lean over to the dresser so that I can put on my glasses and then, wrapped up in Tate's tan arms, I stare at the view some more.

"Nice, huh?" he says, bouncing me on his lap as I take it all in. Obviously I could feel the crunch of the snow beneath my boots when we arrived last night, but under the cold morning sunlight it looks like a whole other planet out there.

"Let's go outside for a minute, okay?" he asks, and my eyes instantly shoot to his.

"Aren't we... I thought we were going to..." I attempt to roll his boxers down my hips whilst simultaneously running my palm over his length. It's been two weeks since the last time he could visit me on campus so now that I have him beneath me I feel desperately hungry. I'm Oliver Twist with his little bowl of porridge. *Please sir, may I have some cock?*

He kisses my neck consolingly and says, "I just want to show you one thing first."

I pull a face but I trust him, so I let him move away to shuck on a pair of briefs and his jeans, quickly sliding the tongue of his belt through the thick metal buckle, and then throwing on a shirt and a jacket. He pulls me by my ankles to the edge of the mattress, pushing his pyjama pants up my legs, but he does stop for a minute after he glances at my chest, running his fingers over me before taking me in his mouth. I clutch him tightly to my body but he groans and pulls away, looking around to find another shirt and my winter coat, and then we walk to the patio doors to put on our socks and boots.

He pushes open the door and I'm met with the crisp soundless air, snow twinkling up at us from every available surface. He gives my ass a firm little spank and I yelp out of my reverie, scowling up at his annoyingly attractive face with narrowed eyes and a frown. He grabs my cheeks, already frozen pink, and smashes his mouth down onto mine, a laugh reverberating in his chest as I bite him petulantly. I push him away and trudge sulkily through the snow to the edge of the lake. Okay, it's beautiful, but it could have waited another fifteen minutes. Or another twenty-five minutes. Or even another hour, I don't care, I've missed him, alright?

I stand at the water's edge, waiting for him to come up behind me, and I look down at my reflection in the crystallised surface. My hair is spilling around me in thick curls and waves, mussed up from the night before, and my eyes – although feigning irritation – are bright like the sky above me. I almost startle as I watch myself because my expression is so full of hope and wonder and love. I breathe out a sigh, and it mists in the cold air around me. I don't think that I could be any happier than I am in this very moment, and what a nice feeling that is to have.

"Tate?" I ask, not feeling his body behind me. I turn around to see where he's gone to and my breath catches in my throat. My lungs empty. If my boots weren't impaled ten-inches deep in the snow I would have probably fallen over.

Tate is down on one knee, his hands clasping a little leather box, and when my rounded eyes flash to his, the fingers with my name inked across them gently ease open the lid. Sat inside a plump cushioned bed is a large twinkling diamond, so bright and multifaceted in the winter sunlight that it sends millions of refractions sparkling across Tate's sun-kissed skin.

"I've wanted to do this since you were fourteen years old," he says. My eyes sting as I hold back a sob. "And I needed it to be perfect for my girl, so I thought I should write a speech."

My vision blurs, so I quickly push up my glasses for a moment and wipe the heels of my hands over my eyes. Ever since Tate told me about his dyslexia he has been trying so hard to improve all of the things that he didn't prioritise during high school. I love him so much, and my heart constricts painfully when I think about him putting pressure on himself like this.

I readjust my glasses so that they're back in place and he jerks his chin to my coat.

"Check your pocket, baby," he says, eyes on the silver zipper.

With shaking fingers I pull down the zip and put my hand inside. When I feel a little piece of folded paper I can't keep my tears back any longer. They're streaming down my face like a waterfall as I choke out, "Please tell me that this isn't what I think it is."

He waits for me to pull it out and when I open it up I clutch my chest in anguished heartache. It's a marriage proposal – and it's handwritten. My eyes trail to the neat black question mark at the end of the last sentence and I can barely see for my tears.

I shake my head and I hear Tate's quiet laugh as he stands up to pull me against his chest. I clutch my fingers into the fabric of his coat as he caresses my head with his free hand, his biceps securing my body to his.

"Want to read it later?" he asks, a smile in his voice.

I nod and tilt backwards so that I can look at him. He sees my face and pulls an adoring expression, stroking the backs of his fingers over my salt-stained skin.

"I need to say the important bits now though, okay?" he asks, before pressing a kiss to the tip of my cheek.

"Okay," I whisper, wrapping my arms around his waist.

He smiles at me and says, "I've loved you forever baby, and I have no intentions of stopping. You made me a better man than I ever thought I could be, and I want to live the rest of my life with you. Only with you. So please will you do me the honour of being my lawfully wedded wife?"

I pull his lips down to mine and he instantly exhales with relief and pleasure, sliding his tongue against my own with long unhurried strokes.

After a minute he murmurs against my mouth, "Is that a yes, baby?"

I laugh and bite my lip. "Yes," I say excitedly, butterflies fluttering in my stomach. "Definitely, definitely yes."

He draws my mouth back to his, and he fills me so deeply that I feel him everywhere. I gasp at the intensity.

"Need to get this ring on you," he murmurs, pulling away only so that he can get back down on one knee, take my shaking hand in his, and slide the diamond up my finger. He bows his head and kisses the back of my hand, and my legs tremble at the sight. He gets back to his feet and lifts me so that I can wrap myself around his waist as he walks us back up the shore to the chalet.

As soon as we're back inside with the door clicked shut Tate is ripping the clothes from my body, growling as he crowds me backwards towards the bed.

"Only the ring," he says as he tugs his pants down my legs, his teeth grazing the insides of my thighs. "Want you wearing only the ring."

When I'm suitably stripped he moves to undress himself but then I suddenly realise, "Wait, my socks!"

We both look down at the baby pink bed socks on my feet and Tate breathes out a laugh, pressing my naked skin against his jacket and jeans.

His hands roam to my ass, kneading roughly as he says,

"Okay, the ring and the socks – you're not getting cold feet on me, baby."

I crawl backwards up the mattress and I watch him as he tugs the clothes off his own body. Coat: gone. Shirt: gone. When he gets to his belt he studies me with hooded eyes, gauging the fast-paced heaving of my bare chest. The buckle jangles as he unsheathes the leather tongue, and he yanks his button open and his fly down. My eyes trace over the ink on his bicep and the letters on his hand, and I squirm agitatedly on the soft quilt. He pulls his jeans and briefs down over his hips and I sink my teeth into my lip in anticipation.

He takes a condom from the box on the floor and leans his body over mine, the hard leather and denim digging into my thighs. "Want me to keep them on?" he whispers as he pulls my hips down to meet his.

I nod slowly like a woman possessed, and then I run my left hand languidly across my throat. His eyes flash down to the ring and a flame ignites behind his irises. He interlocks our fingers and presses our hands down into the bed, using his other hand to bite open the foil packet, sheath himself in the condom, and then align his body against mine.

I move my free hand to his cheek and I caress it sweetly. He meets my gaze and presses a slow kiss to my lips.

"I love you so much, baby," he murmurs. "I can't wait to make you my wife."

I kiss him again, running my fingers up the thick column of his neck and into his hair. "I love you too."

Then, with one more kiss, he rolls his hips into mine and we pick up where we left off.

ABOUT THE AUTHOR

Sapphire is a debut author writing New Adult and contemporary romance stories. She has a degree from Durham University – wherein she graduated with a First Class Honours Bachelor of Arts degree in English Literature and Education Studies – and a degree from Cambridge University – wherein she graduated with a Master of Philosophy degree.

Her favourite hobbies include buying books, reading books, and writing books.

You can find out more about the author on her website: www.sapphireauthor.com

For more updates, Sapphire can be found on TikTok and Instagram: @sapphiresbookshelf

Made in the USA
Las Vegas, NV
24 June 2023

73838789R00163